The GRAND HOTEL

"Behold a palace of madness and desire, its crimson corridors home to a gallery of the damned. Kenemore's novel tours the mysterious recesses of the human soul and what we will do in the name of fear, of love, of vengeance. In the tradition of the great canon of weird tales, *The Grand Hotel* generates its own dark light, its own cold flames."
—Laird Barron, Bram Stoker Award-winning author of *The Beautiful Thing That Awaits Us All* and *The Croning*

"Kenemore has strung a series of enchanting and horrifying stories like dark pearls on the thread of a mystery that leads us onward to an inevitable and totally satisfying end—a masterful voice whispering into the dark. *The Grand Hotel* is the best book I've read this year! Highly recommended."
—John Hornor Jacobs, author of *Southern Gods* and *The Twelve-Fingered Boy*

"With an assuredness that never missteps, Scott Kenemore's *The Grand Hotel* intrigues and delights. It's a book singing with voices—at once charming and bizarre and frightening. It deftly wraps puzzle around puzzle, drawing you deeper into the dark passages and hidden doorways where nothing is as it seems. *The Grand Hotel* masterfully celebrates the truth and mystery inherent in all great story-telling."
—Simon Strantzas, author of *Burnt Black Suns*

"*The Grand Hotel* is essentially refined shivers from another era. Gothic, funny, even old fashioned . . . it is a book to be read by the fireplace with your dog (and a big dog is best) who rests loyally and unknowingly at your feet. Imagine the writers of Creepshow hanging out with a tipsy Mary Shelly, a bottle of Absinthe half empty, a rainy day willingly declaring itself."
—Steven Schlozman, author of *The Zombie Autopsies*

"*The Grand Hotel* is Scott Kenemore's best novel to date, hands down. Here he commands a gallery of horrors, and fills his nightmare hotel with the voices of the damned. Every story, every lonely, damaged soul, is another turn deeper into the labyrinthian horror Kenemore has created. This is easily one of the best books I've read in the last five years. Powerful and beautifully haunting, *The Grand Hotel* gets my highest recommendation."
—Joe McKinney, Bram Stoker Award-winning author of *Plague of the Undead* and *Dead World Resurrection*

The
GRAND
HOTEL

SCOTT KENEMORE

TALOS PRESS

Talos Press books may be purchased in bulk at special discounts for sales promotion, corporate gifts, fund-raising, or educational purposes. Special editions can also be created to specifications. For details, contact the Special Sales Department, Talos Press, 307 West 36th Street, 11th Floor, New York, NY 10018 or info@skyhorsepublishing.com.

Talos Press is an imprint of Skyhorse Publishing, Inc.®, a Delaware corporation.

Visit our website at www.skyhorsepublishing.com.

10 9 8 7 6 5 4 3 2 1

Library of Congress Control Number: 2014941974

Cover design by Rain Saukas
Cover photo: Thinkstock

Print ISBN: 978-1-940456-08-9
Ebook ISBN: 978-1-940456-16-4

Printed in the United States of America

For Molly

"For good reasons did the ancient magicians express their prophecies in images rather than in writing. For who dare tell the naked truth to a king?"

—Paracelsus

*"Undaunted, the king reached those burning grounds
That loomed in front, in swirling smoke enveloped,
Complete with a whole array of horrors;
The most hideous place imaginable on this earth."*
—Sivadasa, *The Five-And-Twenty Tales of the Genie*

"Is what?" I asked, not grasping the meaning of this
unfamiliar word.
"Is goophered—cunju'd, bewitch'."
—Charles W. Chesnutt, "The Goophered Grapevine"

The Grand Hotel lies at the end of a desolate, mist-shrouded street.

The columns that frame its entrance have old and peeling plaster. The crenulations along the walls are covered in ancient ivy, most of it dead. Filament still burns in the copper fixtures above the door, but the resulting glow casts little light. Some of the windows are broken. All of them are dark.

Visitors creep inside tentatively, unsure what to make of the place. They are a nervous bunch . . . intrigued, but unaccustomed to trespassing. (How long have they stood outside, daring one another to go in? I often have difficulty telling. Time has a way of passing strangely for me.) The visitors wonder aloud if the building is abandoned. Some clearly fear discovering vagabonds squatting within its crumbling lobby. Others expect only mice and rats. But certainly—all of them feel quite sure—this place cannot be a functioning hotel.

It is my job to disabuse them of that notion.

When I look up from my desk, it often gives them a start. I keep the lights rather dim, you see, which tends to render me quite invisible. It is not uncommon for my guests to gasp or even, occasionally, scream when I finally raise my head. (Though he remained silent, I once had a grown man faint dead away.)

Yet after this initial shock, my countenance usually reassures them. I smile broadly and lift my brow. My demeanor projects propriety and taste. I have seldom been called "handsome," but some have said my features confer feelings of trustworthiness—a notion which pleases me inordinately.

"Welcome, welcome," I say to them. "I'm sorry for giving you a fright."

This is not true.

"Oh, we didn't see you there!" they will say, some still gasping in surprise. "What *is* this place?"

"Ahh, so you are tourists, then?" I inquire.

They nod. Of course they are. They always are.

"Are you in town for the culinary festival?" I wonder aloud. "Or the museum opening, or—yes, of course—the equinoctial celebration?"

Oh, they wonder. Was there some sort of celebration?

I smile silently, divulging nothing.

"You have come to the Grand Hotel," I inform them. "The building may not look like much to seasoned travelers such as yourselves, but I assure you, in its heyday this was a remarkable place to be. To see and be seen, as they say. Kings and queens have stayed here. Presidents and Prime Ministers from countries all around the world—including, I believe, some of your own—have sequestered themselves within these walls. We've had film stars, champion sportsmen, four-star generals, top scientific minds. . . . The history of the Grand Hotel is *really* quite remarkable."

At this point, braver members of the party will venture a query as to the nature of *my* position. Am I a security guard, keeping watch over the sleeping structure? A docent? Or even a tour-guide? (Perhaps an official one—licensed through the city tourism office—or perhaps an *un*official one . . . working for tips, thankyouverymuch.)

Here, I must disappoint and astound them in the same breath.

"No," I say softly. "I manage the front desk."

Manage the front desk? (I can almost hear the gears turning inside their thick skulls.) The front desk of the hotel? Then that would mean . . .

"Oh, yes," I clarify. "The hotel is fully operational. My shift covers the evening and overnight hours. If you desire a room, I believe we just *might* have a vacancy."

Here they will exchange a look.

"Let me see . . ." I say, consulting the ratty, timeworn ledger in front of me. "Here we are, then. The Honeymoon Suite is available, I see . . . though that might not suit a mixed group such as your own. There are also two single rooms, but—drat—nothing with much of a view. Our western balconies get a remarkable panorama of the city at sunset. Unfortunately, all we have tonight are a pair of rooms facing east."

Now I see them looking at me and whispering. Sizing me up. Who *is* this strange man? In the difficult light, his height, age, and even race are tricky to discern. (A safe guess might characterize him as tallish, middle-aged, and healthily tanned.) Moreover, they wonder, how can he project such pride—and exude such fastidiousness—amid the ruins of a dump that must be a hundred years past its prime?

I smile back at them, allowing the inspection.

About this time, a heavy tread in the hallway above betrays the presence of others. My visitors realize that I am not kidding about the vacancies. If only three rooms in this vast hotel are empty, then the rest of them must be . . .

"How many rooms does this place *have*?" a member of the group ventures.

"Aha!" I answer energetically. "That's an interesting question, with a long and equally interesting answer. But it's more fun if we make it a game, don't you agree? How many do *you* think there are?"

Oh, the answers I have heard over the years. Oh the answers. Some are risibly low. Forty. Fifty. Sixty. (I think I once got a twelve.) Others hit the opposite end of the spectrum. Thousands of rooms. Millions. (These guesses usually come from children, true, but one does well never to underestimate a child.)

I like to conceal the actual figure for as long as possible. Sometimes I do not divulge it at all. But if the group is attentive and halfway respectful, I will usually let it slip.

"The Grand Hotel has exactly three hundred thirty-three and one thirds rooms."

They smile politely, as if I have told an unfunny joke.

Sorry, I tell them. It's no joke. 333.33.

"That's silly," one of them will say dismissively.

"How can you have a third of a room?" another usually asks. "Who stays in it? A third of a person?"

Here I open my mouth to speak, but always think better of it.

"You know . . . if you don't have any pressing engagements this evening, you *could* join me on a brief tour of the building," I tell them. "I would be happy to conduct it personally. I'm not supposed to leave my post at the desk, but I've been here so long that management has grown rather *flexible* on that point."

The adventurous members of the group are instantly interested. They cajole the more timid ones.

I simply stand and smile.

And wait.

It never takes very long.

Mr. Pence

Many nights, we are interrupted at this point by a delivery person—typically entering the lobby bearing a package; an arrangement of flowers, perhaps, or a prepared meal. For me, he is a familiar face. (We exchange grins, and I always wish his wife well.)

When this interruption occurs, I will elect to begin the tour with Mr. Pence.

"Thank you," I say, accepting the package. "Have a good evening."

The deliveryman exits.

"We are in luck," I announce to my guests. "We now have an occasion to visit one of the Grand Hotel's oldest residents, Mr. Pence."

They look at one another, but I can tell that most are already on board.

Cargo in hand, I conduct the group across the lobby, our feet making *tik-tak* noises on the tile (theirs rather more than mine) as we go a little deeper into the hotel. The visitors look around cautiously, examining the dim expanse of the inner lobby, with its high ceiling and exquisite latticework. Upon the north wall, an oil painting of one of the hotel's founders frowns down at them. (His eyes are remarkably lifelike and hypnotic. I have stared into them for hours on end.)

"How do you *see* in here?" a brave or impertinent member of the group may query. "It's so *dark*!"

"Oh, there's no trick to it," I tell them. "I open my eyes and look around, just like anyone else."

Of course, looking and seeing are not the same thing.

My answer is *not* usually satisfactory, and I frequently receive a "Harumph" in reply.

When we reach the red carpet of the royal staircase, I like to stop and let the vision before us sink in. I've worked here longer than I care to remember, and yet familiarity has not diminished its ability take my breath away.

The staircase really is magnificent. Ten feet wide with an elegant slope from left to right, it is one of our hotel's most impressive features. Artists have come from halfway around the world to paint models ascending or descending this staircase. It is has been featured in the pages of architecture and design magazines. (When money is no object, a builder suggests to his billionaire client a staircase modeled after the one in the Grand Hotel.)

Overweight members of the group—particularly Americans, it seems—have been known to sigh ponderously at the thought of all the steps before them.

"Come, come," I say in these instances. "I climb it several times a day . . . seemingly with no ill effect."

This line always earns me dirty looks.

We begin our trip up the silent, velveteen staircase. We become like ghosts, our footfalls muffled completely by the thick red carpet. (Only the exaggerated breathing of the Americans gives any clue to our presence.)

"Is this the only staircase in the hotel?" one of the guests wants to know.

"Oh, by no means," I respond. "But it *is* the grandest."

Upon reaching the top, we see that the carpeting unfolds down the hallway in front of us. In fact, most of the hotel's hallways are covered in this same cruor stain. Though it makes our individual footfalls silent, the odd floorboard nonetheless creaks in protest.

Past the staircase, we begin to encounter doors to private rooms. Each has a heavy brass knob and a single keyhole. (Contemporary hostelries have converted to keycards, true, but at the Grand Hotel we find the old ways are best.) Some doors still have visible room numbers, yet many bear no demarcation at all. Mr. Pence's room is the very first. A good place to start.

My guests seem disappointed when I stop in front of Pence's door. They were hoping to venture deeper, to see more.

"This is really as far as we're going?" one of them asks.

"For the moment," I reply.

Some members of the group look expectantly down the darkened hallway ahead of us, or else back down the staircase into the lobby below. They are nervous, curious, impatient.

I shift the delivery item to my left arm and prepare to knock on the door.

Here—most times, at least—I take a final, mischievous glance back at the visitors clustered behind me. After this, there is no going back.

When I knock on the door, it begins.

★ ★ ★

Knock, knock

"Oh Mister Pence," I announce. "A delivery of flowers for you this evening. They're lovely and fresh. Tulips, I think."

Horticulture has never been my forte.

I gesture for the visitors to back up, then open the door.

The reaction of a group—upon beholding a sight like Mr. Pence—is usually a good indicator of how the rest of the evening will go. Some stand their ground, struggling to make sense of what they see. Some turn around and leave the hotel forthwith, stomping out wordlessly. Others have threatened to call for the authorities, or threatened me personally with violence!

There is no typical reaction.

As I throw wide the door to Mr. Pence's quarters, we are greeted by the pleasant smells of aftershave mingled with fresh night air. Mr. Pence keeps his windows open at all hours. It is dim inside the room, but still brighter than I keep the lobby. After a moment, it seems laughable to my visitors that Mr. Pence keeps any light on at all.

He hasn't any eyes. They have rotted out of his head. The flesh on his face is sunken and sallow. His teeth have gone to a dirty black, and his mouth hangs open in perpetual expectation. His hair is thin and his nails are long.

Mr. Pence reclines in his bed. He wears a nightshirt, and a blanket covers him to the waist. The linens are freshly cleaned, and there is no cadaverous smell.

"Mister Pence," I say. "Here are your flowers. Shall I set them by the night stand, or . . . yes, here on the end table. I trust you are keeping well. Do let me know if I can shut your window. I haven't forgotten how you like to keep it cool."

Mr. Pence smiles (as he always does) while I place the flowers on a table beside his bed.

"We have a tour group this evening," I explain. "Perhaps you would care to say hello?"

Here, a moment of tension.

The group regards me, one another, and most assuredly the desiccated man in the bed before us. Will he move? Will he answer? The more fantastically inclined members of the party wait expectantly for the corpse to draw breath and wish us all a grand good evening.

I merely smile at Mr. Pence as he remains, quite unmoving, before us in his bed.

"This group will be around for a while," I say to the body. "We are just beginning the tour. I will, then, leave you for the moment, Mister Pence. Do ring down if there is anything you require."

I do not enjoy being regarded as a madman. However—as I back out of the room and quietly close the door—that can be the only meaning in the looks these visitors cast my way.

"How *could* you?" one of them often asks.

"I say, is this a put on?" another typically wonders. "Because it's in very bad taste."

Once, a loud American was the first to break the silence with a resounding "*WHAT* in the serious *FUCK*?" (O, how it made me laugh!)

I take a deep breath.

Accounting for Mr. Pence is tricky . . . but always can be done.

It makes me feel like a lawyer with a good case, but a particularly dull jury. I do my best to bring them around, one step at a time. They get there in the end . . . most of them.

"These are the facts about Mister Pence," I say, turning to face the group. "He moved into the Grand Hotel fifty years ago, nearly to the day. Overnight, he became one of our most well-liked guests. All our long-term residents know and care for gentle, generous Mister Pence. As age came upon him, he *did* find himself significantly less mobile than he once might have been. We saw less and less of him around the hotel."

"Was that before or after he died?" one visitor quips.

I ignore this impudent japery.

"Mister Pence always pays his bill on time, and has never once occasioned a complaint from another guest—a distinction that far too few of our permanent residents can claim."

"But he's dead!" one of them will stammer. (Usually, she is an overbearing, upper-class matron, tending to the portly side.)

I bite my lower lip and nod thoughtfully, indicating that I feel the visitor's consternation.

"Whatever the state of Mister Pence's body, he stays in regular communication with us," I say carefully. "Each month, a check for the amount of his accumulated hotel bill is delivered to my desk. The funds from the bank account in his name are always adequate. Every piece of food brought to Mister Pence's room manages to become eaten. Leave him a chicken leg at noon, and you will return to find it a bare bone by two-thirty. And though he does not use the telephone—or our somewhat dated intercom system—he regularly sends written notes to the front desk when there's something he needs. We like to think of the Grand Hotel as providing the classic service of another era, you see? Whenever I can satisfy the requirements of one of my guests, I am always happy to oblige."

"What kind of things does he ask for?" one guest wonders in a tone suggesting she still expects this to be a joke.

"Oh, you know," I say, running my hands through my hair. "This and that. Trinkets and trifles mainly, but not always. Just last month he asked a model fire engine be requisitioned for his great-grandson's birthday. I am proud to say I found the perfect one in a shop on Mott Street. Mister Pence was, from every indication, quite pleased with the result. In fact, he grinned at me all day."

"But he's dead!" one of them cries, waggling his head as if to shake off a pall I have cast.

"As you say," I respond quietly.

At that moment there is a very loud creak from the floorboards behind them. Many in the group give a start. (I do not. I could see what was coming . . . or rather, whom.)

The visitors turn to find a hunted-looking man in a high collared shirt approaching along the hallway. He is very thin and has a forehead full of wrinkles. His open mouth betrays blocky, gravestone teeth.

"Good evening," he says in a hard-to-place accent.

"Good evening, James," I return.

They regard him cautiously.

"Something from Mister Pence," he says, proffering a hand-written note from within his coat. I accept it.

James then brushes past us, stalking down the royal staircase and disappearing into the dimness of the lobby beyond.

I glance at the note, smile, and put it away. Then I look at my visitors. A moment before, many of them appeared as if they were thinking of leaving the hotel. Now they are curious once again.

"'Ere, what's that?" a British visitor says.

I wave the question away.

"No, seriously," rejoins a teenage American. "Tell us."

I point to the pocket where I have secreted the note, and raise my eyebrow to make sure I have heard them right. I have.

"Well . . . it is a note from Mister Pence," I tell them.

"How can that be?" asks one.

"What's it say?" asks another.

I remain perfectly still for a few moments. Then I bring the note back out of my pocket.

"It says thank you for the flowers. It also says tonight's group is lovely, but observes that the young man in the off-yellow vest is a pickpocket who has removed my wallet."

Everyone in the group glances at the man in the vest. He quietly looks at the floor.

"I had hoped to speak with him privately, you see," I continue, lowering the note. "Yet, Mister Pence has forced my hand, has he not? Incidentally sir, I do hope you will return my property without further ado. As you'll find shortly—if you haven't already—it contains no money. The stitching, however, is immaculate, and it holds some sentimental value."

The man in the vest returns my wallet without looking up from the carpet.

"Thank you," I tell him. "No hard feelings."

The rest of the group takes a moment to process what is happening. A few of them edge away from the pickpocket.

"'Let me see that note," a bold visitor says. I offer it willingly. The visitors crowd around and read over the shoulder of the one who holds it. They see that it says, more or less, exactly what I have described.

"How'd you do that?" one asks. "The man who gave you the note was outside of the room."

"Are you in on this?" one of them asks the pickpocket. He is tempted to lie. I can see it on his face. I stare him down hard. After a moment under the weight of my gaze, he relents and admits we are not in collusion.

A kerfuffle breaks out amongst the visitors. They are not sure what is happening, or who is being straight with whom. (For some reason, this is always paramount upon their minds.) Some members of the group clearly feel uncomfortable and violated. They accuse me of trying to deceive or rob them. (The very idea! When, of course, it is *I* who has most lately had his wallet pilfered.)

It is time for me to bring out—as they say—the big guns.

"Perhaps then, we should stop the tour here," I say, raising my hands like a shopkeeper who is tired of haggling with a customer. "If I have upset or offended any of you, I am truly sorry. It was never my intention. If I have made you uncomfortable somehow, then I apologize for that too. Yes. Yes, I do believe we ought to conclude the tour now. We ought to go no deeper inside the Grand Hotel."

They fall silent. Some look bashful. Others, apologetic.

"But I am not a liar!" I say loudly and dramatically. "I have at no time lied to you. Nothing I have shown you or told you has been untrue in any way. Even so . . . I can accept that the Grand Hotel may be a bit . . . *much* for some."

I slump my shoulders wearily, looking crestfallen and disappointed in them. (I must bite my tongue to avoid smiling. In truth, I am nearly trembling with pleasure. Sometimes I actually *do* tremble, but the group mistakes this for shudders of despondence, which works out just fine.)

"We're sorry," a spokesman—or woman—will invariably declaim. "We didn't mean to hurt your feelings, sir. We would very much like to see the rest of the hotel."

"Do you. . . . Do you really mean that?" I ask, knowing full well that they do.

"Oh yes," they agree in a chorus.

I shrug to indicate that, thus united, there is little I can do to resist them.

I straighten my posture, allow a smile to return to my lips, and lead the group deeper inside.

Mr. Orin

The design of a hotel can tell you important things about it. The *fundamental* design, that is. The core arrangement of bricks and mortar and wooden beams can give you a powerful clue to the original vision of the builder. What feeling was it intended to convey? Was the goal to impress and dazzle the guests? Was it instead built with a strictly utilitarian comfort in mind, an easy-in/easy-out rest stop for the exhausted traveler? Or was it perhaps constructed as a rendezvous for those with dark and secret liaisons in mind?

The placement of doorways, halls, and balconies. The fact that certain spaces in the hotel exist . . . or do not exist. These are the things from which it is beyond the poor power of an interior decorator to add or subtract. These are the immutable, unchanging truths of a place. However many times a hotel "reinvents" itself, this core being never changes. The vice dens of Las Vegas stretch to sell themselves as "family friendly" destinations, but the addition of clowns and acrobats to betting pits does little to change a casino's soul. The flattened televisions and electronic music piped into the venerable hotels of ancient cities allow for new marketing strategies and the application of words like "boutique," yes . . . but the dimensions of the rooms themselves show no alteration. Neither do the number of steps from the lobby to the door or the amount of time one spends waiting for the elevators. Some things are fundamental. Some things are fixed.

Most guests have little inclination to delve beyond a hotel's latest, most-contemporary presentation. They are uncurious. They are trusting. They like to believe a thing is what it says it is. Yet at the same time, they are often struck by an uncanny feeling that something about a place is somehow . . . *off.* That a deeper, more primordial version is struggling to squeeze through the ventilation shafts and seep out from underneath the brand new wallpaper.

Inside the Grand Hotel, our well-worn carpeting and decades-old fixtures make it appear that we are clinging to the sensibilities of another time; that we have no interest in following contemporary trends. Yet it would not be entirely accurate to say that everything inside the Grand Hotel is precisely what it seems. My visitors—every one of them—eventually find that out for themselves.

One way or another.

★ ★ ★

We step away from Mr. Pence's room, working our way down a slightly stale but well-lit hallway lined with wooden doors. At the hallway's termination, the way before us opens into a sunroom. Depending on the time of day, it is either bathed in glorious natural illumination or lit by several tastefully shaded lamps. It holds an arrangement of dark leather couches, venerable wooden chairs (nearly blackened with age), and positively ancient card tables.

"I never heard of a hotel with a sunroom at the end of the first hall," says one of the guests.

"Yeah, weird," another offers.

"What's a 'sunroom'?" tries a third.

"Does it have vending machines?" a fourth wonders. (The visitors are always concerned about replenishing themselves. I suppose this is not entirely misguided. We are just starting a journey, and adequate provisions are important.)

"Shhhh," a member of the group wearing a camera and "fanny pack" musters. "I hear something."

They fall silent and look around. I smile and watch. How long will it take them to figure it out?

"It's somebody laughing," one of them states.

"No," says a little girl with red hair. "It's somebody crying. How sad."

"Very *good*," I say to her, giving off a smile.

The red-haired girl is young, perhaps eleven or twelve. She does not return my grin. Something in her expression comports a mix of displeasure and anxiety. There is, of course, no "right" or "wrong" reaction to the Grand Hotel. Yet it displeases me that someone so young should have made up her mind about the place—in either direction—so early in the game. (I had not noticed this girl before. I also find that I'm unable to tell which of the adults is her chaperone. Certainly, she bears no marked resemblance to anyone else on the tour.)

"Wait," one of the visitors cries loudly, stealing my attention away. "Now it's stopped."

I exhale through my grin. I have let the mystery linger for long enough.

"My dear Mister Orin," I call. "Are you in a storytelling mood tonight? You've gotten our visitors curious, as always. Could you hear us coming down the hall?"

For a moment the air is still. Nothing in the room appears to move. The visitors look at me expectantly. I motion with my hand that they should remain patient.

Momentarily, a figure rises from a high backed leather chair in the corner. He is small of stature and easily concealed. His eyes are red and his lower lip protrudes forward into a frown.

My visitors look upon him piteously. Little do they know that this is all a part of Mr. Orin's act—which, over the last few years, I have learned to find amusing rather than annoying. The demons that haunt Mr. Orin want to come out. They *want* him to speak. I believe it is his only relief.

"Ladies and gentlemen, this is Mister Orin," I announce as the small man draws closer. "He has been a guest of the hotel for some time now, and the sunroom is his favorite place, day or night . . . and, luckily for him, it is always one of the two."

"Mister, are you okay?" one of the visitors asks. Her tone indicates that she finds my introduction of Mr. Orin somehow insensitive. She shoots me a glare to confirm this, then turns a sympathetic smile back to Orin.

He burbles anew, pleased at the attention. I can only roll my eyes.

"Perhaps," I say after a deep sigh, "you would like for Mister Orin to tell you a little about himself. Mister Orin, would *you* like that?"

The small man turns to me, tears in his eyes, and nods appreciatively.

I encourage the group to assemble the chairs from around the sunroom into a half circle. (Mr. Orin himself—I have learned—prefers to stand. I believe this is for dramatic purposes.)

When the appropriate seating arrangements have been made, Mr. Orin begins his tale.

We had always been poor, you see.

My parents were poor. They had other problems too. They were screwed up in lots of ways. Screwed up people. Always fighting. One of them was always drunk, and the other was running around.

But I thought: "I won't be like them. I'm not screwed up. I'm a sober, sensible person. When I grow up, I'll not be poor. That's the difference."

Little did I know that our poverty was like a blood virus, and I already had it.

As I grew older and made my own way, I realized that my parents fought and drank and committed adultery only to numb the pain of the virus. Their vices were not the cause of their penury. The vices were a way to deal with the frustration of knowing they would never be able to do anything about their station in life. It was the poverty that had screwed them up, and not the other way around.

I had a wife and a kid and we tried hard. I didn't drink or screw around. But I stayed poor.

Then somebody told me that you could make a lot of money in Alaska.

The amount of money . . .

Let me just say that, to *me*, it was a lot of money. For a doctor or a lawyer or a stockbroker, it wasn't very much at all. But to me it was a lot, what they offered.

It was cold, hard work at a government research station far to the north. I would have to leave my family for a year and would mostly be alone. But when I came back, we would be out of arrears and I would have more than a regular year's pay saved. That would mean a lot to my family.

I got up there. It was grim. Disorganized and grim. All the people had something wrong with them, as far as I could tell. Mentally, I mean. They were nice enough on the outside. Friendly, sure. But that part of your brain that tells you that spending your life in a cold research station in the middle of nowhere is probably not the way to live was totally gone. I decided I must have been missing that brain-part too, because there I was.

I was a maintenance engineer. A janitor, really. I maintained a building where the government had set up a powerful telescope. I hardly saw the researchers. They were looking at stars and planets far away.

Aside from the government employees, there were some fishermen who used an nearby inlet to repair their boats. There was a big metal warehouse there where you could keep a boat dry in a snowstorm. There were also some Inuit locals in the area. I never saw more than a couple or three together, snowmobiling around. I wondered where they went after it got dark. I wondered where "headquarters" was for an Inuit.

In late fall, it got colder than the coldest winters back home. Go outside without a scarf over your mouth and your throat could freeze. When you'd spit, it would crackle. Your nose felt hollowed out from the cold and you got ice boogers . . . and it technically wasn't even winter.

Also, one thing you realize is that the news in the lower forty-eight is not like the news up there. When a twister destroys a little town in the Midwest—or New Orleans floods, or California has an earthquake—it's big news everywhere. National. They get right on it, the news people do.

Up in Northern Alaska, stuff goes crazy all the time. The weather goes wrong and causes big disasters. Fishing boats get sunk or little towns get buried in snow. And you never hear about it down there.

It was only November when the storm blew in off the water. It was on one of the long weekends when people were gone, and I had the research station to myself. Just being isolated like that could be scary enough. But I was still young and my health was fine. I never worried about being stranded and having a medical problem. But accidents could still happen. Did happen. So did crime. Alaska has way more crime than most people think. If someone wanted to bust down the door and steal what we had in the research station . . . well, let's just say it wouldn't be too hard. I didn't have a gun. I hardly had anything.

The last Saturday afternoon in November, the sky got dark and green, and not in a fun, Northern Lights kind of way. It made me sick to look at. Black clouds and a swirling green eye in the middle, like it was looking at me. Lightning and wind, too. So much wind.

All day, the gale got stronger and stronger. I sat in the little first floor lounge of the research station and looked out the window and worried. I ate junk food and drank soda and stared into the billowing whiteness outside. There was no new snow coming down—the temperature had dropped too low for it—but the wind whipped up what was already on the ground. Any window you looked out of, it looked like the windshield of your car if you were doing eighty in a full-on blizzard. A swarm of little white flecks that came and came and never stopped.

When dusk arrived, the station started to seriously creak. It had always creaked a little. The scientists and other workers told me not to worry about it. But this was a new kind of creaking, like the roof of the place was going to lift right off. I imagined steel girders bending. That kind of sound.

Just as it got dark enough for the exterior security lights to come on, the glass window in the first floor lounge exploded. I had already put my coat and hat on, in case something like this happened, but I was still terrified. I thought about making for the second floor of the station. Then I heard a noise like footsteps on the roof. "What can be up there?" I thought. Then I realized it was the roof itself peeling off. A few moments later I heard the loudest *CRASH* of my life and realized the giant tele-scope had exploded in the cold.

Snow was blowing all through the station and accu-mulating on the floor. The inside had become the out-side just like that.

Do I just sit here and die? I thought to myself. You'd think I'd be thinking about whether or not it had been worth it to come here just for the money. Honestly, that never crossed my mind.

Then I remembered the metal warehouse where the boats got repaired. I hadn't seen any boat traffic in a while—too cold for it—but I thought there might be people inside who could help. To boot, the warehouse looked stronger than the research station. The rear door had a keycode thing, but everybody who worked here knew the combination.

I staggered outside into the wind. Jesus, it was blinding. I didn't have goggles, either. I pointed myself in the direction of the warehouse and started walking with my eyes mostly closed. The wind blew me over a couple of times, and blew away my tracks in the snow almost immediately. It was easy to get disoriented. Finally, I saw the security lights glowing above the warehouse door ahead of me. It felt positively miracu-lous that I'd found it.

By then I couldn't really feel my fingers, but I punched in the keycode and the metal door opened. I stepped inside and shut the door behind me. The wind was still powerful, but I felt like the warehouse walls were going to hold. They were creaking and cracking to beat the band, but the snow and wind stayed out. For me, at that moment, it was enough.

Now the problem was the temperature. It was still bitterly, bitterly cold inside. Frozen and dark. Ice crystals everywhere. I didn't know if there was a way the warehouse heated itself, but it didn't feel like there was. I got some of the lights to turn on. The main light above me was on a cord, and it kept swinging when the wind rocked the building. That made the shadows move.

I called out, but nobody answered. The place was empty. There were no boats being worked on. Most of the tools and equipment had been put away. Everything packed up for the winter.

I started frantically looking around the warehouse. I wasn't thinking straight. Do I even have to tell you that? It was so, so cold. I didn't know what I was thinking. I didn't know what could happen next. Maybe I was just looking for a place to die, like an animal.

There was a room in the back of the warehouse with a metal door, like a freezer. It had a blinking light right above it. I walked over. Maybe the blinking light meant I should die there?

The door wasn't locked. I walked right in.

Inside, there were a bunch of long back tables, with lights hanging above each one. It made me think of a mortuary. I think the tables were for cutting fish.

In the back of the room was a clear container, like a fish tank. There wasn't any water in it, but there was a fish. Or a squid. It was hard to tell. The thing was all squished up in an awkward position. It was as big as me and spilled out of the top of the tank. I went over to take a closer look. At least I would get to see an interesting fish before I died.

The thing was gray and brown and had scales. Its head was like a normal fish head, but it had three holes in the top. In the middle of its back was a stalk with something on the end that looked like an eye. On the sides of the fish were wings. Really large wings, like on a skate or manta ray. At the aft of the fish were spindly things, long and green. They would trail after it as it swam, I guessed.

Why was this crazy fish here? Had they kept it for some reason? I looked at it and shivered. Maybe this container was where they kept things they wanted to show each other. Weird things.

I looked around the rest of the warehouse. There was nothing. No heat source. I didn't know what to do. I opened the outer door and took another look. The storm had not abated. If anything, it had worsened. I went back inside the room with the fish. I looked at it some more.

Here, Mr. Orin pauses. He appears uncomfortable and runs his fingers through his thinning hair. His mouth hangs open and he looks away. (It is a performance I have seen many times, and it's all

I can do not to laugh out loud. Sometimes I do produce a small titter, but usually manage to play it off as a cough.)

After a full minute, Mr. Orin regains his "composure" and continues.

This next part, I don't expect you all to understand. I can only tell you what happened.

I was dying, and trying not to. Freezing. Not thinking. There were no blankets. Nothing I could see to keep me warm. Nothing but the fish.

With the last of the energy in my body, I pushed over the tank. The fish-thing spilled out onto the floor.

I got on the ground and laid down next to it. I pulled one of the fish wings over myself like a blanket and I curled up underneath. It kind of worked. I felt a little warmer. I was worried it would smell, but it didn't. It was all too frozen. Nothing smelled like anything.

I wondered if falling asleep meant freezing to death. Probably any action I did meant freezing to death. The storm outside showed no signs of stopping, and even when it did, it would take the government hours or days to get a team back up to the research station. There was nobody important here to rescue— only me.

I decided that if anything I did meant dying, then I would do what I wanted to do. Which was to sleep.

I pulled even more of the fish-thing onto myself and closed my eyes.

Before I knew it I was dreaming. I was standing in some kind of marsh or bog. The water was up to my waist. There were tall trees all around, but they looked like no trees I'd ever seen. Instead of proper leaves, they had long ribbon-appendages that dangled down from the branches and blew in the wind. The water in which I stood was hot, almost like I'd pissed myself. The air was hot too, and there was a glint of sunlight coming off the bog. I looked up through the branches and ribbons and saw a red sky with seven suns.

Then I looked down at myself, and saw that I was the fish creature that I had been using as a blanket. I was standing up on one end. My chest had puffed out like a barrel. It was slowly expanding and contracting as I breathed.

I saw a thin green tentacle bobbing near my chin. The end of the tentacle was wrapped around something shiny and black, like an animal's horn. The tentacle— which I began to suspect was my own—brought the horn up to my fish-lips. The gills on my sides opened and began to propel air. It turned on like I was some kind of vacuum cleaner. Air went up through my gills and out through my mouth, and into what I realized was a flute.

The noise was not like a sound you would make intentionally. Not like music. It was more like the by-product of a crime. A horrible, high squeal.

I stood there with the flute in my fish-lips, feel-ing stunned by the sound. Then I saw that other fish-creatures had joined me. Good God! Was that what I looked like? A tentacled, winged monster with a chest cavity expanding and contracting with an obscene, almost sexual urgency as its body forced air through a glistening black horn? It must have been so. It can only have been so.

I began to count them—the creatures. It was hard to see with all of the trees, but I was past twenty when the bubbling began in the water below us.

The entire marsh was thick with it. Little bubbles came up everywhere, but a circle of huge ones made a concentrated funnel at the center of the marsh. Something deep and enormous had been released.

The bubbles intensified and soon a giant black tree began to rise out of the water. Moments later, I understood that it was an appendage. The ground beneath the swamp shook as other parts of the slimy behemoth emerged from beneath the waterline. They were multifarious, defying description except collectively. The suns were soon blotted out as the creature rose thousands of feet into the air. Creaking, wet, and clearly sentient, the titan bristled to the music of our flutes.

Gazing up into its immensity, I could make out a single yellow eye—idiot and flat . . . yet also incandescent—pulsing in the darkness the beast had brought up with it.

Then, all at once, the omnipresent piping stopped. My gills relaxed and my chest deflated. I looked up into the yellow eye. I think the other fish creatures did as well.

There was no sound but the sloshing and dripping of the wet giant. Its tentacles slowly extended down over each one of us.

Suddenly, a great flash of green and purple obscured my vision, and a sound similar to a thunderclap echoed across the marsh.

Then it was gone.

The marsh, the giant with the yellow eye, the other fish-creatures. All gone. Nothing but blackness. I could see nothing, smell nothing, hear nothing. A powerful, raw nausea overtook me. I felt overheated, like a man who has sprinted with all his might and then stopped frozen in his tracks.

Minutes might have passed, or they might have been days. I began to make out an ugly, grey light, and to feel cold. Gradually, I discerned an underwater scene. A fish eased by and seemed to notice me. Undersea vegetation floated past.

I swam toward the light above, up through the depths. I reached the surface and stuck my head out just enough to see, my gills still breathing in the water below. A single luminous sun burned overhead. The air was cool and sweet,

In one direction, I saw nothing but empty ocean. In the other, a shoreline and a small city with chimneys billowing healthy black smoke. In the harbor was a wooden ship. On its mast was an American flag with fifteen stars.

Then everything went black again. I was in a state between wakefulness and dreaming. I began to hear voices.

Someone clearly said: "It's a half man, half fish!"

Then another voice grumbled: "You dummy. It's a man *and* a fish. Looks like they died fighting each other."

"Really?" said the first voice. "Is that what you think happened?"

I looked up and saw two men in modern military uniforms. I was too cold to move, but I moaned.

One of them said: "What was that? Is the fish talking?"

"No," I said. "I'm talking."

And I was.

The visitors are quiet as Mr. Orin concludes. Many of them lean in hopefully, as if anticipating a punch line still to come. Others smile in a different way—uncomfortably, anxiously—like they're waiting for an idiot to finish babbling so they can excuse themselves and walk quickly in the opposite direction. Some have no reaction at all.

For his part, Mr. Orin looks utterly spent. Wordlessly, he turns away and retreats to his camouflaged corner of the sunroom. He finds the familiar chair and sinks down, as if he is becoming a part of it. In the shadows, it is hard to distinguish exactly where he ends and the chair begins.

The guests wonder if it can truly be over. Erasing all doubt, I exhale and give the group a hopeful smile that says *Well then . . .*

Slowly, the visitors stand and replace their chairs.

"What was the point of that?" asks one.

"Yeah, I don't get it," says another.

"Some kind of sicko or something," decrees a third.

I gesture to the hallway on the other side of the sunroom leading off to yet unexplored regions of the hotel.

The group looks at one another.

Once again, they find themselves at a crossroads. Do they follow me? Do they continue with the tour? Do they go deeper? Searching for an answer, their eyes gloss over the dusty tabletops of the sunroom. They consider the wallpaper, aged and peeling in many places. They look at the dust on the molding and the dead insects in the lighting fixtures. They wonder if it is worth spending any more of their evening here.

Then there is the unmistakable sound of jumping on the next floor. Noises clearly made by a dancer. The gentle creak of well-worn shoes. That unique bob-and-bow of feet that tread the boards.

An older lady raises her eyebrows and smiles.

"Oh, dancing? I *love* dancing."

I try to contain my smile.

"The grand ballroom is on the next floor," I say, as if it is only an incidental matter. "The orchestra shell is in need of some repair, but the chandelier is one of the finest in the city. A salvage from the destroyed opera house in Vienna, I believe."

"There are dancers there now?" one of the visitors asks.

I have only to nod.

★ ★ ★

By coincidence—or perhaps not—I find myself next to the red-haired girl as we begin our journey down the far hallway and away from the sunroom.

I wonder . . .

"What did you think of Mr. Orin's story?" I ask. "Quite a tall tale, eh?"

She takes a moment to respond.

"I think it means a lot to Mr. Orin," she answers carefully, showing the tact of a much older person.

"Do you really think so?" I reply. "He is a rather dramatic fellow, if you hadn't noticed. You certainly don't *believe* him, do you? What he said? A smart young lady like you? And I mean . . . even if it *were* a true story . . . what can he possibly *do* about it?"

With unnerving patience, she considers my questions thoughtfully before making any kind of response. For a moment, there is only the soft tread of our footfalls along the carpeted corridor, and the whispered conversations of the guests around us.

"Mr. Orin knows there's nothing he can do about it," she answers. "*That's* the thing."

"Is that what you *really* think, child?" I ask.

She is wise enough to remain silent.

Ms. Kvasov

Everything in life is a test. You just don't know it at the time.

School is the only place where somebody tells you "There will be a test," or "This material will be on the test," or even "This *is* a test!"

I wonder if—in this respect—educators do more harm than good. Conditioning our youngest and most impressionable to believe that evaluations present themselves only when boorish cat ladies scrawl "REMEMBER—TEST THIS FRIDAY!!!" on the front of a chalkboard is clearly a disservice.

That is what the visitors to the Grand Hotel do not yet realize. This, like everything else, is a test.

Like it or not.

★ ★ ★

The corridor soon terminates in a wooden staircase leading up. We begin our ascent. The stairs twist through sloping, wood-paneled hallways where timeworn paintings hang. Some are portraits, but most show landscapes or crowd scenes. The visitors look the paintings over quickly, trying not to make eye contact with the portraits. I always want to say: "If you're looking at the *faces*, then you're missing the point." But I don't. Of course I don't.

The staircase ends and the corridor straightens out again. (We've taken so many turns that it's quite difficult to guess the direction in which we now proceed. Several of the visitors remark on this. I do not supply any clarification.) The paintings remain, but now take a turn for the fanciful. The canvasses show cavorting acrobats, magicians gesturing with wands, and dancing circus elephants. The subject matter is so carefree, almost none of the visitors really stop to look at the figures represented. In their hurry to get to the next thing—a side-effect of modern life, I am told—they fail completely to notice the consternation and existential terror on the acrobats' faces. The anguish of the elephant forced to perform against its will. The dark, insidious smile of a magician who knows his next trick will ensnare the souls of the children in his audience.

"Aww, look at the elephants," one guest says, after the most cursory of glances.

Yes, look at them. But never too closely.

Soon, we begin to hear the percussive footfalls of a dancer hammering a tango into well-worn floorboards. We can also detect the tinny playback of recorded music on a phonograph.

"Down that way," I encourage the group. "The ballroom is just around the corner."

I shoo them along.

"We won't be interrupting a performance, will we?" one of them asks. She is clearly so excited to see the ballroom that nothing will stop her, yet poses this question to appear considerate.

"It is possible," I say evenly. "But I can guarantee that your presence will be appreciated by the performers."

This brings a wide grin to her face and she advances with renewed enthusiasm. The music grows louder, and louder still. One begins to detect the smell of chalk and oil.

"Ooh, I see people," says a woman at the front of the pack.

"Dancing people!" cries another.

All at once, they rush forward to where the bright ballroom beckons.

And there they pause. Their expressions grow cagey as they survey the immense space beyond and the unmoving tuxedoed figures within. They say nothing, waiting in vain for something to explain the strange sight. After a while—this becomes a pattern, of course—they look back to me make sense of it for them.

I clear my throat.

"This is Ms. Kvasov," I say, indicating the woman in the center of the ballroom with her arms wrapped around a life-size tuxedo-wearing figurine. Probably in her late sixties, she is clad in a dance leotard and a frilly hat with a flower. Her face is made up and her hair is tied back.

"And these," I continue with a sweep of my hand, "are her dance partners."

The room is full of wooden mannequins dressed for dinner. There are thirty-three in all. Instead of feet, their fixed maple legs terminate in wheels.

Ms. Kvasov takes in the audience and smiles. A painted eyebrow arches skyward. She leans into the nearest mannequin and sensually trails her fingers across its featureless face. Then, suddenly, with a practiced motion, she pulls the figure close. Its oiled wheels roll in absolute silence.

Ms. Kvasov poses dramatically with her partner, eyeing the audience. She gives them a look as if to say "Yes?"

Kvasov has her own story to tell, but the performance always comes first. To move things along, I step to the side table and replace the phonograph's needle. The band strikes up, and the dancer springs to life. Or should I say dancers? The unique power of Ms. Kvasov to imbue her mechanical partners with the appearance of life is positively uncanny.

Moving to the center of the ballroom, Kvasov and her mannequin sway and twist to the music. At times she leads, but just as frequently it seems the wooden man is leading her. The illusion is remarkable. As she switches from partner to partner, the maple figures do more than dance. She gives each one a personality. Some show great alacrity to command her. Others appear timid, and it is up to Ms. Kvasov to cajole them along.

Time passes quickly in the thrall of such a spectacle. After what feels like only a few short moments, the song winds down and Ms. Kvasov disentangles herself from the figures. She does not breathe hard, but a healthy sheen of sweat now glistens on her brow. She smiles through her made up face.

The visitors quickly recover from their stunned silence and erupt into applause.

"That was amazing!" one of them says.

"I've never seen anything like it!" offers another.

"Oh, thank you for bringing us here," one says appreciatively to me.

Then someone finds the temerity to address Ms. Kvasov directly: "Where did you learn to dance like that? With these . . . things as your partners?"

An inelegant phrasing, but it gets the job done.

Ms. Kvasov looks to me. I curtly nod back. She may proceed.

Her lipstick twists into a smile, her eyes unfocus, and suddenly she is far, far away.

In an accent thick enough to strain the ear, the master dancer begins to speak.

When it happened, I was a young student at the Royal Ballet School in England. I had grown up poor; a serf's daughter in the Russian countryside. I was, however, lucky. Lucky and gifted at dance. Attending a serious ballet school in England would open doors that a girl of my upbringing could seldom hope for. It was my only ticket to a better life, and I knew it. Accordingly, I undertook my studies with the greatest of seriousness and discipline.

My lone friend at the Royal School was another outsider—Irina, a gypsy girl from near Bucharest. Like me, she was just fifteen years old. Unlike me, her English was very good. She could speak fair Russian too, and because of this I often relied on her.

It was rare for us to have time to ourselves, but whenever we did, Irina and I would almost always spend it together—usually in the countryside just outside of town. One summer afternoon we walked deep into the northern forest to have a picnic atop a hill we both liked. After we had eaten, Irina took a nap while I walked down to the valley to gather water from a stream.

No sooner had I dipped my jar into the babbling brook than a hunting party rode up on the other side. There were three riders, all men. Two were old and bearded and wore unpleasant frowns. The third, however. . . . He was the most beautiful boy I had ever seen! He could not have been more than two or three years my senior. He had broad shoulders, thick black hair, and electric green eyes. He looked me over and smiled.

"Gavin," barked one of the old men, warning him to pay me no attention.

And so I knew his name.

As the noblemen dismounted and let their horses drink from the stream, Gavin and I stole glances at one another. He seemed as desperate to speak to me as I to him, yet instead he only fidgeted, brushed his horse, and counted the bullets in his knapsack. Never had a young man made me feel like this. My chest fluttered, and my knees felt weak. I was desperate. I knew I must see this boy again . . . but how?

When the horses had had their fill, the old men began to ride away. Gavin looked at me one last time. Then he whistled and clucked his tongue. His horse turned and followed the old men, and they rode out of sight.

Distraught, I returned to Irina and told her everything that had happened. Or so I thought.

"You silly girl," Irina said when I had finished my tale. "He plans to see you within the week!"

"What?" I said.

"Tell it to me again," Irina pressed. "Tell me exactly how he fidgeted? Show me precisely as you did before."

"Like this," I said, repeating his motions.

Irina shook her head as if I were a fool.

"By hooking his finger in his mouth like that, he was telling you his family name: Liphook," Irina said. "They are famous. The wealthiest in the county! By touching his gun and his grey horse, he sought to bring to your mind the Greyshot Festival which begins in only three days. By waving his finger once, he gave you the date of your meeting: the first night of the fest. As he rode away, he whistled and clucked to tell you your meeting place: The Whistling Cock. It is a public house with rooms to let, not a mile hence."

Irina's interpretation seemed far-fetched, but her English was much better than mine. Also, I desperately wanted to believe that she was right. Irina encouraged me to be brave and meet Gavin Liphook at the proposed rendezvous. I did not need much convincing.

On the first night of the Greyshot Festival, I crept out of the dormitory and stole my way into town. I found the Whistling Cock just where Irina had said it would be. And I could hardly believe it, but Gavin was waiting for me outside!

The dashing young man approached and grasped my hand. I smiled, unable to hide my pleasure.

Gavin took me to a room at the inn, and there we spent the night together. I was not experienced with love-making, but it did not seem to matter. We made love four times, each time in a different position. It was nearly dawn before we ceased. I have never known such passion. I was exhausted, sore, and, for a while, quite unable to speak.

At this point I take a careful survey of the faces around me. So often, tales tending to the amorous make my visitors uneasy. As in so many things, this is especially true with the Americans. (I sometimes worry that their tendency to fixate on sexual situations may cause them to miss the point of a story entirely.)

On this night, however, the group seems willing to tolerate the racier aspects of Ms. Kvasov's tale. If any of the visitors are scandalized, they do not let it show.

I return my gaze to Ms. Kvasov, and our narrator continues.

As the sky threatened to lighten, Gavin said to me: "So, you were able to figure out my little message? Such a bright girl!"

Without thinking, I answered him truthfully: "Actually, it was my friend Irina from school. I described your actions to her, and she deciphered their meaning."

"Ha!" roared Gavin, slapping his side. "Then I owe that girl dearly! She must have a show of my appreciation. Does she have a favorite food?"

"She adores chocolates," I answered. This was true.

"I'll send her a selection of the finest Belgian chocolates as a reward," Gavin promised.

As dawn broke, I hurried back to the dormitory in a daze. My head was swimming with thoughts of the handsome British boy. Even so, I stayed sensible enough to remain in the shadows and elude detection. Only Irina noticed as I crept back in through the dormitory window.

At breakfast, I told Irina everything that had happened. Though only a girl of fifteen, Irina was quite worldly and did not seem impressed when I told her of our four ways of lovemaking. I believed that Irina's worldliness came from her gypsy upbringing. She frequently spoke of things she had seen in her parents' caravan that seemed beyond the ken of most fifteen year olds— things to do with sex, yes, but also with the larger world. In addition, she knew how to tell fortunes with a strange deck of cards she always kept in her backpack.

The next day, I returned to the dormitory after classes to find Irina holding a large box of chocolates tied with an elaborate bow. The other girls were whispering that Irina had a secret admirer. When she saw me, Irina took me by the shoulder and forcefully walked us outside.

"These are obviously from your boyfriend," she said when we had reached the empty clearing at the back of the school. "But they are addressed to me."

"Oh, yes," I said brightly, and told Irina how Gavin had promised to send chocolates to thank her for deciphering his signals.

Irina's expression turned foul. It was as if someone had poured ice water down her back. Her hair visibly bristled.

"What's wrong?" I asked.

"These chocolates will be poisoned," Irina said flatly.

"What?!" I cried. I was dumbfounded. If anyone else had said this, I would have insisted that they were joking.

But Irina had a way of knowing things, and I had never heard her make this kind of joke.

Still, I refused to accept it.

"No," I insisted. "Gavin would not do that. He wishes to thank you. He is wonderful. He is my lover. He—"

I was cut off as Irina put two fingers in her mouth and whistled. Moments later, one of the feral dogs that lived in the woods behind the school loped into view.

Irina untied the ribbon and opened the box. The chocolates inside looked normal enough. Irina carefully plucked one from the gold-foil lining with her thumb and forefinger. She turned it this way and that—inspecting it closely—then threw it to the approaching animal.

"Irina, no!" I said. "Chocolate is bad for dogs."

With a voice like ice, Irina replied: "This chocolate, especially."

The canine ate the treat so fast it was like it had disappeared. The dog looked up at Irina for more. Irina's expression stayed cold. She motioned for me to wait.

Moments later the dog coughed. It seemed to lose interest in getting more chocolate. It lowered its head and walked twenty paces away. Then it lied down at the edge of the forest and stopped moving. Within five minutes it was dead.

Irina smiled. It was a smile that was terrible to see.

I did not want to believe what my own eyes had just shown me. I walked over to the dog and turned it over with my foot. The beast was no longer in the realm of the living.

"My God," I said to Irina. "How can this be happening? Why would Gavin do this?"

"In a way, he acts out of love for you," Irina explained coolly. "It would be disastrous for both of you if your love-making were discovered, no? You would lose your scholarship. And he? Who knows what punishment awaits him? The risk of being disinherited, I should think, at the very least."

"But how could he do this?" I asked. "It's murder!"

Irina seemed to grow distant. Her face assumed the strange aspect it held when she read fortunes on her cards.

"The rich and powerful live in a different world," she said. "You may think you understand them, but you do not. Their way of seeing things would not make sense to one such as yourself."

It was all too horrible. I needed to think.

I left Irina and walked into the woods where the wild dogs lurked. There I stood for several minutes, pondering the way forward. When I had made up my mind, I returned to my classmate. She was still standing in the clearing beside the dead dog, silent and pensive.

"We have to do something," I told her.

Irina nodded. She knew I meant that we must get revenge.

Inside the school, a bell sounded. It was time for our evening meal.

"This is what you must do," Irina said matter-of-factly. "You must write him a letter. Say that you ache to see him again; that you are driven by desire. Do not mention me or the chocolates. He may be confused when you do not allude to my death, but he will still be curious. Say that you will meet him again at the same location, next Thursday night. Do not give any specifics or sign the letter. Tell him to burn it after reading."

"And then what?" I asked.

"Trust me," said Irina.

I did as she advised. In the week that followed, Irina divulged no additional details of her plan. However, when Thursday morning came, she rose early and took me out to the clearing behind the dormitory once again.

"Tonight, you must go to Gavin and make love with him once more," Irina said.

"What?" I responded. All week I had been hoping that Irina had hired a tough Gypsy hitman who would be waiting to garrote him. The thought of lying down with a would-be murderer made my skin crawl.

"You must," Irina repeated. "And during your lovemaking, you must scratch him—hard—right next to his testicle sack. Three scratches, just like this."

Irina drew three lines with a stick in the dirt.

Here, again, I glance at the Americans. A few wince at the anatomical mention, but most seem to be taking it in stride.

"Your fingernails are long," Irina continued. "Leaving a mark will be no problem. Afterward, tell him you were carried away in the throes of passion."

"Then what?" I asked.

"You will bring a bottle of wine," Irina said. "After you lie with him, you will produce the wine and propose a drink. You will pour the glasses, and into his glass you will slip this."

Irina looked left, then right, and then handed me a small vial with clear liquid inside.

"Poison," I announced confidently. "But why not simply poison him first? Why do I have to sleep with him again?"

"What I have in mind . . . will be better," Irina said mysteriously. "That is not poison, besides. It is a laxative. Very fast acting. You will give him the wine with the laxative. He will drink it, and within five minutes he will excuse himself to the bathroom and close the door. He will leave his clothes in the bedroom with you. Ignore his pants, but take his underwear. Also, take anything embroidered, and anything with the name of his school or his family on it. If he has jewelry—"

"He wears a distinctive gold chain!" I announced.

"Yes," said Irina, nodding and narrowing her eyes. "You must definitely take that."

"Fine," I said. "And then what?"

"You will leave him while he is still locked in the bathroom," Irina said. "You will return to the school before dawn—in through our window just as before—and you must give to me the things you have taken. You must ensure that nobody sees you on the road."

"And then?

"Then I will do the rest."

I could hardly stand the thought of being with Gavin again. I had once felt I might be falling in love with the boy. Now I knew that his soul was rotten. Sleeping with him again would be like eating my favorite food after it had been left out for days and was covered in squirming maggots. A distressing thought. Part of me hesitated to go forward with Irina's plan at all. But no. I had seen the dog die with my own eyes. There could be little room for doubt. Besides, Irina was wise and, moreover, my best friend. She would not betray me. I would do as she said.

That evening I crept from the dormitory and once again found Gavin waiting at the Whistling Cock. He said he had received my letter. Though it hurt even to gaze upon his face, I smiled and tossed my hair as though nothing were amiss.

Inside his room, I forced myself to think not of what our bodies did, but only of the mission. Soon, his hands were upon me, his mouth was on mine, and our clothes were off. The week before, I probably would have agreed to elope with him, had he proposed it. Now it was as if I were going to bed with a monster.

When he was fully distracted in his passion, I scratched him as Irina had instructed. My nails were long and sharp, and suddenly he had three long gashes on his inner thigh. For a moment he flinched and grabbed my hand away. I was afraid he would kill me, but no. He only laughed and made love to me all the more vigorously.

When it was over, I remembered the wine. I poured two glasses and put the laxative into his. I brought the glass to Gavin. He drank it down in a quick gulp and asked for more. While I was pouring the second, a look of anxiety crossed his face. I could hear his stomach gurgling from the other side of the room. When I turned back around, he was already running for the bathroom. He dove inside and slammed the door.

Working quickly, I took his gold chain, his underwear, and his socks—which were stitched with his initials—and put them in my handbag. Then I left the inn and ran back to the dormitory as quickly as my feet would carry me. It was a moonlit night, but the roads were nearly empty. I hid behind a tree whenever someone came close.

I arrived back with time to spare. Irina was awake and waiting for me.

"You have been asleep all night," she said to me, accepting the underwear, chain, and socks. "This boy, Gavin? You have never met him before. Do you understand?"

"Yes," I told her. "Whatever you say."

It was two days later that it happened.

Irina went missing. She did not show up for morning studio, and by the afternoon the instructors were on the point of calling the police.

Then she emerged from the woods looking like a zombie.

Her presence was announced by screams from the girls milling in the back of the school. Her clothes were rent and muddy, and her face was bloody and bruised. She looked numb. Insane. She was taken to the headmistress's office and did not come out for many hours.

The last time I saw Irina again was when she returned to the dormitory to gather her things. One of the instructors was with her and helped her pack. She did not even look at me. Her face stayed blank and cold.

As she left, she hugged me goodbye. In the instant it took us to embrace, she whispered: "Thank you." This was the only clue that told me she was okay.

It did not take long in the subsequent days for us to hear gossip that Irina had been assaulted by a local boy. Apparently, his family was among the wealthiest and most powerful in the community. The authorities could have been called—and many thought they should have been—but the school wished to avoid a scandal, as did the boy's parents. At first the young man had denied the crime. Yet Irina had seemed to provide indisputable proof—identifying intimate defensive marks made during the attack, and producing shreds of the boy's clothing and jewelry.

The gossip went that the young man's wealthy father had insisted to the headmistress that something could be "worked out." If the issue went no further, he was prepared to make large donations to the school and to Irina's family. Both Irina and the headmistress were quick to agree, and Irina returned to Bucharest a wealthy young woman. Though word of the crime spread privately through the community, it stayed out of the newspapers. The boy's family must have considered this a victory. It was the kind of scandal that, in a few years, would pass out of memory entirely.

For my part, I never heard from Irina again. Except once.

On the occasion of my retirement from the Royal Ballet—what? nearly thirty years ago, now—I received cartloads of gifts from my fans and admirers. One of them—an inconspicuous looking package postmarked from Romania—contained a very large sum of money, with no card or explanation. I did not have to wonder who it might be from. On a whim, I used the money to commission the dancing figures you see before you.

Of course, hardly a day goes by that I do not think of Irina. And wonder, privately, if the boy's chocolates were actually poisoned by her.

Silence.

With the story concluded, I turn back toward my guests.

It is not unusual for Ms. Kvasov's tale to raise objections in a "Now, see here—" sort of way. I brace for them as one might raise an umbrella in anticipation of a sudden summer squall.

"Why that's horrible . . ."

"I don't even like to think about things like that!"

"I guess that's how people behaved. You know, back in the old days."

I smile at this final notion, as if time were something that tempered the harshness of the universe. As if it could!

Ms. Kvasov, it should be said, is also used to these disagreeable reactions. It's clear that she does not take them to heart.

I quickly thank her for indulging us and motion to indicate the door on the far side of the ballroom. I've found that if I do not urge the visitors to move along, they may attempt to press Ms. Kvasov for additional details. They so wish to discover the truth of what happened, suddenly fancying themselves a flock of Sherlock Holmeses.

"Come along, everyone!" I announce. "We have so much of the hotel yet to see! We must leave Ms. Kvasov and her partners to their important rehearsals. They have a performance upcoming, and a lot of work still ahead, I'm sure. If you would kindly follow me in this direction . . ."

I conduct them across the room—away from Ms. Kvasov and her thirty-three friends—and we begin to trudge down the darkened hallway beyond. (Though the visitors are reluctant to go, the unfamiliar environs do make them tend toward obedience. At this point, I'm confident not a one could successfully navigate his or her way back to the lobby. Without their tour guide, they are completely lost.)

Already, I feel the guests at my heels. Good. Whether or not they want to, they follow the lead dog.

I turn slightly, and see that the one closest to me is the redhaired girl.

Dare I?

I dare.

"So, what did you think?" I ask nonchalantly as we creep down the corridor.

"A sad story," the girl says evenly.

"Yes," I say. "An old one, too. Ms. Kvasov . . . I mean. She is not young."

"Still sad," the red-haired girl insists.

"But you know . . . I'm curious about something," I say, stroking my chin pensively. "So many people behaved poorly in that tale. Who do you think behaved the most poorly of all? Surely it was Irina, with her plot to extort money from the tragedy. Or else the headmistress of the school, keen to accept a bribe in exchange for concealing a ghastly crime."

"It was the boy's father," the red-haired girl answers without hesitation. "The father of the rich boy, Gavin. He behaved the worst."

"Ahh, of course," I say. "For offering to pay to keep the crime quiet. I see your point."

"No," the girl corrects me. "For making such a grave decision so quickly, without due consideration. The evidence of the crime was counterfeit, but he just accepted it as true. He should have been more careful."

"Mmmm," I reply thoughtfully. "A grave decision, indeed. Speaking of the grave, at least no one died in Ms. Kvasov's story. That ought to count for something, no?"

"The dog died," she answers.

She says nothing more.

We continue in silence down the hallway.

This one. I must watch her closely.

Detective Click

A small detour takes our group to the western balcony.

Considered by many to be one of the hotel's winningest features, the balcony emerges halfway up the side of the building. The westward-facing vista gives guests a stunning panorama of our fair city, especially when the sun is low in the sky. The balcony is also quite large; it has been able to accommodate entire wedding parties, and many other festive and well-attended events.

The gigantic wooden doors that open out from the hotel onto the balcony are inset with windows, but these are kept covered with long velvet curtains. I pause in front of these curtains and wait for the visitors to accumulate. When all have finally caught up, I pull aside the curtains and throw the doors wide in one dramatic movement. A cool breeze rushes in. The curtains ruffle furiously. Most of the visitors smile. They have been feeling a little bit claustrophobic, and fresh air is just the antidote.

"Please join me outside on the balcony," I say with a grin. They don't have to be told twice, and spill past me in a rush.

"Do be sure to stop at the railing," I call after them. "If you don't, there is a bit of a drop."

When the last visitor is through, I turn and follow them out onto the enormous cantilevered platform. All at once, it is plain that the time of day has gotten away from me. This is not uncommon, but the presence of guests usually mitigates my handicap to a certain degree. Yet as I stare out over the marble balustrade, I see that I have erred profoundly. I had so hoped to present my guests with the glistening acronychal vista of a city tinged by the last embers of sunset. However, the sun has passed away entirely. The sky is black, with no stars that I can see. All that remains is a thin blue line radiating at the horizon's edge.

My visitors are taking it in—despite the darkness, I suppose it may not be an entirely disappointing sight—yet they cluster together in the center of the balcony and do not approach the far edge. After a moment, I realize that this is not because they are following my instructions, but because a stranger lingers there. That is, a stranger to them.

"Detective!" I beam, striding over. The visitors part to let me pass.

Detective Click remains motionless, staring silently out into the distance. With one hand he holds a freshly lit Churchill. With the other he grips the marble railing.

"We have disturbed your evening cigar," I observe. "An unforgivable transgression. For it, you have my apologies."

"No problem," he says in his gravelly voice. "It's a beautiful night."

"Indeed," I tell him. "Detective, as you see we have visitors. Perhaps you would like to say hello."

For a moment he remains motionless. Then, when he moves, it is only to bring his cigar to his lips. Detective Click deliberates.

"Hey," says an impatient voice from somewhere in the throng. "Where are all the lights?"

"Yeah," says another. "What's going on?"

For a moment I do not understand them. I edge my way to the railing and stare down into the nearly abject blackness below.

"They mean the city lights," Detective Click says softly, indicating the scene with his cigar.

"Exactly," responds a visitor. "All the buildings must have their lights off."

"It doesn't even look like the same city!" says another.

I turn back to the guests. Those who had not noticed the phenomenon before are certainly noticing it now. It's true that there are no streetlights twinkling beneath us. Even the ambulatory illuminations usually thrown by automobiles are strangely absent.

I open my mouth to account for this discrepancy.

"A power failure," Detective Click says before I can speak. He turns, now, to face the group. His thick black beard glistens in the cherry glow cast by his cigar.

"Ah, yes," I say, smiling. "That must be it."

"The entire western grid, I'd lay odds," says the detective. "They ought to have it back up in a couple of hours. The folks at power and light are a bunch of jokers."

"Because it looks like the wrong city," one of the guests insists rather aggressively.

If there is any trait I despise, it is rudeness.

"Detective Click is one of my closest colleagues here at the Grand Hotel," I say loudly. "A former officer on the Chicago police department, he now serves the vital function of providing our private security. He is trusted with all matters requiring discretion, and I have never known a situation in which his assessment could not be taken as the absolute gospel truth."

"Well . . . I still think the city down there looks wrong," the wag bleats.

"It was a night just like this when I made up my mind to leave the police force back in Chicago," Click says. "A night like this that brought me here."

"Oh," I say, as if surprised. (I am not surprised.) "Surely that must have been a coincidence. A power failure and your decision to leave, I mean. Power—all sorts of power—can fail unexpectedly."

Click looks at me for a long moment.

Despite his celebrated deductive skills, Click has never shown any sign that he has discovered the real, underpinning truths of the hotel. I do not say that he has not discovered them—only that he has shown no sign. In fact, I find it likely that he has. No one spends very long within these walls—especially alone, as Click often is—without a few things becoming bracingly clear. I can tell that Click is deeply and innately clever. Perhaps he is clever enough to understand that some mysteries are better off left alone.

Click takes another puff on his cigar and begins to speak.

There used to be a house just off 47th Street on the south side of Chicago in a neighborhood called Kenwood. It had a high circular turret on one corner. I did an overnight job there. It looked abandoned, but the police department had rented it to keep tabs on a drug gang next door. From the top window of that turret, you could see right into their house.

I was in narcotics. I had a partner named Lindale. He was a real piece of work. Looked like a buffalo in a gun belt. He was older than me, but had been demoted twice for shooting his mouth off. He always said he envied the Chicago cops of the 1960s who got to beat hippie kids at the DNC, and the cops of the 1910s who had truncheoned people—black and white, but mostly black—during the race riots. He'd been born too late, he always said.

Lindale had problems.

We got assigned to the overnight shift on the house in Kenwood. The thing had started as a short-term bust, but that changed when half the south side gang leaders started showing up for meetings there. No longer was the plan to charge in and get a few collars and hold up some drugs for the TV cameras. Now the idea was to wait for the next meeting of the kingpins. Catch them all at once and decapitate a bunch of gangs simultaneously.

Lindale and I heard bad things about the house from the start. I didn't think much of it, because the complaints mostly came from slackers and bellyachers. Guys and gals who just wanted to meet their quota and go park underneath a tree and take a nap. Those kind of cops.

They said that the house was "fucked up." That it gave you "the heebie jeebies." Probably, I thought, this was simply code for a place where it was hard to not do actual police work.

I remember the moment Lindale and I first walked inside. Our shift started at eleven at night. We brought coffee and snacks. In the car on the way over, we tried to keep our spirits high. When we got there though, the faces of the cops we relieved said it all. They were oyster-eyed and dour. They wordlessly brushed past into the hot summer night, just happy to get out of there.

We settled in and tried to get comfortable.

"What do you think the problem is with this place?" I asked Lindale. "Everybody talks bad about this assignment."

"Well . . . to start, it's hot," Lindale observed thoughtfully, sipping his coffee. "No A/C."

"We want the gangsters to think it's abandoned," I said. "Of course there's no A/C."

"It smells bad, too," Lindale observed.

He was right he house had that old, ghetto smell you reliably found in public housing.

Until recently, Chicago had kept most of its poor in high rise developments. Places like Cabrini-Green and the Robert Taylor Homes. The social scientists had thought they would provide a good option for poor families with no place else to go. Instead, they concentrated poverty and hopelessness and violence. Made it all worse.

At the end of the last century, the sociologists finally wised up. They realized that you wanted to do the opposite of what the high rises had done. You wanted to sprinkle the public housing in little apartments all over the city. Don't let it concentrate and feed on itself. Keep it isolated so it can't get momentum.

In the early 2000s, the city knocked down all of the high rises. Moved the residents to smaller buildings throughout Chicago. It was a tremendous and sudden displacement.

"Do ya think this was one of those houses?" Lindale said, reading my thoughts. "One of the places where they moved . . . those people?"

Lindale was a man who did not try to hide his disdain for the poor.

"Could be," I said.

We sat and drank our coffee and watched the house next door. There was very little to see. Mostly, I thought about the weird smell.

"Do ya think it's coming from the walls?" Lindale asked at one point. "I feel like it's coming from inside the walls."

"Uh, yeah," I said. "I guess."

I didn't really have an opinion on the matter.

A little after one o'clock, I walked to the back of the house to take a piss. I was thinking about what Lindale had said about the walls. In the back of the house, where the john was, the smell was even stronger.

On my way back, I stopped to look in the kitchen. It was empty, with no tables or chairs. There was a stove that looked like it might explode if you turned it on. I saw cockroaches scuttling in the corners.

The wallpaper in the kitchen was peeling, especially above the range. I thought maybe it was from the radiant heat over all the years. I stood there and picked at the wallpaper absently. I brought some of it up to my nose and smelled it. Lindale was right. It was the walls.

No wonder the other cops didn't like being here.

I turned around to leave the kitchen and heard a voice. Clear as day. Clear as you're hearing me now.

"I know your type," it said. "I plugged him at the Ludlow Room. He died easy."

The accent was out of a different time, like someone doing a bad gangster impression.

I looked around for the TV or radio that was obviously on. Detecting nothing, I called to the front:

"Hey Lindale, you hear that?"

"Hear what?" he whisper-shouted back.

I looked all around. Nothing. Was one of the cops from an earlier shift messing with us?

I crept back to our perch by the window.

"Somebody left his radio back there," I said to Lindale. "Or a phone. I heard it talking."

Lindale nodded and looked into his coffee. He peered into its murky brown depths like a seer convinced it might hold portent.

We looked across the street at the house. A light went on, then abruptly shut off. There was no traffic. Some clouds spread over the moon, and suddenly it was very dark.

Then, behind us, I heard the voice again.

I thought maybe only I had heard it, but when I raised my head, Lindale was looking at me.

"That was a voice, right?" I asked.

Lindale appeared uneasy, but nodded.

"Somebody's radio," I continued. "Or a TV or something. It sounded like an old gangster movie."

Lindale put his hand on his service weapon, and crept to the back of the darkened apartment.

"Right there by the kitchen," I told him. "It's coming from somewhere around there."

Lindale returned empty handed.

"Smells awful," he said.

"It's the walls," I told him. "There was a section where the wallpaper peeled off. It's really bad."

"Ludlow Room," Lindale said.

"Huh?" I said.

"It sounded like the voice was saying something about the Ludlow Room."

"Yeah," I told him.

Lindale relaxed.

"Must have been an old movie, then," he said. "My grandpa used to talk about the Ludlow Room. It was right around here, but eighty years ago. Some kinda pool hall."

A few minutes later, we heard the voice again. Lindale was talking, so we missed what it said. It sounded as if someone were right there, ten or fifteen paces behind us.

Lindale stopped talking and we looked at one another.

"Maybe the lighting fixture?" he said. "Or the wiring? Sometimes it can pick up radio stations."

A sudden movement across the street caught my eye. Lindale saw it too. One of the dealers had eased himself outside. He was looking anxiously down the block like he was expecting somebody.

A few moments later a car pulled up. The driver gave a signal, and the man reached through the passenger window and took out something that looked an awful lot like a stick of dynamite.

Lindale had time to say: "Is that. . . ?"

The man hurled the stick through the window of the drug house and it exploded. Moments later, there were gunshots from inside. The driver stuck a MAC-10 out of his window and sprayed the front door when someone tried to open it.

Our radio started squawking like crazy. Lindale drew his weapon and galloped toward the back of the house. I kind of watched him go. I tried to stand up but instead fell to one knee. I looked down and saw a single bullet hole low on my abdomen.

I eased myself over onto my side. Then everything went black.

Power failures happen in the summers in Chicago . . . especially in poorer neighborhoods where the grids aren't good. Enough people running their window units at full blast, and—boom—a ten block radius goes down for the rest of the night. It took me a few seconds to realize that was what had happened.

Outside, it went to total chaos real quick. I could hear an automatic, and at least three distinct handguns.

The energy went out of my body, and I kind of curled up. I tried to turn my head toward the doorway. I hoped that if some paramedics came in, I would be able to see them and call out.

After a few seconds, the shooting quieted down. One final braaaaaaappp from the MAC-10 and it ceased completely. I could already hear sirens in the distance. With my free hand, I put pressure on the hole in my gut.

Then I heard someone trudging up the wooden stairs. I didn't think it was likely to be the gangsters, but I fingered my Glock just in case.

The footsteps reached the top step, and a shadowy figure loomed into view. With all the electric lights and streetlights dead, it was very difficult to see. I began to bring up my weapon—which had somehow become ponderously heavy—but stopped when I figured out it was Lindale. He took a few cautious steps into the room and the moonlight hit him in the face. He wore an expression like he'd just seen his parents having sex.

"Lindale," I called.

He didn't respond. The summer breeze blew through the shattered window and rustled the curtains above me. He said nothing. Didn't even look at me.

Lindale walked to a low bench at the side of the room and sat down. It took me a few moments to realize that he was dead.

The sirens outside drew closer. So many sirens. Like the whole Twenty-First District was descending.

Then there was indistinct movement from the back of the house. I squinted and rubbed my eyes. I was really fading now. Blood was pooling on the floor underneath me. It was a challenge just to hold my head up.

But I still saw them.

A group of five or six people, all men. I could barely make them out. Something told me I could have shined a flashlight straight through them if I'd had one.

The men walked over to Lindale. He kept his head low, like he didn't want to look up at them. They were a strange crew. A couple wore dirty suits and fedoras. One was dressed like an old-time policeman in a plain blue uniform with big gold buttons. Another appeared to be a contemporary gang member, with tattoos up his neck and a bandanna around his head.

They stood beside Lindale. The two men in suits gripped him under the armpits. Lindale didn't resist, but neither did he seem entirely to understand what was happening. They helped him up. It was like watching a concussed athlete getting taken off the field.

Slowly—careful step after careful step—they walked him into the darkness at the back of the house.

Lindale looked over at me once. His eyes met mine. His expression held a terror beyond what I can describe. Then the antiquated policeman gripped his chin hard and turned Lindale's head to face forward again. Then the policeman looked at me. Where he should have had eyes were just holes.

Lindale and the strange group disappeared into the darkness. A few moments later, the lights outside flickered and turned back on. I heard footsteps and a uniformed policeman ran up the staircase with his weapon drawn. I used every bit of strength I had left to call out a nonsense syllable and hold up my shield.

I woke up in the hospital. Some officers led my wife into the room. I hugged her and we both cried. The officers told me my partner "didn't make it." I said I knew that already. A few hours later, the police superintendent and the mayor showed up and shook my hand. The superintendent was stoic and boring, but the mayor was fun and got me to crack a smile. I guess that's how you get to be mayor.

It was a month before I got up the guts to tell my wife what happened.

"Don't say anything to the people you work with," was her immediate response.

I nodded. If I said I'd seen ghosts, I might have to go in for a psych evaluation.

"But is there anyone I can talk to?" I asked her. "I've met some of those local 'ghost hunter' people before. They don't seem like real experts. I want a real expert."

My wife put her chin on her fist like she always did when she was thinking hard. Then she said: "What about Alec Kuttlewitz?"

"Who?" I said, knitting my brow. That name was familiar.

My wife reminded me that Kuttlewitz was a local author who'd become famous by writing books about life in Chicago's toughest housing projects.

"If anybody's seen things in those neighborhoods, it's him," my wife said.

I decided it was worth a shot.

Kuttlewitz had become a professor at the University of Chicago. I looked on the school website and found his address and office hours. I wanted to go in person. Years of police work had taught me that a cop standing in your doorway was harder to ignore than an email.

I went the next day, arriving at Kuttlewitz's office just as a student was leaving. Kuttlewitz was middle aged and wore thin, John Lennon glasses. He had two tufts of hair on the sides of his head, but was otherwise bald. The shelves of his office were filled with copies of his best-selling books. He apparently liked to keep the place dark; the only electric light came from the computer monitor.

"Professor Kuttlewitz?" I asked. "I'm Sergeant John Click from the CPD. Do you have a moment?"

He smiled and said he did. I rested my crutches against the wall and sat down.

"Did you happen to hear about the shootout near 47th and Greenwood a month ago?" I asked. "CPD officer killed. Another gutshot?"

"Oh gee, it was during summer exams . . . but yes, I remember," he said, nodding.

"I was the one gutshot," I told him.

He looked sympathetic for a moment. Then his eyes searched their sockets as he strained to remember more details.

"Quite a few young men were also killed that evening—some by Chicago police—as I understand," Kuttlewitz said icily. "You neglect to mention them, I note."

This was the point where I would normally keep asking questions to stay in control of the conversation. But—as the ivy-covered walls outside reminded me— Kuttlewitz wasn't a perp and this wasn't a traffic stop. I couldn't make him tell me anything he didn't want to.

"That's correct," I answered. "I didn't shoot anybody, though. I was hit right at the start of things. Never even drew my gun."

The writer frowned as though this made little difference.

"What can I help you with, Sergeant?" he asked. "What's the reason for this visit? Did you absolutely need to see me in person?"

Now he was the one trying to question me to death. Perhaps he knew the tactic. The thought made me smile.

"I think we may have gotten off on the wrong foot," I told him.

"Oh?" he said.

I took another glance over at Kuttlewitz's wall of books.

"I'm here today because when my partner was killed in that shootout, I saw his ghost," I said. "We were in a strange old house, and we'd been hearing voices there all night. When my partner died, these ghosts kind of showed up and took him away."

Kuttlewitz said nothing.

"I came here because you're supposed to be an expert on the south side of Chicago," I continued. "In all the research you've done—all the years you've spent in the roughest parts of the city—did you ever see anything like that?"

Kuttlewitz looked straight ahead. He opened his mouth to speak, then closed it and reconsidered. Then opened it again.

"Sergeant . . . I'm a professor of creative writing," he said, as if this fact should end the matter. "I use this office to talk to students about their stories and poems."

"I'm just asking for information," I told him. "Like maybe you saw something once—in a house or in a housing project—that wasn't part of your research. So you might not have written it down. It's not useful to your books, right? But here's the thing: it might be useful to me."

Kuttlewitz took off his tiny glasses and rubbed the bridge of his nose between his forefinger and thumb.

"Of course I've seen things, Sergeant," he said quietly, like a man resigned. "Of course I have. Why would you even need to ask?"

"Like what?" I pressed.

"As you say, it's not part of my research. It's not part of yours either, bye-the-bye. Some things on the south side . . . it's not going to do you any good to go digging them up."

"But . . . you . . ." I stammered. "If you've seen things, can you please tell me? Were they like what I saw? Am I crazy?"

If the lights in Kuttlewitz's office had been on instead of off—or if there had been slightly more sun shining through the two large windows—I would have completely missed the thing that happened next.

The writer's face contorted in annoyance. He furrowed his brow and frowned. As he did this, a distinctive red light began to emanate from his eye sockets. At first, I mistook it for the reflection of his computer monitor. But no. He had turned around. The monitor was behind him now. There were discernibly beams of red light coming out from his eyes.

"These things go deeper than you know," Kuttlewitz whispered. "It is not your place to ask why things happen here. Know your place, little policeman. Go back to wherever you are from."

I sat there, looking into his glowing eyes. They were like small, red coals left in the fire on an overcast day. After a few moments, I stood and collected my crutches. Then I ambled back to my car.

Weeks passed, then months. Eventually I went back on the beat. My new partner was a talkative, rail-thin lesbian named Martha. She was nice. I tried not to think about Lindale more than I had to.

I'd like to say that having a murder in a building would keep anybody from wanting to rent it out, but that's not the case in Chicago. Eventually, though, other forces conspired to undo the place where Lindale died. Suddenly the nation had a president who lived just a few blocks away. Developers wanted to tear down the old house and put up some mixed-use buildings. Pretty soon, that was what they did. The local alderman came and made a speech. It was a big to-do.

A few months after that, I started hearing about what they found when they knocked the place down. Bodies in the walls . . . generations of bodies. Apparently there had been an opening up in the attic where you could drop something—like a corpse—into a crawlspace that ran down between the rooms. Chicago gangsters had being using it since before Capone. They found bodies in there that went back to the 1800s.

When I learned about this, I asked my wife: "Where do the ghosts go when you knock down a haunted house?"

She shrugged and said: "Where did the people go when they knocked down the housing projects?"

I think she had a point. I'm still not sure what it is.

Detective Click takes a long draw on his cigar and falls silent. A gentle breeze blows across the balcony from the dark vista beyond.

"Well, that took a long time," one visitor whispers.

Almost in the same instant, the lights in the city beneath us come back on. The entire party appears cheered by this development.

"There, you see?" I announce reassuringly. "The detective was right, just as he always is. Our municipal engineers now have the matter well in hand."

The group surveys the illumination below.

"Undoubtedly, we have distracted the good detective for long enough," I continue. "The view from this balcony is certainly beautiful, but I think you'll also enjoy the Grand Hotel's reception room. We'll head there next. It doubles as our portrait gallery. While it may lack the majesty of an outdoor setting, some of the portraiture has been known to elicit quite powerful responses from visitors."

I stride over to the doors leading back inside and extend my hand. Most of the group takes the hint and shuffles through. One or two stragglers linger next to Detective Click at the railing.

"I'm just not sure," one of them says. "It doesn't look like the same city from up here, even with the lights back on."

"A trick of perspective," I offer. "Consider how different things look from the window of an airplane."

"Yes, but . . ." the visitor tries.

"I'm quite sure that's what it is," I insist more forcefully. "Now run along, or you may be left behind."

The tarrying visitors take one final, doubtful look over the railing. Then they relent and follow the others back inside.

I give Click a nod. He hesitates, then returns it.

Good old Click.

Once more inside the hotel, I direct the group down the hall toward the doors to the reception room. They swing freely on their hinges, like the entrance to a Western saloon.

"I had a professor with red eyes, once," a member of the group confides. "Suffered from albinism, poor chap. Very sad."

"Oh!" another announces brightly. "Why my cat has the very same condition."

The two smile at one another. In their tiny minds, a bond has been created. I am not above being amused by this, though the pleasure is passing at best.

Then I turn and see the red-haired girl standing next to me. She is smiling as well.

"Did you like Detective Click?" I inquire.

We pause at the doors to the reception room and allow the rest of the group to file past.

"He seemed like a perfectly nice man," she answers. "I think he's confused by his own story, though. He's turning it over in his mind. I bet he figures it out eventually."

I smile.

"I have no doubt that the walls of many Chicago buildings contain bodies," I tell her. "It is a bare, bleak city, with murder often on its mind. I'm sure Click saw much of that in his time as a patrolman. The portion of his tale concerning the writer is difficult to credit, however."

"Yes," the girl replies without hesitation. "But even if that part's exaggerated, Kuttlewitz is still the villain."

The breath nearly goes out of me.

"Truly?" I ask in an astonished tone. (I am less astonished than impressed.)

"Yes," the red-haired girl responds.

"Why?" I ask. "All he did was sit at his desk."

She thinks.

"Because he's . . . fundamentally uninterested in assigning blame."

I cross my arms and frown at her, as if this reply is close to being inappropriate.

"I mean . . . it's not nice to blame people for things," she adds quickly. "It's not polite. But maybe if you're at a university, it's part of what you're supposed to do. Kuttlewitz writes books about problems in the poor part of town, but he never says who created the problems. The leaders and politicians and whoever. He never points to the people who benefit from keeping the poor people poor. He just . . . I don't know . . . says that bad things are bad."

"So maybe he should be a bit meaner?" I wonder, uncrossing my arms. "Meaner . . . and more specific?"

The red-haired girl nods vigorously and smiles.

"I think he makes people feel like the problems will always be there, and you can't do anything about them. But really, you can . . . if you're impolite and point out who is causing them."

I say nothing, but nod thoughtfully.

"Are you okay?" the red-haired girl asks.

"Perfectly fine," I assure her, though my voice is distant.

"I thought I might have said something wrong."

"You did not."

"Oh," she says. "Good."

"I was just thinking . . . it might be fun if you and I played a little game—going forward—for the rest of the tour. Would you like that?"

"What kind of game?" she asks. Her tone indicates caution, but her grin tells me that she is nonetheless intrigued.

"How about this . . ." I begin. "After every stop on our tour, I get to ask you a question. It will be a question about something we have just seen or heard. If you give me the right answer, then everything is fine and the tour continues. Unfortunately, if you give me the wrong answer, I shall have to end the tour then and there. Though that shouldn't be too much of a disappointment, I hope. At this point, you've already seen the hotel's best features. Going forward, I'm afraid it gets a little bit . . . obscure."

"If I'm wrong, does the tour end just for me," she asks, "or for everybody?"

"Oh, it will end for everyone," I tell her.

"That sounds like a big responsibility," she says.

"Well, if you are not up to it . . ." I begin with a sigh.

"I'm definitely up to it," she replies confidently. "This will be fun. I'll see how long I can keep the tour going for."

Despite her decision to end a sentence with a preposition, I am pleased with her enthusiasm.

"Exactly," I tell her. "And if you keep the tour going all the way to the end . . ."

"Yes?" she says expectantly.

I smile.

"There will be special reward," I say.

"What kind of reward?" she asks.

"I think that by the end of the tour—if we get that far—you will probably be able to guess what it is."

This seems to please her. With no prompting, she strides through the swinging doors and into the reception room. I watch her go. A shiver runs though me that has nothing to do with the night air.

Now it begins in earnest.

It has been years since I've had a real contestant for this game—ages—but it all comes back to me now. Very like riding a bicycle. You get right back on.

If the girl answers me incorrectly, it is over. For all of them. Everything ends.

But if she continues to get things right—to see the point of the places and people I am showing her—well . . . that is almost too exciting to think about.

Thus galvanized, I take a deep breath and stride purposefully into the reception room where the tour group is waiting.

Ms. Konig

What is it—precisely—about a gallery of portraits that so contains the power to unnerve us?

Paintings are just paintings, no matter how lifelike. They are oil on canvass. They are immobile. They cannot touch us or speak to us. We hang them on the wall at our pleasure and whim. We can cover them with a cloth, if we like. At every point, we are the ones in control.

And yet. . . .

Their uncanny effect upon us never quite dissipates.

When entering the reception room that serves at the de facto portrait gallery of the Grand Hotel, one cannot help but be startled when the coterie of framed faces first comes into view. The reception room is almost perfectly circular, you see, and so the portraits lining the walls tend to give one the feeling of being surrounded. The expressions on the painted figures vary, but most typically indicate mistrust. Smiles are rare. Genuine-looking smiles, even rarer.

Though they seem uniformly suspicious of the first-time visitor, the portraits are homogenous in perhaps this aspect only. Some members of the gallery are recent additions, painted by artists who are still very much alive, showing subjects that are likewise living. Others portraits give the appearance of possessing great antiquity, and must almost certainly predate the hotel itself.

Because I am sometimes asked, I often start by admitting that the provenance of the paintings in our gallery is not uniformly known. A guest once pointed out that a canvas showing a pale boy bathing in a creek seemed to match the description of a long lost Vermeer. Another swore that the portrait of a wealthy landowner—whose worldly possessions arrayed in the opulent salon behind him seemed to dance in the air as if possessed by spirits—was a dead ringer for a stolen de Gelder.

Errant Dutchmen aside, it is true that most of the paintings predate my time at the hotel (and therefore my knowledge of the circumstances surrounding their respective acquisition). From what I have heard, the reception room became our gallery organically, over time, as different works were hung within. One person placed a portrait, then a different person placed another some years later, and so on. Yet even though the origin of many of the works is mysterious, the collection never gives the impression of a random arrangement. To the contrary; it is clear that the paintings in our gallery have been very carefully curated. The faces that line the walls complement one another with eerie regularity.

Here we see the fat, clowning buffoon, clad in medieval garb, an archaic conical hat adorning his head. Directly adjacent to him, the portrait of the smiling schoolgirl with her head tilted to one side. Her expression seems a direct response to the portly man's antics. To the westernmost side of the gallery, we see a terrifying crone who bristles and bears her teeth like an animal surprised. The figures in the paintings to either side seem to turn away in disgust. Directly across from her on the east wall, a princess or noblewoman from the eighteenth century wrinkles her nose. (Perhaps she finds the hag's appearance distasteful, or perhaps she is unsettled by the knowledge that the opposite canvas shows her own future, however distant.)

Each time I sidle through the swinging doors, the strange panopticon effect of the encircling portraiture is not lost on me. It is as if—even after all these years—I still have not completely earned their trust. They stare back at me silently with the same haunting suspicions.

Yet it is something deeper that brings me unease; the true reason that portraits are so jarring. It is, of course, the possibility that we are the portraits. Perhaps we hang on their walls. In that initial instant of confrontation, we wait for the face in the wooden frame to begin moving and speaking, and to find ourselves frozen into place. That they are the ones in power, and that we must be still forevermore.

Predictably, most visitors have gathered around the largest canvas in the room—a life-sized rendering of a Turkish sultan standing beside a Caspian tiger. The Turk's sword and turban are both cocked at jaunty angles, and the expression on his face is brooding and mysterious. It is the face of the tiger, however, that has always seemed to me the centerpiece of the work. The confusion and madness in the animal's eyes give a clue as to what must have happened moments after this picture was made. The sultan's sword appears more decorative than functional, and there is no reason to believe he was skilled with it. Thus, I think it safe to conclude he gave the giant feline very little trouble when it pounced and began to devour him.

Yet the group is transfixed by the enormity of the canvas. They look it over and nod approvingly, as if expansiveness somehow corresponded to importance. . . .

"This is our reception room, which, over the years, has come to double as the hotel's informal portrait gallery," I announce.

"Ooh, did all of these people stay in the hotel?" asks one woman.

"Don't be daft," says her companion. "There's paintings here from the Middle Ages or before. The hotel didn't exist back then!"

I suck my lips into my mouth, forcing myself to stay silent.

"I've never seen a portrait gallery with the faces in a circle like this," says another. "It's like we're passengers in some sort of ship and they're all looking in through the portholes."

Several cluck in agreement with this description.

"Are any of these paintings valuable?" asks a heavier, middle-aged fellow. "That is, are they painted by famous artists?"

I allow my lips to relax.

"I have been told that some of our works are valuable, yes," I say carefully. "But I'm afraid I'm personally not much of an art historian. I don't know which ones would fetch a high sum at auction, and which hold merely sentimental value."

"Can you tell us anything more about the paintings?" another visitor asks, perturbed by my lack of knowledge.

I bite my lower lip and exhale through the side of my mouth. My expression indicates that I regret not being better acquainted with the pieces on these walls. Suddenly, my eyes go wide as something occurs to me . . .

"I may not be an expert on these canvasses," I answer, "but there's one portrait here that can tell you about itself."

The visitors exchange an uneasy glance.

"What do you mean?" one says cautiously.

"It's a piece of interactive art, I suppose you might say. Allow me to show you."

I direct the group's attention to the southwest corner of the gallery. There, a plain black frame holds a painting of what appears to be a contemporary astronaut. The pleasant-looking woman in early middle age wears an orange and blue spacesuit, and holds a spherical helmet in her lap. The large metal lip of her collar encircles her neck like a medieval ruff. This lends an almost regal air to her appearance. She wears the short, plain hair of a practical scientist, and there is very little makeup on her face. The landscape behind her shows a rocky terrain almost completely obscured by darkness, but the sky above glistens with a vast, endless starscape.

"Ooh, she looks important," one visitor stammers.

"An astronaut . . . why, this must be the most recent picture in your gallery," another helpfully concludes.

I try to conceal my shudder.

"This is a portrait of Isabelle Konig, the famous space traveler and scientist," I explain.

"Never heard of her," one of the visitors says, as if I am too freely assigning her celebrity-status.

"If you look closely at the painting, you may see something that provides a clue to her unique accomplishments," I tell them.

From the corner of my eye, I see that the red-haired girl is now paying close attention.

"The planets behind her are wrong!" a middle-aged man finally cries.

"Very good!" I tell him.

I cast a look at the red-haired girl to say 'Where were you on that?' But then I smile. It is all in fun. (Or so she should believe.)

"You're right!" a second visitor chimes. "There are two moons, and . . . is that the Earth?"

"Indeed it is," I say. "I believe Ms. Konig sat for this portrait directly prior to her celebrated voyage to the red planet. The artist has fancifully positioned her atop the Martian landscape. You'd be surprised how many people never notice, if I fail to point it out."

The visitors nod thoughtfully, but a few crane their necks as though they may have misheard me.

"To Mars?" asks one. "Have we gotten there yet?"

"Oh," I say, as if genuinely puzzled. "Have we? This painting certainly seems to think so."

"I think I heard someone was going," an elderly woman declaims. "You know, one of those space-exploring countries. Perhaps they went already and I missed it? I always seem to be losing track of the spacemen . . . and women too, now. The things they can do with science . . ."

"Quite," I allow after a long pause. "Now if you'll all direct your attention to the wall beside Ms. Konig, you will see a feature that makes this portrait unique."

They look.

Set into the wall directly adjacent to the frame is a small white button. Beneath it—camouflaged in the same color as the wall—is the mesh netting of a speaker cabinet.

"Should we press it?" one of them asks.

"Please do," I tell them. "It plays a message Ms. Konig recorded not long after her return to Earth, intended to accompany the portrait."

"I still haven't heard of her," one of the visitors says. "And I don't remember anybody going to Mars."

"Well . . . try pushing the button," I suggest. "Who knows? The narration might help to refresh your memory."

The skeptical looking man glances all around the group, smiling as though this is silly. Yet he is the closest to the button.

"Go ahead," someone urges him.

"Yeah," says another. "It can't hurt."

He still hesitates.

Then the red-haired girl steps forward.

"Here," she says. "I'll do it."

The young lady walks to the portrait and depresses the round white button. She glances up at me. I silently mouth the words "thank you."

At first, there is nothing but the prolonged *sssssh* of tape hiss. Then we hear the sound of recorded trumpets, as though announcing the arrival of royalty. Then the bright horns fade, and Ms. Konig begins her tale in heavily-accented English.

> The first manned journey to the surface of Mars took three hundred and thirty-three days, from launch in French Guiana to return touchdown in the Indian Ocean. Our vessel was the *Fafnir-2* Mars Exploration Module, propelled into space by a six-stage rocket. The two astronauts aboard were myself, Isabelle Konig, and Njall Thorfinsenn, who was also my husband.

"A husband and wife in space?" one of the guests quips. "Now I've heard everything."

"Please!" I say to shush him. "There is no rewind function on this recording. If you speak over it, we shall have to listen to the entire thing again!"

"A husband and wife in space?" you may be asking… Indeed, it was so. However, we were not selected because of our marital status. The competition to participate in manned spaceflight is great—as perhaps you already know—but Njall and I were both exemplary candidates. We each had two doctoral degrees, spoke five languages, and were in perfect physical condition. We had no children or other attachments here on Earth. It is true that the European Space Agency *may* have smiled upon our being an international couple—I from Germany and he from Iceland—because it spoke to the spirit of solidarity between nations that had made the mission possible. Yet this would not have prevented one—or both—of us from being disqualified if we had been found lacking in any way.

Our selection for the mission was announced in Paris in the fall, with the launch set to take place the following spring. In the time between, we became two of the most famous people in the world. Njall and I would be the first humans to walk on Mars. Overnight, this made us exceedingly interesting to everyone, whereas just days before we had been almost totally unknown. Now people wanted to learn our opinions of every matter—large or small—and our pictures appeared on magazines next to pop singers and diplomats! It was most surreal.

This was, of course, before the tragedy . . .

With spring approaching quickly, it seemed that Njall and I spent every waking moment together. We trained during the days and shared the same bed at night. Privately, we joked that this would be good practice for the long voyage. Three hundred and thirty-three days was a considerable stretch of time to spend with someone in a space capsule—but not entirely unprecedented. A few Russians and Americans had already done more than four hundred days at a stretch on the International Space Station. Yet there was another aspect that made our mission more harrowing. We would be traveling a greater distance from Earth than any human had ever gone.

Spring arrived, and after two launch delays, there was finally an opening in the weather in late May, and the Fafnir-2 successfully took off amid great fanfare. Rocket separation—the most dangerous part of the voyage— went off without a hitch, and once through the Van Allen Belt we settled in for an uneventful journey of about one hundred and fifty days.

We filled our time preparing scientific equipment for the experiments which would commence after landing, yet we could work at a relaxed place. Mostly, we kept up these preparations to stay busy and feel occupied. After the first two weeks, the novelty of floating about and brushing one's teeth in zero-gravity largely abates. There was plenty of time to look out the window at the passing stars.

It was in one of these idle moments that I first spotted the asteroid group. We had passed many in the course of our journey. That was nothing new. Yet something in the arrangement of this cluster of floating space-rock caught my attention. I radioed back to Paris to ask about it.

"It is part of the Oog-Thurmburster Cluster," Mission Control assured me. "Perfectly harmless. It won't come anywhere near you."

"Strange to see such a tightly grouped bunch, no?" I asked.

The scientist on the other end laughed politely.

"You have seen nothing yet," the voice said with a titter. "Just wait until you get to Mars."

I put down the transceiver and peered again out the window at the space rocks beside our vessel. Behind me, Njall emerged from the chemical toilet. That was when it struck me.

"Njall," I said intensely. "That cluster of rocks. It looks like you!"

Njall squinted and smiled, as though I must be kidding around.

"Seriously, come have a look," I told him, pointing to the window of the spacecraft. "It looks like your face in profile. That dark rock halfway down is your nose. The four rocks above make your eye socket. The ones to the left form the crown of your head. It is most convincing."

Njall took his time getting over to the window.

"Um, I don't see it," he said.

"Well . . . the rocks are moving," I told him. "It looked a lot more like you a second ago."

We stared out the window together. Now I had to grant it did not look much like my husband anymore.

"I think you are letting your mind wander when I am not around," Njall pronounced playfully. Then he kissed my forehead.

We stood there like that, looking out of the window for a while. Njall tried to see the rocks the way I did—or rather, the way I had—for quite some time. He was that kind of husband.

Four months later, we descended to the surface of Mars in the Mobile Landing Unit. While the bulk of the Fafnir-2—now unmanned—orbited above, the MLU would land, sprout its wheels, and help us conduct a month's worth of scientific investigations.

The descent through the atmosphere inside the MLU was loud and violent. Our months of preparation had taught me what to expect, however, and I stayed reasonably calm despite the wild jostling. There was one window in front of us through which we could see the red orb getting bigger and bigger below us. I was watching the craters and ancient lakebeds come into view when I saw a cluster of mountains that, for the second time on this trip, appeared to form a portrait of Njall. It was not a perfect version of his face—no, the rocks gave his brow

odd, bony ridges, and his expression looked uncharacteristically cadaverous—but the ultimate impression left
no room for doubt. It was Njall!

"Look there," I called to him, gesturing wildly at the
mountains as our seats bucked beneath us.

Njall looked at me, alarmed, and then peered
through the window in confusion. He thought I was
indicating an instrument failure, or the need for us to
alter our course. I gestured again . . . but now the face
was gone. Just as suddenly as it had appeared, the
formations below ceased to make an outline of my
husband.

I felt silly and did not know what to think. In the
moment, I believed my eyes had been playing tricks on me.

Subsequent events, of course, convinced me to
reevaluate that idea.

There is a pause in the narration, and then a quiet shuddering
sound. Many of the guests will mistake it for more tape-hiss. It has
taken several listenings for me to become absolutely certain that it
is, in fact, the sound of human whimpering.

Moments later, the noise ceases and the narration begins
anew.

In the weeks that followed, we performed numerous scientific experiments, explored over 600 square kilometers
in the MLU, and planted the flag of the European Union
on the planet's face. We spoke via satellite to the political leaders of the world who congratulated us on our

accomplishment. Footage of us on the surface of the planet was beamed to every news outlet on Earth.

It was also during this period that Njall's sputtering cough became noticeable. At first I attributed it to our new daily exertions. Some of the tasks after landing included operating a heavy drill, for example, or transferring large equipment cases to different parts of the MLU. Even though our weight was greatly reduced on the Martian surface, there was still some gravity, and in its pull I could tell that our muscles had atrophied during the voyage.

When it became time to drive the MLU to the edge of Gale Crater—a survey of the giant indentation would comprise the balance of our fourth and final week on the planet—Njall finally began complaining of a generalized weakness.

We put our heads together. What could it be?

There was little chance of his having contracted a virus or bacteria that might have lain dormant for five months. He and I ate the same prepackaged food and breathed the same re-circulated air. There was always the chance of hitting a heretofore unknown radiation belt. But, again, I had had all the same exposures as Njall and felt completely fine.

Mission Control diagnosed generalized exhaustion and told him to rest for forty-eight hours. He managed to stay in his cot for about half of that time, and then insisted the enforced rest was making no difference and returned to work alongside me.

In our final day on the planet, Njall donned his spacesuit and walked to the rim of the great crater alone to collect the last sample of basalt and iron from the deep burrowing drill. Usually, we stayed in regular radio contact when one of us left the MLU, but Njall was uncharacteristically quiet for the duration. I worried a bit—because of his sickness—but respected his wish to work in silence. I hoped that the journey home would afford him the opportunity to recover from whatever ailment he had.

Njall returned to the MLU with the rock samples, yet he remained uncommunicative, hardly acknowledging me as he doffed his spacesuit and retired to the laboratory. Most disconcerting, however, was the look on his face. His eyes were round. Haunted. He had seen something out on the crater that he did not wish to share.

I had an inkling of what it might be. His own face. Represented either in the rocky landscape below, or the stars above.

Several hours later, we made final preparations to leave the red planet. After securing our equipment and cargo, we launched the MLU into the atmosphere where it reconnected with the Fafnir-2. My husband remained silent and increasingly sickly throughout this process. Soon after the initial docking, he collapsed and I put him in a cot. Mission Control advised that they would monitor his vital signs and urged me to continue the preparations for the voyage back to Earth.

After two days of working alone, the ship was in readiness for the journey home. The master thrusters fired on schedule, and we left Mars's orbit. Now, theoretically, I could relax. I hoped to spend my time attending to Njall, who slumbered fitfully in his cot around the clock. Mission Control assured me that his condition did not appear serious, yet they remained puzzled by his sudden weakness and decline.

Six days into the journey home, Njall died while I was asleep.

I was heartbroken. Frustratingly, the situation forced me not to dwell on his passing, but instead to fixate on the new logistical problems it created. Because of the processes involved in disconnecting and reconnecting the MLU—and also the numerous surface samples we had loaded onboard—there was now considerably less room inside the module than there had been on the outbound journey. With the exception of a small privacy door on the lavatory, there was only one small area for sleeping, eating, using the exercise bike and resistance bands, and maintaining the ship. Landing the Fafnir-2 without Njall's help would not be an issue. Probably, Mission Control could have done that remotely, even if both of us had passed away. However, my concern was that I would have to spend the remaining 144 days beside his dead body.

"We've worked out a way you can move some of the carbon samples into the Command Cabin," Mission

Control advised me. "You'll have to Tetris-around the hold containers, but you'll be able to clear out enough space for Njall."

"Okay," I told them. "I'll think about it."

"We're certain there will be room," they advised. "We figured it out exactly, and the computer has checked our work."

"Okay," I told them. "But first I need to sit with Njall for a while."

Mission Control had no response.

The effect of space upon a fresh corpse had not been studied. I can tell you that it was very strange indeed. Njall's sleeping straps kept him in his cot, but his arms and legs still sometimes flailed. His eyes and mouth often opened. Sometimes his teeth would come together with a mighty *chock* sound. It was very disturbing.

I was beside myself with grief and confusion. He was so young. The best doctors in the world had certified him as healthy. Why had he been taken from me so mysteriously? What had happened? What space-sickness had killed my husband, but left me unmolested?

Again and again, I thought of the times I had seen Njall's face—first in the floating space rocks, then in the mountains on the surface of Mars. For several days, I was unable to perform my basic functions aboard the ship. The vessel piloted itself, but several science experiments went entirely neglected.

When Mission Control asked me what was wrong, I replied that I was grieving. Other times, when they radioed to check on me, I simply failed to respond. Sometimes I stared at Njall's body for hours, watching it flap ever so slightly in the weightlessness, almost as if some small part of him were still alive.

After a week, I received a call from Mission Control and chose to pick up. The voice on the other end carried an uncharacteristic formality.

"Isabelle? There is someone here who wants to speak with you."

I was kneeling on the floor of the cabin, just a few feet from my husband's corpse. My eyes were closed. I had been trying to think of nothing.

"The in-craft cameras and recorders have been turned off," the voice continued. "There will be no record of this conversation."

Now I was curious.

I opened my eyes and floated over to my captain's chair. After a few seconds, a new voice came through the speakers. It was Vaclav Wroclaw, the President of the ESA.

An aloof administrator, Vaclav had not touched base during the mission except to congratulate us after touchdown.

"Isabelle, we were not going to inform you of this until you had landed," Vaclav began. "But after considerable deliberation, we have decided that you need to be told. As I think Franz just made clear, we have turned off all shipboard recording devices and cameras. No part of this conversation will ever be known to history. Do you understand?"

I said that I did.

"As we've always maintained, you and Njall were independently selected for this mission because of your remarkable achievements and immaculate qualifications," Vaclav said. "Though it makes for a nice news headline, your status as a married couple was never counted for or against you."

"I know that," I replied.

"You also know that competition for the two positions aboard the Fafnir-2 was as fierce as has ever existed in the history of spaceflight," Vaclav said. "Possibly as fierce as has existed in any human endeavor."

"Yes," I told him. "I know that's true . . . but your tone makes it sound as if the environment was cutthroat and filled with negativity. That was never my experience. There was considerable collegiality between those of us in the program. Everyone wished to be the first on Mars—yes, of course—but there was always a friendly attitude of 'May the best person win.'"

I heard Vaclav exhale deeply.

"There may have been a darker side than you saw," Vaclav said. "You were our first choice for the Fafnir-2, but Njall was not the second. He was, in fact, third, behind Lars Mortensen of Denmark. We were near the point of informing both you and Lars privately—with the formal announcement soon to follow—when Lars's weekly bloodwork unexpectedly came back positive for high renal function. We thought it was a lab mistake, and tested it again. The same result came back. Our doctors were baffled. Lars had been perfectly healthy the week before, but was now showing symptoms of early to moderate kidney disease. We shipped him off to a private medical center and they confirmed the results. With such early detection, the chances for a positive health outcome were very good, and Lars began treatment immediately. His position on the Fafnir-2, however, would have to be forfeited. With Lars out of the picture, we turned to our next choice, which was your husband."

"I never knew that," I said to Vaclav. "I'm glad to hear Lars's disease could be treated. But he must have been absolutely crushed to miss the mission."

"And so he was," Vaclav said. "A few weeks after your touchdown on Mars, he took his life."

"Oh my God!" I sputtered. "How horrible."

"Yes, well . . ." Vaclav said. "There is more to it. A few days ago, a conspirator here at the ESA was wracked with guilt and came forward. He was a scientist who was friends with your husband. He said that when the selection committee's decision was made—but still private—he told your husband what had been decided. Together, they conspired to knock Lars out of the running. They secretly gave him a mild toxin—not enough to kill him, but enough to create serious questions about his physical soundness. Your husband paid the scientist a large sum of money for his assistance in this matter."

My jaw dropped. It seemed impossible.

"No," I cried. "Njall was a decent soul. A kind man. He would never—"

Suddenly, the main display monitor in the Command Cabin blinked on. The screen showed what looked like security footage from a stationary camera mounted on the ceiling of a changing room. There were walls of lockers and long wooden benches set into the floor. A man briefly walked into shot, and then back out again. He was completely nude except for a white towel over his shoulders. A few moments later, another nude man walked into frame. It was Lars Mortensen.

Vaclav continued: "The conspirator shared with us when and how the transmission of the kidney disease was accomplished. We found the video footage to confirm it. This is from inside the men's locker room at the ESA fitness facility."

As Lars toweled off, Njall walked into shot. He was fully dressed, and wore a coat and gloves. He spotted Lars, and approached him. There was no audio, but the men appeared to greet one another. They chatted briefly, then Njall turned to go. As he did so, he appeared to slap Lars jovially on the rump. Lars started, but smiled at Njall and shook his fist in jest. It was all a game.

The video suddenly stopped, and rewound itself to the moment of the playful slap. Then it zoomed in.

"If we look closely at this moment, we can see the injector extending out of your husband's glove," Vaclav said. "A small needle, but impossible to miss from this angle, no?"

For several excruciating seconds, the image lingered on the screen. I could not have sworn to it, but it did appear that a tiny protuberance stuck out from Njall's glove. Then, mercifully, the screen went black once more.

Vaclav continued.

"We are confident that you had no knowledge of this plot, Isabelle. In fact, the conspirator verified that it was Njall's wish that you should never be aware. We now believe that your husband's untimely passing aboard the Fafnir-2 may have been a result of accidental exposure to the poisoning agent, perhaps during the preparation of the injector device. We will not be certain until we can autopsy the body."

Vaclav paused. I stayed silent. I did not know what to think.

"Do you understand what I have told you today?" Vaclav asked.

I nodded. Then, remembering the cameras were off, I said "Yes."

"Do you have any questions?" Vaclav asked.

"When we land. . . ?" I began.

"For the sake of the reputation of the space program—and its funding—it is our preference to keep this matter private. The public will be told that Njall passed away from natural causes during the return flight home. The confessed conspirator has agreed to make a large financial restitution to Lars Mortensen's family, and to serve a term of imprisonment under an assumed pretense."

There was a long pause.

"Would you be willing to support this version of events?" Vaclav asked.

I wondered if I should feel something at a moment like this, but, truly, I felt nothing. My whole world had shifted. There was little to consider.

"Yes," I said flatly. "That sounds fine."

There was another pause. I think the administrator was trying to decide if he believed me or not.

"Thank you," Vaclav eventually managed. "We'll leave the cameras off for a while, in case you need some time to process this. Just buzz if you need anything."

"Okay," I said. "Thank you."

I sat in my captain's chair for several hours, thinking. Now I had so many more questions with no answers. What did this mean for me? For the legacy of manned spaceflight? And what did this say about my choice to love someone like Njall? I knew he was not perfect—no man is—but never had I imagined him capable of something like this. My mind felt numb. I tried not to think at all. Not long after, I fell asleep.

I awoke some hours later to an embrace from Njall.

He was standing behind me and had placed his arms around me in the chair. I could smell his smell and feel his familiar hands on my body.

I turned and looked around the ship. What was happening? Had the last few hours all been a dream? Had we been to Mars yet, or was that a dream too?

In a few stomach-turning instants, it became clear.

This was no dream, none of it. Njall was a conspirator who had used sabotage to get his place aboard the Fafnir-2, and now he was dead as a doornail. Surveying the Command Module, I saw that his body had simply come loose from its sleeping restraints. By pure chance, it had floated behind me and assumed the position of a lover's familiar hug.

I rose from my chair and turned to face the body.

As previously remarked, the effects of zero gravity on the deceased have not been exhaustively probed. I did not know that in the weightlessness of space, a man's arms could part so plaintively, as if intending to show regret. That his eyes could open, and that his mouth could curl into a frown that begged—begged!—for my forgiveness.

My dead husband floated in front of me like that for a full minute. When I did not respond, the longing seemed to leave him. His eyes closed, one after the other. His arms went down to his sides, and he bowed his head as if in shame.

There is tape-hiss and some audible sniffling.

I took Njall's corpse by the wrist and pulled it to the storage bay at the back of the Command Module. Mission

Control had said something about my needing to remove equipment to get him to fit inside, but I found that if I pushed Njall hard enough against the storage boxes and kicked his floating limbs in after him, I was just able to shut and bolt the door.

This accomplished, I told Mission Control they could turn the cameras back on, and informed them that Njall had been stowed.

There is another pause and more tape-hiss. The astronaut's tone changes, as though she has already found the end of her tale.

The remainder of the journey home was mostly uneventful. A time or two it seemed that I heard Njall's body clattering against the door of the storage bay—regular and rhythmic, almost as if there were some intentionality to it. Yet the banging never lasted more than a few moments.

When I forced myself to return to the shipboard scientific experiments, I found it possible to ignore him quite completely.

The tape-hiss continues for a few moments more, then that too falls silent. The visitors look blankly at the quiet speaker set into the wall, then up at the painting again, then, finally, over at me. Most of them are sow-faced, unsure if the tale is finished but afraid to ask.

Off to the side, a large, wide-shouldered visitor—he looks more like a bull than a sow—finds the temerity to offer an objection.

"This is some kind of stunt!" he growls. "We haven't been to Mars. Nobody has. This is a put-on. Either that, or you've got a painting of a lunatic hanging in your art gallery."

"Good sir!" I object, raising my hand.

But he continues: "This is some kind of test for dupes! You bring people here and get them to believe crazy things. Then I suppose you make fun of them later. Well that's just mean."

"Sir, please," I try again.

Other visitors help.

"Look out!" one says.

"Mister! Behind you!" tries another.

Yet, alas, the gentleman will hear no objections. Even as the life sized painting on the wall behind him—a head-to-toe portrait of a Templar leaning against his sword—begins to dangle forward on the wall, and then to descend in earnest.

"Well I don't appreciate—" is all the man has time to add before the heavy frame connects with the top of his head. There is a loud, reverberating crack as the wood splits, and then a second shuddering sound as canvas and splintering wood fall to the floor together.

The man does not appear seriously injured, though he is clearly startled. (His eyes *do* cross momentarily.) The other visitors are shocked into silence. Several cover their mouths with their hands. The large man slowly brings his fingers to the top of his head and comes away with a trace of blood.

I rush to his aid.

"Oh dear," I sputter. "I'm so terribly sorry. I've said for years that these paintings were not always hung with sufficient care. It was only matter of time, really. This is simply awful!"

"You people should be more careful," the man says, a bit disoriented.

"I'm a nursing student; let me take a look," a young female volunteers. I stand and watch anxiously. The man bows his head and she inspects it.

"A nice long cut," she pronounces. "Not very deep."

"Ehh, it doesn't feel too bad," the man says, rubbing at the wound.

"I appreciate your assistance," I say to the young lady, "but we really must have the opinion of a licensed professional. This is how lawsuits happen. Come, we will consult the hotel's attendant physician."

I can be quite persuasive when I have to. The group quickly understands that they have no say in the matter. Taking the injured guest by the hand, I lead him forcefully through the swinging gallery door. The red-haired girl props the fallen Templar's canvas up against the wall, then hurries after me.

The other visitors take one final look at the portraits encircling them. Their uncomfortable stares are returned. Then they too hasten out of the room.

* * *

We head to the Grand Hotel's ancient infirmary, deep within the bowels of the building. Along the way, the lighting overhead becomes sparse. The deeper we go, the greater the distance between overhead fixtures. It is apparent to all that we are now "backstage." That is to say, in a place intended for hotel employees only. The doors along the walls no longer lead to guest rooms.

There is a musty, moldy smell in the air. We take several winding staircases, all of them going down.

In the middle of one such staircase, I notice a familiar face on the step behind me. I clear my throat to indicate that I would like to speak with her.

"It may well be that Ms. Konig was entirely blameless in the tragedy which befell her mission . . . but, despite myself . . . I always come away from that recording with the feeling that she is . . . confused . . . about one or more aspects of her experience."

"Is that your question?" the red-haired girl inquires.

I smile.

"Could Ms. Konig have done anything to prevent the death of her husband during their voyage?"

I glance back at her.

"That is my question," I say.

She considers it, but has an answer by the time we reach the bottom step.

"Yes," she says.

"Yes?" I say.

She stares at me expectantly. I furrow my brow.

"But how could that be?" I ask. "Surely, he had committed his horrible crime of sabotage *before* their craft lifted off. He was already doomed. Cursed. What could Ms. Konig possibly have changed?"

"She could have known her husband better," the girl replies. "She could have talked to him more about the faces she saw. If she had done that, she might have even gotten him to confess."

"And that would have saved him?" I ask.

The girl considers for a moment, then manages: "It's possible."

"You know . . ." I tell her as we continue down the poorly-lit hallway. "I am inclined to agree with you."

She smiles. I pick up my pace and urge along the injured man at my side.

The timeworn carpet beneath our feet gives way, and soon we are walking on bare floorboards. The guests are uneasy. This part of the hotel is unnerving. (I myself am not entirely immune to the sensation, and make a point never to venture down where the doctor lurks unless I absolutely have to.)

At the far end of the hallway is a very large mirror, reflecting back the way which one has already come. From a distance, it tends to give the uncanny impression that the corridor goes on forever. I have reached the mirror a time or two—by mistake, always, because there is nothing to access at the terminus of the hallway—and recognized myself as the strange, dark figure approaching from the opposite direction. It is always exceedingly unpleasant.

Fortunately, we reach the modest, unassuming door to Doctor DeKooning's office long before the corridor's end.

Doctor DeKooning

The visitors stare at the door for a long moment. It is old-looking, grimy, and covered in dust. The knob has been painted the same dull grey as the rest of the door. One might suppose it to be a storage room or janitor's closet, were it not for the small placard set into the wall adjacent.

"Doctor's Office" it reads.

Now there is new reluctance on the part of the injured man.

"Really?" he says, eyeing the placard doubtfully. "Is all of this absolutely necessary? The bleeding has stopped. It doesn't even hurt anymore."

"With respect," I tell him, "neither one of us is a licensed medical professional. And as I value my position within the Grand Hotel, I cannot do otherwise than consult our resident physician. There is protocol to follow. Now if you would all please move aside . . ."

The group which has clogged the slim hallway—similar to lipids that conspire to block an artery—now moves just enough to allow access to the door. I knock loudly. DeKooning is rather deaf.

"O Doctor!" I shout. "There is a patient here to see you! If you are not indisposed, could you please open up?"

My tone indicates that I address someone who is hard of hearing or easily confused. Or both. This does not inspire confidence in the gentleman with the head wound.

There is the sound of movement behind the door. Then something crashing against the ground and rolling for a bit on the floor. Then an unrepeatable profanity is uttered—in German, which protects most of the group—and then the door is unlatched and opened.

Dr. DeKooning stands before us, a gentle man with a gentle face and disposition. He is all of eighty-two years old. His hair, though thin, is still extant. His nose is like a wizened apricot, and it supports a tiny pair of wire-rimmed spectacles. He wears black trousers, a white dress shirt, and a pair of red suspenders that look as timeworn as he.

"Yes, hello, come in," the doctor says with a smile.

"Forgive our disturbing you at this hour, Doctor DeKooning," I say as the entire group begins to shuffle inside his combined office/examining room. "We have visitors, as you see, and one was just struck by an unstable portrait up in the gallery."

The doctor tents his fingers and nods, as if this sort of thing happens all the time.

I point to the injured man. Somewhat embarrassed to be the center of attention, he bows before DeKooning to show his wound. The doctor adjusts his spectacles and begins rooting through the man's hair like a gardener searching for a lost implement in the grass. The tail end of the tour group enters and the last one closes the door. Because the quarters are so tight, they are forced to encircle the doctor and his patient quite completely.

"It is nothing," the doctor replies after a moment. "A few stitches only are required."

"Oh," says the injured man. "Should I find a hospital?"

"No," DeKooning says absently. "That, I can do here. After three weeks, you will—as they say—'follow up' with your own physician to have them removed."

"Oh," the man says uneasily. "That's nice of you. Thanks."

The visitors move aside as DeKooning slowly leads his patient to the back of the examining room. There, a metal table and several cabinets filled with medical supplies are waiting. (There is a door beside one of the cabinets which leads to the doctor's private quarters, but there, I have never ventured.)

DeKooning bids his patient sit on the table. The man obeys, and DeKooning pulls on a pair of gloves and activates a bright overhead lamp. Then he adjusts the light close to the injured man's head, giving him something of a corrupted halo effect.

"This table looks antique," the patient says as the metal groans beneath him.

"I am confident that it will support your weight during this short procedure," the doctor replies, now going for a needle and some thin, black thread. "At least, probably it will . . ."

DeKooning gives the rest of the tour group a wink. Many of the visitors smile back. One even guffaws. Yet at least two of them do not smile at all. They are the ones concentrating on the glass specimen jars on the shelves behind the doctor.

"'Ere," says one. "What's that 'orrible thing?"

"Mmm?" intones the doctor, not looking up.

"Those jars behind you," another says. "They've got what look like dried up body parts floating in them. The one on the top shelf has an entire head! And there's a jar of eyeballs . . . most of which are staring right at me!"

"But look 'ere," says the original objector. "That big jar on the middle shelf. It's got a little baby in it. And what looks like manure. And plant roots. And crawling worms. And…a bunch of other stuff…I don't even know what! That's 'orrible, it is!"

We all look. The objecting guest is—more or less—correct. A small lifeless newborn appears to reside within the large jar, surrounded by all manner of strange organic material—some of it moving. The injured patient attempts to look as well, but DeKooning gently restrains him by the head.

"Please sir," the doctor says. "I must ask you to remain still during the procedure. You can look at my specimen jars after-wards, yes? My hand already shakes somewhat, you see. So it is better if you do not move at all."

"Okay," the injured man says doubtfully. "But tell me what everyone else is looking at."

DeKooning adjusts the overhead light once more.

"*Homunculus,*" the doctor intones. "It is a relic of another age. Early European physicians believed that a tiny human could be grown external to the womb of a woman if the correct combina-tion of organic factors were introduced."

"Wot, leaves, and mud?" one of the visitors asks skeptically.

DeKooning appears unfazed.

"Yes," he says. "And Mandrake root. And the ejaculate of a man who has died by hanging. And other things yet. You see, I am something of a collector of items from different schools of medical thought."

"Just make sure you use the modern stuff on me," says the man on the table.

"'The modern stuff'?" DeKooning replies as he threads a needle.

"Yeah," the man says. "You know. The new stuff. What they use now."

"Ah," DeKooning says, carefully attaching needle to thread. "And you shall have it! But it may interest you to note that it is only in recent years—given the long span of humanity—that 'modern medicine' has been associated with 'most superior medicine,'" DeKooning adds cryptically.

"What?" the patient says. "Everybody knows that each year medical science gets better. It improves bit by bit. It's always a little better than it used to be."

"Mmm," DeKooning hums noncommittally, surprising the patient with the application of an antiseptic salve to the wound. "Yet it was not always so. Many were the classical physicians who envied knowledge lost to antiquity. In the time of homunculus, the physicians of Europe were quite aware that healers in previous eras had skills that far surpassed their own. Avicenna's work in the ancient Arab world is one example. Or the learned doctors of the Venetian Empire at the turn of the first millennia. Even the ancient Greeks—when it came to certain diseases and conditions—were known to have superior curative powers then lost to the Medieval doctors."

The man on the table makes no reply, but it's clear from his expression that this idea does not still well with him. DeKooning finishes cleaning the wound.

Then, from just behind me, the red-haired girl pipes up.

"Is there anything they knew how to do back then that we still don't know now?"

DeKooning is poised above his patient—needle and thread in hand—like a conductor ready to signal the opening note of a great symphony. Yet the girl's question seems to disarm him, and he lowers his implements.

"That," DeKooning says, "is a very interesting question. And a very bright one. Who knows, young lady, you may have a future in medicine."

The red-haired girl glances over at me, pleased with herself. I roll my eyes and look away. It takes less than she imagines to amuse DeKooning and, besides, we were all once "future doctors" at some point, were we not? Usually just after receiving slightly above average marks on a remedial science exam.

"If you like, I can relate my own modest experiences with that question," DeKooning continues. "It might be a good idea if I do. I find that talking aloud, even to myself, places me in a kind of trance in which my hands become much steadier. For, as it stands . . ."

DeKooning extends one of his hands. Indeed, a small tremor soon becomes discernible.

"Anything to keep him steady, I say do it," opines the man on the table.

"Very well, doctor," I say. "It appears the floor is yours."

With the visitors crowding around in a circle—very like ancient medical students observing a master in an operating theater—the doctor begins his surgery, and his tale.

When I was young, my family purchased a small estate on the edge of the Black Forest near Lahr in Southwestern Germany. The lands had once belonged to a rustic nobleman. Judging from the stories and tales passed down by the local peasant families, he must have been a very evil man.

Most of the accounts were far too fantastic to believe—that he bathed in the blood of murdered girls, that he held banquets in his great hall attended by devils and demons, that he used a maleficar to place a curse on a rival family causing their children to be born disfigured; missing eyes, fingers, and toes. These local yarns were obviously farmers' fantasies, but they likely hinted at the actual misdeeds this blackguard had committed hundreds of years ago. He had almost certainly had his way with peasant girls, and there were extant records of the crippling taxation he had imposed on those working his lands. The fact that those subject to his wrath had chosen to embellish a bit was certainly no surprise to us.

When my family moved in—myself, my mother, my father, and my only brother, Hans—we committed ourselves to making the old manor a place of light and joy. We consecrated it with wonderful parties, festive community gatherings, and loving acts of charity. My dear parents did their best to dispel any ghost that might have remained from the old days of the wicked nobleman. And it seemed we had succeeded. Even the gruff locals eventually warmed to us.

In the back of the estate, set far against the trees, was an ancient stone well. Other than two small outbuildings and the stables, it was thought to be the only construction on the property remaining from the time of the evil nobleman. The well was mossy and overgrown with weeds. It no longer drew any water, and my brother and I were cautioned—perhaps over-cautioned, it now seems—never to risk falling into it.

My tale really begins in the summer of my twenty-second year, when I was home from my medical studies in Bonn. Four years my junior, Hans was likewise home from school. Though I very much thought myself a grown man—many in the community already addressed me as 'doctor'—seeing Hans always had the effect of making me feel thirteen again. No sooner were we both returned to the estate than we resumed a regimen of horseplay, jokes, and athletic contests. We rode together in the mornings, played football with the local boys most afternoons, and stayed awake late into the night sharing stories—most of them exaggerated—of women and derring-do.

The fateful day began like any other, with a morning ride through the forest. Then, after lunch, Hans bet me his new hat—which I very much fancied—that I could not hide in any location on the estate and remain undiscovered by him for more than an hour. His bet was that if he found me, I would be responsible for the upkeep of his horse for the remainder of the summer. But if I remained undetected, I could have his hat.

It felt like a safe bet, and I agreed without deliberation. Enlisting a butler to act as our referee, we decided that Hans would wait in the dining hall under the butler's watch while I was given fifteen minutes to hide. Then he would be released to come and find me, and the butler would keep the official time. In return, Hans wished that I should whisper the location of my hiding place into the butler's ear. This would prevent me from cheating by moving to different locations over the course of the hour.

"Come on, brother," Hans said, giving me a playful slap on the back. "You don't mind a rule to keep it honest, do you?"

I assured him I did not, but then paused to think. Where would I hide for an hour undetected, and so obtain my brother's hat?

Hans and I were natural explorers. Throughout our childhood, we had searched every inch of the enormous house and its lawns and outbuildings. Moreover, we always shared our findings with one another. Whenever one of us independently discovered a new opening for a servant's entrance or an interesting old tree stump in the forest, we could never keep it a secret. In fact, I could think of only one place on the grounds where I had been and Hans had not. And it was perfect for this contest.

One summer when I was fifteen, I had carefully lowered myself into the ruined well at the edge of the forest. Hans had not been with me that day, but rather in his bed fighting a flu bug. So while Hans sipped chicken broth and dozed, I crept down the mossy opening and explored the darkness beyond.

It was rather disappointing. A flick of my flashlight showed me a bed of uneven stones at the bottom, and I stood on them with little difficulty or peril. Some of the larger stones looked intentionally placed in a sort of star-shape. Presumably, this had served an architectural function back when the well worked. To one side of the well's wall was a small nook—roughly man-sized—containing only mossy rocks and mud. No pirate treasure. No dragons. Nor any of the other exciting things that a fifteen year old boy's reading list assures him are to be found in unexplored subterranean depths.

Disappointed, I extricated myself with no great difficulty, and never breathed a word of it to anybody.

But now, the rules of our contest forced my hand.

Dare I? Though we were now grown, beer-drinking, womanizing men, our parents would still be furious if they knew what I proposed to do.

But that hat! The elegant leather trim; the bright flash of the brass buckle; the gentle indentation in the crown. I had to have it!

"I will hide for the next hour in the old well on the edge of the forest," I whispered in the butler's ear.

The butler, who knew the family rules, cocked his head to the side and raised a hairy eyebrow in concern. I raised my own eyebrows—both of them—and stared down my nose, wordlessly reminding him I was almost a doctor and would someday be head of this very manse.

And if he should desire to remain employed here after my parents passed on. . . .

The expression seemed to work. The butler shrugged once, and nodded to Hans. Hans smiled and asked the butler to begin timing. Then Hans shouted "Go."

I went. The game was afoot!

Still struggling to digest the heavy lunch in my stomach, I left the dining hall through the kitchens at a good clip. Many corridors led away, so this did not provide Hans with any clue to my ultimate destination. I exited the estate through a side door and I looked at my watch. Thirteen minutes left. It would be no great challenge to go straight for the well before time elapsed, but it had rained the previous evening, and my footfalls would be visible in the wet grass. Such an error would lead Hans directly to me. Thus, I took a circuitous route. I headed first to the stables, then to the garage, and then made for the edge of the forest at a point over a hundred yards from the well.

Once inside the treeline, with my steps unnoticed amongst the leaves and detritus, I picked my way over. Looking at my watch again, I saw that my deceptive backtracking had taken more time than I'd first supposed. My fifteen minutes had just expired. Drat, I thought. If Hans chances to look out one of the rear-facing windows, the entire jig will be up! And no hat and a whole summer of mucking-out the stable of a horse that isn't even mine!

I sprinted the rest of the way to the well. Briars poked me and branches scraped my forearms, yet I hardly felt it. I concentrated only on my final destination. Now and then I looked up to check the windows of the mansion, offering silent prayers that I would not see Hans's face staring back at me.

With a great sense of relief, I sat down on the ancient lip of the well and swung my legs inside. My feet dangled for a moment over the pile of jutting rocks which I would use to descend into its depths. Then, suddenly, a section of wall gave way beneath me. I tumbled forward, sustaining several injuries, including a painful blow to the forehead which caused me to lose consciousness.

Our branch of the DeKooning line has always tended toward corpulence. My years away at school had involved considerable amounts of sausage and bread and beer. Who was I to think that the stone lip of the well—that had barely held my weight seven years before—would support me? It was the act of a fool, and I paid dearly for it.

The cessation of consciousness was quick and utter. When I awoke, I had no sense of what was happening—or, indeed, what had happened. I knew I was at the bottom of a well, but it was several minutes before I could recall the game with Hans that had led me to my current state.

It was also disorienting to find that there were several feet of water nearby. By chance, my tumble had launched me into the mossy nook at the side of the well, which was now just above the waterline. With some horror, I realized that my accident had nearly been a fatal one. A few inches in the wrong direction and I surely would have drowned.

I had no memory of my parents saying they planned to bring the well back into working order, but I had very little memory of anything at that precise moment. Perhaps they had told me in a letter and I had forgotten.

I inspected myself and found nothing beyond a few bruises and scrapes. I probably had a concussion, but counted myself fortunate that nothing more serious had befallen me. The sky had grown darker, but was not completely black. Sunset. I had been out for many hours. Hans and my family would be alarmed. I must go to them immediately.

I began to use the pile of craggy rocks that spilled down the side of the well to climb back out. Here, I encountered my first considerable surprise.

From halfway up the pile, I could see that the lip of the well had been repaired. Instead of broken or breaking mortar, it now featured brand new walls of stone. I could not understand. Had someone rebuilt the well while I slumbered below? Had I been out for longer than I thought? For days?

This gave me an eerie sensation, yet it was nothing compared to what awaited as I hoisted my frame up from the darkness and gazed out across the familiar lands beyond.

Most of my family's estate was, quite simply, not there. The main house had been replaced with an oblong structure like a medieval longhouse. The wooden horse stables remained, but the garages were gone entirely. Several large tents had been erected around the edges of the property, and several unfamiliar looking people were cooking inside one of them with what I presumed was a firepit. The glow was most distinct.

I stared for a long, long time. Obviously, I had fallen into the well on my parents property and then . . . been transported to another well, on property that looked similar to the grounds owned by my parents? Or something like that?

After a few moments, I realized that a person far across the grounds was waving at me. I panicked, and ran into the woods.

Here, another horror, for the woods were *my* woods. There could be no doubt. These were the same hills and trees that I had played among since childhood. And yet they were changed. What I knew as an empty creek bed was a free-flowing stream. The land was thick with trees, but they were not quite the ones I knew. Towering pines and strange, twisted beeches covered the Earth where they had not been before. Yet the landscape itself remained somehow familiar.

Then I came upon the injured man . . . and my predicament began to make an awful sort of sense.

It started with a moan. A human moan. As the sun threatened to set and cloak me entirely in darkness, I heard what was distinctly a human groaning in pain somewhere ahead. Much alarmed, I searched until I found a gentleman in early middle age slumped at the base of a tree. He had a badly dislocated shoulder, probably as the result of a fall. He was looking up at the sky, seemingly unaware of me.

In the oncoming night, it took me a moment to discern his strange clothing. His brown, muddy trousers were made of the crudest fabric and stank. His shirt was held fast by a rudimentary button as a child might design. On his head he wore a knitted cap with large flaps that hung over each of his ears.

I stood there, wondering what to do, until the man's eyes found me. He looked me up and down. Then, most troubling of all, he began to speak.

His words were not gibberish, but they were not entirely German. His accent was beyond placing. I took him for a foreigner, struggling to communicate in half-remembered words of my language. I tried English, French, and Italian, all to no avail; the man shook his head at each one, continuing to speak in his pidgin-German and occasionally to gesture at his injury. Plainly, I had to help him. I was not a full physician then, but popping an arm back into place was within my abilities. Further, if I did not assist him, he might come to more serious harm. These woods were full of wolves that could savage a wounded man. Even as the thought occurred to me, I seemed to hear them howling in the distance.

I crouched beside the man and made clear through gestures that I meant no harm. Up close, his stink was enormous. What was his story? A homeless person who lived in these woods year-round? A mentally handicapped escapee from an asylum? Clearly, this gentleman needed to have his faculties examined by a professional as soon as possible.

I took the man's arm in both hands, braced my foot against his side, and tugged hard. The errant limb slid easily back into place.

After an initial cry of pain, the man seemed pleased with the result. He tenderly rotated the arm in his socket, testing it. I wanted to caution him not to overextend himself or pop it out again, but it was difficult to communicate this idea. Mostly, I patted his shoulder and made gentle, pacific noises. The man shook my hand and began to babble again in his strange half-tongue.

My good deed accomplished, the unpleasantness of my situation came crashing back. Where was I? What had happened to my surroundings? Was I on my parents' property or not?

As the strange man continued to spout effusive thanks, a cold realization crept over me. I suddenly focused on his words with great intensity. He was not speaking a pidgin-version of my own language, I realized, but rather Middle High German! That version of the tongue had not been used for five or six-hundred years.

My legs went weak and I leaned against the tree. The man saw this change in my demeanor and put out his hand to steady me. It all made sense now. The reduction of my parents' estate to an ancient-looking longhouse. The restoration of the crumbling well. The strange man's garb and tongue and odor.

It could all be explained . . . yes . . . by my having traveled back in time.

"Ow!" the man on the table objects as DeKooning completes a stitch. "That one hurt. Watch your shaking hands, eh?"

"My hands are quite steady now," the doctor returns. "I believe that you moved."

The patient's expression indicates he knows this is fully accurate.

"Yes, well . . . time travel?" the man on the table says. "You can't expect me to be still when I find out the guy stitching up my head believes in time travel, can you?"

"You have not heard the end of the tale—or even the middle," the doctor observes, lifting his hands away for a moment. "Perhaps a rational explanation exists after all."

"Outside of you stumbling into a one-man Renaissance Fair, I don't see how it can," the patient objects, shaking his head.

"Do you trust me?" the doctor asks with a grin to the on-looking group.

"What choice do I have?" the man says. "You've got a needle and thread still in my noggin."

"Yes," DeKooning agrees. "I do. Now please remain as still as you can for the remainder of the procedure. I will try to impart any further surprises as gently as possible."

His patient thus cautioned, Doctor DeKooning continues.

For the second time, I lost consciousness. The enormity of what had befallen me was so great that I fainted dead away.

I awoke on the back of a wooden cart. It had been pulled to the door of a ramshackle hovel with a thatched roof and circular door. The man who had dislocated his arm stood in front of the house, talking to another man with a long white beard and a skullcap covering his bald head. I assumed that I was the subject of their conversation, for they gestured at me, and at one point the first man seemed to pantomime my pulling his arm back into place. The other nodded thoughtfully. After a moment, they noticed I was awake.

I rose from the cart and scanned the scene for any new evidence that it was not the year 1400. To my dismay there was only more to confirm it. The cart beneath me was exceedingly crude and made use of wooden pegs instead of screws and bolts. The small house bore no trace of an antenna or utility connection. The road was well trod by horses and men, but not paved. Most damningly, our only light came from candles and torches.

The two men approached. The bearded one opened his mouth to speak, but what emerged was, again, the nearly incomprehensible German of the early Middle Ages. Though I could make no sense of what he said, his tone was gentle and something about it put me at ease.

Stunned—and still somewhat concussed, I think—I allowed myself to be helped into the strange little house.

Inside, it was dark and hard to see. A one-room arrangement, there was a bed, a firepit, two chairs, and even a small library of books. Against one side of the room was a great collection of jars with large cork stoppers. They contained everything from feathers to mushrooms to moss. There were small knit sacks of what looked like grain or salt or gravel in the corners. The beams of the roof were low, and small metal totems dangled down from them on strings. The house smelled earthy, like a forest floor—not unpleasant, but somewhere in the mix of scents I also detected the odor of a sickroom. Soon, I saw why.

There was a straw pallet tucked against one of the walls. Lying on it was an old person with yellowing skin.

The man in the skull cap was a doctor, or what I understood passed for one in these dark times. My History of Medicine course in my first year of medical school had not dwelt long on the Middle Ages. What I could recall was reflected in the trappings of this one-room physician's practice. Magnetism and metals used to treat venereal disease; the known intercession of devils and the spirit world into a patient's wellbeing; and, of course, the underpinning notion that most maladies arose from an imbalance of the four humors, blood, phlegm, and black and yellow bile.

Indeed, as I looked more closely at the person on the pallet, I spotted a dish of red liquid on the floor nearby; he or she—it was impossible to tell—had been recently bled. In the moment, there was no way for me to diagnose what might actually be wrong with this person. However, whatever ailment lingered, bleeding was only likely to shorten the patient's life.

While I took in the strange sights around me, the first man departed and the doctor began to mix a series of compounds with a mortar and pestle. Moments later, he approached me and—still wearing a kindly smile that I have no doubt was genuine—attempted to apply it to my many cuts and scrapes. Again remembering my History of Medicine class, I shrunk away.

The "tonic" applied to wounds by Medieval physicians was usually a mix of bird dung, mummia (crushed dried corpses), and herbs. This was one of the worst things you could do for a wound, but—to the Medievalist fractured way of thinking—it made a kind of sense. These primitive doctors had never seen a serious wound that did not grow infected. Thus, infection was assumed to be a necessary step in the healing process. By prompting the inevitable infection with the help of dung, the physician believed he was only inducing the first step to healing.

The bearded man before me smiled and raised his hands as if to say he would not press the matter. Turning back to the table, he put the mixture away. He spoke in gentle tones, but I made out only the most basic gist of what he intended to say. He wished to help me, he said. And even though I was a stranger, I had nothing to fear from him.

Again, this kindness felt genuine.

I could not stay where I was. Begging the doctor's pardon, I excused myself and left the cabin. Outside was a darkness like I had not seen in years. No manmade lights polluted the sky. The stars above me twinkled with an almost unbelievable incandescence, and the moon's craggy face rose giant and near.

I guessed—accurately, it turned out—that I could not be far from the well. By the light of the moon, I picked my way through the familiar-feeling countryside until I found a valley that led back to my point of origination. My desperate hope was that that if I slept in the well once more, I might awaken back in the present day.

And you know . . . I was right.

I found the well and lowered myself back into its murky depths. I crawled back into the small nook and closed my eyes. There I remained—exhausted and famished, with my eyes tightly shut—until the following afternoon.

When my wristwatch showed that a full day had passed since I had first hidden in the well, I allowed myself to roll over and observe my surroundings once more. The bottom of the well was dry again, and I could see the strange pentagram stone arrangement. The wall above me was as crumbling and decrepit as I remembered. I carefully climbed out and was thrilled to behold my family's familiar mansion rising from the grounds again.

No sooner did I exit the well than I saw Hans stalking across the lawns. I hailed him with an enthusiastic shout and ran over. He stopped and looked at me with a strange expression.

"Hans!" I cried, running up to him.

"Decided not to play, then?" he asked, puzzled.

"What?" I said.

"You are not hiding. You do not want my hat after all?"

"I . . . I have been hiding for . . ."

Hans indicated his watch and explained that about twenty minutes had elapsed since the butler had told him it was time to begin looking. I would have declared it impossible for anything to leave me more stunned, but this did it. By my own reckoning, I had been gone for a day. To the rest of the world, I had been inside the well for little more than fifteen minutes.

Hans noticed my distracted manner, and also my bumps and bruises. I told him I needed something to eat and drink, and then to lie down for a very long time.

"But . . . we just finished lunch!" he protested with a laugh.

I headed for the kitchen, consumed an enormous amount of ham and cheese, and then fell into my bed as though I had not slept for a week.

For days I wondered if the strange adventure had been but a dream. I had returned with no physical evidence of my journey except the mud on my clothes.

I said nothing to Hans or my parents about what had transpired.

An older and wiser man would have quickly resolved to fill the well with concrete, and to forget all about the matter. I was neither old nor wise. The summer dragged on. My scrapes healed and I grew increasingly bored. Despite my daily exercises with Hans, I soon found I missed women and cities and adventure. Before long, my thoughts returned to the well.

I wondered: If I crawled inside again, would I experience more time travel? Would I awaken back in the same period, or at some other time? Could there even be a risk of going forward in time? Some part of me had to know.

Before the summer had reached its halfway point, I was once more back inside the well. I recreated the conditions of my previous journey as closely as possible. Instead of knocking myself unconscious, I took a powerful sleeping aid. When I awoke from my chemically-induced slumbers, I found myself again inside a restored well with water at the bottom. I emerged from it, and beheld the familiar ancient longhouse in place of my parents' home.

This second adventure, though brief, nearly cost me my life. Moments after I exited the well, a group of men near the longhouse saw me. They began shouting and motioning. When I did not respond, several produced pikes and swords. I ran into the underbrush. Only my knowledge of the nearby caves and crevasses saved me. I hid for the better part of an hour while this team of angry men scoured the forest. When I felt sure they had given up, I slunk back to the well and crawled inside. Another sleeping pill, and the next day I awoke back in the world I knew. No time at all had passed.

I retired to my room, again telling no one of my adventure. Despite the peril, I was thrilled beyond description with this second successful trip. I quickly began to plan a third.

Many in my profession have entertained the fantasy of traveling to a less advanced era when their knowledge of today's medicine would make them seem a demigod possessed with miraculous healing power. As the summer wound on, I realized I had the opportunity to make that fantasy a reality.

I planned it very carefully. Researching the clothing of the era, I fashioned myself a crude approximation of a doctor's garb. In a large burlap sack, I packed all manner of modern salves, medicines, tonics, and surgery equipment. Everything a medical student could get his hands on. On the afternoon appointed, I once again crept away to the edge of my family's grounds and lowered myself into the well. I swallowed a sleeping capsule and laid myself on the mossy nook. Several hours later, I awoke in the early fourteen hundreds.

We are finished, incidentally.

It takes the patient a moment to realize that he has been directly addressed.

"Oh," the man says, rising from the table. "Thank you."

DeKooning carefully places his needle and thread in a metal dish next to him. Then he pulls of his gloves, throws them in the trash, and turns to face the group of visitors. He arches his eyebrows, as if surprised that they are still standing there.

"Yes?" DeKooning says.

The homunculus in the jar looks over one of his shoulders, perhaps an angel or devil, or something else entirely.

"So what happened?" one of the visitors asks.

"Yeah, tell us," says another. "What happened when you went back in time again?"

"Wait, did you actually go back in time?" says another still.

DeKooning waves the questions away.

"But the procedure is over. The wound is closed. There is no need to steady my hands."

Ahh, DeKooning! What a scoundrel!

I wait patiently while the visitors do their best to cajole him into finishing the tale.

"Perhaps . . . if you insist," the doctor relents after more of their pestering. "There may be one or two points of interest in the remainder. Very well."

I exited the well carefully, taking pains to avoid being seen, and made my way back to the modest home of the doctor. I didn't know how much time passed in this other world between my visits, yet the doctor recognized me and I was welcomed back into his home. The person on the pallet was gone, but two new patients were waiting.

In the hours that followed, I tried to explain to the doctor that I was also a man of medicine. He seemed to understand what I was trying to say, but remained cautious—if still good humored.

I turned to his new patients. One was a young woman who had broken her leg. The medieval doctor had done a remarkably good job of preparing a plaster cast, one of the few effective treatments understood by physicians of his era. He had also placed an amulet around her neck with a square of tin tied at one end. Judging by the stains on the corners of her mouth, I guessed he had also had her ingest something, with an eye to speeding healing or controlling pain.

I inspected the doctor's work and nodded repeatedly. Though made from inferior material, the cast had been carefully crafted and was sound and strong. The woman might even walk normally one day. I crushed two powerful pain tablets into a powder, mixed it with some fresh water from a container in my sack, and helped the woman to drink it. The doctor watched carefully, but did not stop me. A few minutes later, the expression of discomfort seemed to leave the young woman's face and she began to slumber peacefully.

I turned my attention to the second patient. An older man, it was clear that his ailment involved the respiratory system. His breathing was labored and his chest quite congested. His forehead and cheeks were stained with deep black grime. I guessed he was a miner, and that years of exposure to subterranean gas were behind his condition.

It was not clear how the doctor was treating him, aside from hanging several large amulets around his neck. I looked at the doctor, who shrugged and bit his lip—a universal way of expressing that there was little to be done for this one. I was inclined to agree—though without diagnostic equipment from my own era, it would be impossible to know for sure.

In the end, I tore part of my burlap sack into a rag. I then placed a healthy dollop of powerful menthol cream on the rag, allowing it to soak thoroughly. The doctor's nose perked up at the minty scent, and he looked on with great interest. Now, quite obviously, he began to believe that I might have some medical knowledge after all. I placed the soaked rag just under the man's nose. His eyes widened, and for a time he did seem to breathe more freely.

I rubbed my chin and considered if there was any-thing else to be done. The amulets around the man's neck seemed as though they might make breathing more difficult, and I stooped down to remove them. Only here did the doctor intercede. He shook his head and gently pulled my hands away. I decided not to press the issue, and left the charms intact.

Through these small actions alone, I seemed to have gained the trust and respect of the old physician. As we feasted on roast rabbits that evening, he invited me to stay with him—effectively to join his practice—so that we might learn from one another. I understood that this was quite an honor. During this time, physicians tended to be secretive about their cures. The medical schools taught ten falsehoods for each truth, and most physicians were on their own to learn what actually helped people. This usually took a lifetime of trial and error. Because of competition among physicians, many took their few effective treatments to the grave.

I did not know what would happen if I stayed in this place and time for more than a few hours. Would I lose the ability to return home? And if I did return, would there continue to be a disconnect between the passing of time here and there? Would medical knowledge I passed to the doctor somehow disrupt the flow of history?

In the end, I stayed with the doctor for almost two months. And it was then that the really fantastic thing happened.

A few members of the tour group let their jaws hang open, expressing incredulity that the fantastic part of the tale is yet to come. DeKooning notices. I make a circular motion with my hand indicating he should hurry along to climax of the tale. He nods and forces himself to proceed.

In the days that followed, I followed the doctor as he called upon a series of patients throughout the community. Half had ailments that were impossible for me to diagnose or treat, but were almost certainly advanced cancers and heart failure. Yet fully half of the others had conditions where we were able to make good progress. Using my simple ointments and salves, we cured numerous infections and sores. We mended broken limbs that had been set incorrectly and constructed superior casts. We cleaned festering wounds and ameliorated patient suffering wherever we could.

I still did not understand the utterances of most of the people we met, but the doctor did most of the speaking for me. I gathered that he introduced me as a visiting expert from some foreign land. In most cases, the patients we saw were too sickly or confused to object to my presence. As news of our string of cures spread across the area, patients began disturbing us late into in the evenings, asking to see the visiting expert.

The doctor did not seem jealous of my cures, or worried that I would supplant him in the community. He was genuinely interested in helping others, and did his best to learn from me. Yet despite my demonstrations of the curative properties of modern science, the doctor insisted on continuing his practice of anointing patients with metals and herbs. He also remained adamant that religious icons and medallions should be used as a defense against spirits. When the doctor seemed talkative and relaxed, I sometimes attempted to engage him on this point. If we were, in fact, living in or around 1400, then spirits would be blamed for sickness for another two hundred years—longer, among the unlearned. It was clear that this physician believed wards and talismans were still necessary. He was immovable on the point. I realized my project to dispel his superstitions would have to be a gradual one.

After nearly two months with the doctor, I began to contemplate returning home. I ferociously craved a warm shower and nourishing food, and felt as though my adventure had more or less run its course.

One day the doctor took me to see a patient who lived in a small cottage deep inside the forest. The day was overcast and a steady rain fell. Between the cloudy skies and the thick branches above us, it might have been evening instead of late morning.

When I attempted to inquire about the condition troubling the patient we were to see, the doctor remained vague. He clucked his tongue and shook his head, but did not elaborate on the exact nature of what we hoped to cure or treat.

I could smell the sickly black smoke billowing from the cottage chimney twenty minutes before the place came into view. It looked cursed. The cottage frame was crooked and low. The roof was in sore need of replenishment; in some places the thatch was so thin that I could see right through.

The doctor knocked hard at the door, and moments later it was opened by a kindly, rotund woman with curly hair. Though her demeanor was warm, the lines around her eyes told the story of someone under great strain. We went inside. The logs on the fire could not mask the smell of sickness. In a cot near the fireplace, we found the patient. Probably the woman's father, this man showed all the signs of being in the final stages of some vast internal sickness. His face was shriveled and waxy. His eyes were glazed. His mouth was nearly crusted over with spittle and plasma.

He had obviously been the subject of many prior ministrations by my partner. A quick survey of the patient found a weak pulse, but also wounds from bleedings by the doctor. The patient also showed signs of having been given a purgative with some regularity. Yet more than anything, the doctor's prior attentions were apparent in the fifteen or twenty magical charms placed around the dying man's neck. On top of this, the man had been anointed with strong-smelling oils, and strange occult shapes had been drawn on the floor in chalk to either side of his cot.

Another clue that something was special about this patient was the visible consternation that came over my colleague's face whenever he was forced to interact with the man. In our sixty days together, I had seen him treat some remarkably grisly conditions with never so much as a wince at the pustules and rot which sometimes literally exploded in his face. But this patient. . . . This one unnerved him even from across the room. And up close? Well, the doctor looked positively frightened of the dying man.

While I ministered to the patient as best I could, the doctor stayed away and chatted somberly with the daughter, watching me work. I could tell that he was wondering if anything from my bag of tricks would be able to save this man. I could also tell that he was relieved at my alacrity to take the lead.

Alas, there was little to be done. Doctors in the present day privately wrote "CTD" on the charts of patients like this. "Circling the drain."

There was nothing to do but make his final days as peaceful as possible. I crushed a narcotic sedative into a fine white powder which I mixed into a paste that he might easily ingest. After helping the patient consume it, I noticed that his breathing was somewhat labored. Now and then he let loose with a cough or gurgle. I turned my attention to the charms and wards upon his chest. Surely, several pounds of metal could not be doing any favors for a man with barely the strength to aspirate. I began to move the medallions. From across the room, the doctor jumped up as if electrified. He shouted something akin to "Stop that!" and physically pulled me away.

We did not want to disagree in front of others, and stepped outside the cottage to confer. The rain had intensified, and there was gentle, rolling thunder in the distance.

The doctor and I tried to discuss the matter in civil terms—at least at first—but our language barrier made this tricky. I implored the doctor to understand that his mystical charms were unnecessary, and that their position only made his patient's final moments more uncomfortable.

The doctor grew increasingly frustrated with me. We argued for the better part of an hour. I became annoyed, then positively angry. I considered my own reasons for having traveled back in time. Was not the disproving of superstitious charlatans a central component of the fantasy? For this adventure to remain amusing, perhaps it fell to me to take more extreme measures.

I resolved to give this kindly doctor the dose of harsh medicine he truly required. Before he could stop me, I barged back inside the cottage and stood above the patient. Gripping the strange medallions all at once, I pulled them off of the man's neck. I used the heel of my boot to obscure the symbols that had been traced into the floor. The doctor looked at me aghast as I strode to the door of the cottage and flung the amulets hard into the forest. I stared at him defiantly. He let me know that our partnership was over, and stalked off to collect the charms.

I returned to the house where the daughter was waiting, confused and scared. I did my best to reassure her that I was acting in the best interest of the patient. Already, it seemed the old man breathed more easily. I pointed this out to the daughter, and she nodded cautiously.

An idea crept into my brain. I would stay with this patient and ease his passing. Then I would use the well to return to my present time, but the daughter would be able to share with the old doctor how my ministrations had comforted the patient where his own superstitions had only made things worse. I settled in for the afternoon and began to prepare a second dose of narcotic paste.

The storm rolled in and a powerful wind shook the cabin. Rain began to fall through the holes in the roof. The daughter looked uneasy, but it seemed her fear had little to do with the moistening of their modest possessions. I stayed by the patient and did all that I could to comfort him, regularly examining his breathing and pulse. The storm raged on and the house began to creak. Soon, it was visibly swaying to and fro in the wind. I was reminded that building codes did not exist yet, and thought of how unfortunate it would be if I were crushed and killed under the weight of a peasant's hovel.

Just as I began to seriously entertain heading for the door, the storm relented and an eerie calm settled over the forest. Though the clouds above stayed black as midnight, the rain stopped and the wind died completely. I thought this would settle the nerves of the patient's daughter—it certainly did mine—but she became even more alarmed. She threw a shawl over her shoulders and ran out of the house, leaving me alone with the dying man.

A beat passed, and I laughed. It suddenly struck me how absurd this all was. I grinned at my own foolishness. I was a boy playing games. Did I really hope to teach these Middle Ages folk anything? It seemed a nonsensical, impossible project. What I had been thinking? This was the dream of a fool. It always had been.

I stared down at the dying man once more. I hoped he had consumed enough of the paste that his final moments would be nothing more than a pleasant dream. And that was enough, I realized. Now I needed to stop.

I rose from beside the cot and began collecting my things with the intention of heading directly for the well and back to my own century. The sky outside was turning a sickly green. Perhaps we were in the eye of the storm.

I glanced down to place the last of my creams and pills into my burlap sack. When I looked back up, there was a red devil standing beside the dying man. It looked very much like large crab. It was four feet tall. Its arms were long and disproportionately thin, and they were covered with spiny protrusions. It stood on two equally thin legs. The trunk of its body looked solid and hard like a carapace, and it had no visible genitalia despite its nudity. Its face showed that it was undoubtedly sentient, with a large expressive mouth, wormlike lips, and giant yellow eyes.

In the few instants for which I beheld it, the thing glanced down at the man on the ground with an expression of contempt. It was as if the devil knew him as an old enemy, and this visit was expected. Then, I think, I must have flinched because the thing's eyes—with their beady black pupils—found me despite the shadows.

The devil seemed to understand that something about me was amiss. Its face ran through a string of expressions. It showed surprise, disbelief, and then a terrifying display of *understanding* that crystallized into a horrible and powerful stare.

Nearly losing my wits, I snatched up my burlap sack and fled from the cabin. I ran and ran through the muddy folds of forest, too frightened to scream. I feared looking behind me, for it seemed certain that the devil would be there looking back.

I waited until I had the well in sight before I slackened my pace and allowed myself to verify that the devil was indeed gone. It was. Trembling with fear, I lowered myself inside the well, crawled to the mossy nook, and took a double dose of sleeping pills. When I awakened, I was—thank heaven—back in my own time.

Though my trip had lasted two months, by my family's reckoning I had been missing for little more than a day. Pressed about my absence, I claimed that a school chum had come through town; we had gone carousing and the time had gotten away from us.

My parents seemed to accept this. Hans, who understood me better, never quite knew for sure.

DeKooning stops speaking. The visitors wait anxiously, wondering if the tale is complete. We become aware of the soft hum of the lights above us.

Suddenly, there is a loud bloop from one of the jars behind DeKooning. A large air bubble has risen to the top of the jar containing the submerged homunculus. The displacement causes the tiny human form to give an altogether lifelike twitch.

"Aaah!" exclaim multiple guests at once.

The doctor looks at the jar, smiles gently, and turns away.

"A natural reaction occurring among the organic compounds," DeKooning explains. "No reason to be alarmed."

The guests look on doubtfully, waiting to see if something will prove him wrong. The jars on the shelves behind DeKooning remain still and quiet. So do the things inside them.

"Is that the end of your story?" one of the visitors asks.

"Those are . . . the only parts worth telling," DeKooning says with a nod.

"You're a crazy person," says a heretofore timid, grandmotherly member of the group. (I have long observed that the most reticent guests can often bring forth the most unexpected, poisonous *j'accuse*. This shawl-laden octogenarian proves no exception.)

DeKooning, for his part, seems unfazed.

"You can't travel back in time," the grandmother continues. "Nobody can. It would disrupt everything. And . . . devils!? Devils aren't real!"

"Oh, no?" DeKooning answers kindly, as though he may be mistaken about a small, trifling matter. "I see."

"Well, in religion maybe," the woman grants. "But devils don't come around and look at you. I've never seen one. And I'm very religious!"

The woman seems to grow more cantankerous with each sentence. I physically position myself between her and the doctor.

"Doctor DeKooning, thank you for making yourself available to treat our wounded guest," I announce in transitional tones. "We will trouble you no further. Ladies and gentlemen, if you will please follow me, we will continue with our tour of the Grand Hotel. There is still more to see."

Everybody moves toward the door . . . except the injured man. His hand lightly traces the path of the stitches in his scalp. He does not appear in any undue pain—DeKooning's work was expertly done—but I can already see it on his face. He is not playing any more. He's done. Kaput.

I look him in the eye from across the room with the pleasant smile of an attending waiter. I know what he's going to say before he does. I wait for him to summon the courage.

"Actually," the man begins. "It's already been a long day for me and, seeing as I just had a medical procedure . . ."

"Yes?" I say, willing him onward.

"I think I might like to retire for the evening," he manages. "I don't think I need to see the rest of this place."

The visitors look at me. Their trust in me going forward will hinge largely on my ability to accommodate this request. And accommodate it I do.

"Of *course*," I reply brightly. "We will take you immediately back to the hotel lobby. The entire group will go. There is a direct route through the passageway outside this office. Allow me to show you the way."

The man looks relieved.

"It's just . . . with the jet lag and all," he continues as he heads for the door.

"Think nothing of it," I tell him. "If you feel that's what's best, then I'm sure you've made the right decision."

He smiles, pleased to be validated.

One-by-one, the visitors file out of DeKooning's small surgery. I quietly say my goodbyes to the doctor, then take my place at the head of the tour group. We retrace our steps through the subterranean hallway and take a wooden staircase that forks in the middle. We take the left fork and enter a sort of enclosed tunnel. It is dark inside and very cramped, but realistic paintings of birds have been placed on the walls every few feet. I believe they were intended to distract onlookers from the tunnel's tight constraints, but just as often they have the opposite effect. (One imagines being trapped in a tightly-enclosed space *with birds.*)

Then the avian illustrations fall away and we arrive at an iron studded door with black metal hinges. I give it a heave, and it slowly opens to reveal the lobby of the Grand Hotel. More precisely, that we are standing in an alcove to the side of the royal staircase. The visitors can now see the reception desk where I first greeted them. There are two smaller passageways running off to the side.

I lead the group out of the tunnel and stand a little bit past the easternmost passage. Most of the visitors stick with me, just a few paces off. This positioning is key. We have arrived at a crucial juncture. Just like guests at a party, the members of the tour group are wondering if they too should take this opportunity to depart . . . or if there may still be more "fun" to be had.

I feel a gentle breeze waft down the corridor and into the lobby. I inhale deeply, and feel confident that most will elect to remain.

"As you see, we have returned to our starting point at the royal staircase," I announce. "If any of you are feeling too tired to complete the rest of the tour, now would be an excellent opportunity to—"

I am utterly cut off by the young woman standing nearest to the corridor. She emotes with such volume and so suddenly that I am quite powerless to continue.

"Oh my gaaaawd . . ." she cries, in the accent of the southern United States. "What is that heavenly smell?"

The visitors close their eyes, put their noses to the air, and inhale deeply.

"Oh . . . I suppose that you are smelling food from the hotel kitchen, which is just down that hallway," I say as though it is an afterthought.

"We should go there next!" a rotund man states.

"Will we be able to eat something there?" asks another.

"I . . . well . . . our cook will probably be able to scrounge *something*," I offer.

Without prompting, the tour begins to head down the passageway that leads to our kitchen . . . and to so many other places.

They file past me, one by one. At the tail end of the group I see the gentleman with the new stitches. He pauses, holding his hat in his hand and peering down the hallway after the others.

"That sure does smell good," he says. "And I haven't eaten dinner."

"Our head chef is quite skilled," I say. "Something of a celebrity. Had his own cooking show on television years ago . . . before the accident."

"The accident?" the man says.

"But come!" I say, pointing him to the front door. "As you've said, your head is injured and you need to retire for the evening. I really do think it is a sensible choice on your part. There is the way you came in. I hope you have enjoyed the first part of my tour. And, once again, I do apologize about the painting."

"Yes, well . . ." the man says. He lingers in the path of the kitchen-smell a moment longer, like a cold man savoring the heat from a fire. He casts one final, longing glance down the corridor, then seems to steel himself, nods vigorously, shakes my hand, and walks back across the lobby and out into the night.

I wait until he is completely out of sight before turning back around.

"It sounded like he called you 'Vic-something.'"

The red-haired girl is waiting for me. She leans against the wall with the impudent confidence of a teenager, though she cannot be more than twelve.

"Hmm?" I reply. (Of course, I know full-well what she is referring to.)

"Doctor DeKooning . . ." she clarifies. "When you were saying goodbye to him… It sounded like he called you 'Vic.'"

"Is my name important to you?" I reply.

She considers this, tilting her head to one side.

"I don't think it matters what you call yourself," she says. "People pick their own names. Even if they were named one thing, they can choose to go by something else. You can be named Katherine, but you can go by Kate or Kat or Katie. Or even Kay. You might have been given one name, but it, kind of, evolves over time, depending on who you are."

"I see," I reply thoughtfully. "That makes sense. I wonder if my name has evolved over the years. I shall have to consider that."

The red-haired girl nods. I wait for her to take the foul, vulgar step of asking me what I call myself (or even my original name). Showing the perspicacity that has brought her this far, she remains silent. I stare down at her like a stork. When my gaze lingers on her a little too long, she smiles back innocently.

"I'd like to ask you a question about Doctor DeKooning's story," I tell her. "You will recall that DeKooning briefly alluded to the possibility of going back in time and disturbing events in the future. Changing history and so forth. My question is: Did Doctor DeKooning change history when he went back in time?"

The red-haired girl thinks for no more than a second.

"It's technically possible, but probably not," she says.

"No?" I say. "How can you be so sure? If he indeed went back in time, I don't see how he could *not* change history."

"That's assuming he actually did go back in time," she says.

I raise a single eyebrow.

"But his description leaves little to doubt. If not back in time, then where else did he go? Certainly, the place he describes could not have been the future."

The red-haired girl hesitates, then says: "What if, instead of backward or forward . . . he went sideways?"

I nod carefully.

"To another reality entirely?" I ask. "To an alternate version of the universe?"

She nods.

"That," I say, "is a very good answer."

"Is it the right one?" the red-haired girl answers enthusiastically.

I shrug.

"It will do for now," I allow.

We follow the others down the hallway to the kitchen.

Chef Dunnally

The joy of rising on a Christmas morning surrounded by friends and family; a celebration banquet acknowledging an important professional accomplishment; playing as a child in a grandmother's kitchen whilst unknown but wonderful treats bake nearby in the oven.

These are just a few of the descriptions I have heard of the memories and sensations conjured by exposure to the sights and smells of Chef Dunnally's kitchen at the heart of the Grand Hotel.

When I catch up to the visitors—drawn irresistibly forward by their noses—they are already in full thrall of the place. Probably the best-lit room in the entire building, the kitchen is vast and filled with ovens, stoves, and mixing machines. Some of these contrivances are very modern, while others appear as old as the hotel itself. Food is everywhere. It spills out of cupboards full to bursting, and strains against the doors of refrigeration units crammed to capacity. Less-perishable grains, fruits, and vegetables adorn every available surface. (To my eye, the kitchen has always looked like a classical painting invoking the abstract notion of Harvest or Plenty. But then, my frame of reference is not like everyone else's . . .)

And there in the center of it all is Chef Dunnally. A large, smiling man with a bushy black beard. (Only I know the scars it hides.) Dressed in chef's whites with a floppy hat tilted somewhat rakishly to one side, he smiles brightly as he works a mixing bowl and spoon with his powerful forearms. A handful of assistants labor alongside him, but they do not stand out quite as distinctly.

Dunnally hovers directly beneath the brightest lighting fixture in the very center of the massive kitchen.

A naturally gregarious man, Dunnally is already chatting with a few of the guests as I arrive. At one point he allows an excited young man to stick his finger in the mixing bowl and take a taste. The man's eyes close as he puts his finger in his mouth; utterly transported by the ambrosia on his tongue. Dunnally grins and gives a hearty laugh. (This seems innocent enough, but what would the health inspectors say?)

I push my way through the visitors. Their faces contain a range of emotions, but most show a combination of delight combined with overwhelming peckishness. I hear at least two stomachs grumble audibly as I make my way to the chef. I am not a small man, but Dunnally is still much taller than me and much broader in the shoulders. Given my penchant for darker clothing, I find that if I linger in his shadow, he can quite literally eclipse me. For this reason, I make a point to position myself two full paces away.

"Ladies and gentleman," I say, raising my hand to silence the chatterers. "I see that you have already met our resident celebrity. For those of you without a television or library, I have the pleasure of introducing the head chef of the Grand Hotel, Liam Fairfax Dunnally. You will know him as the author of the best-selling *New Tasmanian Cooking* and *New Tasmanian Cooking Light,* and—for many years—as the star of his own television program on The Chef Network."

I see a new ripple of excitement course through the group. Several cast expressions of "So it is him!" One or two visitors barge to the front, asking if they can have their picture taken. I assure them that there will be time for that in a moment.

"Chef Dunnally probably has the most taxing job of anyone who works here," I continue. "He and his staff accommodate the culinary needs of all our permanent guests—needs which, I assure you, can be quite particular—in addition to preparing the cuisine for the banquets, receptions, and formal dinners held at the hotel. I do not exaggerate to say that he may be our institution's greatest cultural asset. In the ten years he has been with us, we have only ever had compliments."

There are more oohs and ahhs from the crowd. Perhaps sensing their growing ravenousness, Chef Dunnally opens one of the nearby ovens and carefully removes a tray overflowing with fresh dinner rolls. The odor is almost unbearably pleasant, and a great look of relief circulates when Dunnally begins passing them out.

"These are amazing!" a guest pronounces after a single bite.

"Oh emm gee!" says another.

"These are the best rolls I ever had, ever!" cries a third.

Dunnally grins and gives a little bow, then takes up his mixing bowl again. For the moment, the group is completely preoccupied with the task of eating. I allow myself to relish the silence.

Then someone with his mouth half-full asks: "So why didn't you ever get a Michelin Star, eh? Isn't that what famous chefs do?"

Dunnally opens his mouth to speak, but I quickly intercede.

"To accrue a Michelin —or any other accolade from the so-called 'food community'—one must operate a restaurant with open seating and cuisine available to the general public. While the quality of Chef Dunnally's cooking ranks among the finest in the world, every dish made here is a special order and for our guests only. In many cases, the cuisine will arise from private conversations between the chef and our guests. There is no menu for a restaurant critic to analyze, and the vintages in our wine cellar are known to Chef Dunnally alone. While it does not fit the predominant mold, we find this arrangement quite satisfactory. Yet, as you point out, it does mean that we exist outside the wider ranking system."

"That would explain why I've never read a restaurant review of this place," ventures another.

"Precisely," I tell her.

"I loved your television shows," another guest says, redirecting the conversation. "It must have been wonderful making them, no? Getting to travel all over the world? Cooking regional dishes in glamorous locales? I'll bet it was heaven."

Dunnally continues to stir placidly, but I know that an unpleasant knot forms in his stomach whenever the subject turns to TV. (It is only ever a matter of time until the conversation wends its way to that unspeakable final show.)

"And all of the famous people you got to meet!" the guest continues.

Dunnally acknowledges this with a small nod.

"Do you ever think of going back to it?" asks a wealthy-looking man in the middle of the group. "After all, more than ten years have passed since you went off the air."

"Yes," says a woman in a flowery hat. "Ten years, since the . . . since the . . ."

"The *tragedy*," I say loudly and clearly, establishing our preferred term.

"Yes . . . the tragedy," the woman says. "Why surely, everyone knows what happened was not your fault. It was an accident! Terrible, but an accident."

A ripple of confusion spreads through the group. Some of the visitors do not understand what is being discussed. They are discretely asking their neighbors. Among others, there is a general head shaking and recalcitrance, as though the subject is distasteful. Among others still, one hears dark mutterings about a devastating cooking accident.

The crowd is silenced by the sound of someone in possession of the deepest of baritones clearing his throat. The visitors look up and see that Dunnally has set down his mixing bowl and is staring at them. His eyes look tired.

The thick Tasmanian accent, familiar to so many from television, is tinged with a sadness seldom heard on-air. The effect of this unexpected intimacy is rather like seeing a famous person naked. My guests have varying reactions to this frankness.

Mine, of course, is always one of complete pleasure.

It was a time of crisis in the television cooking industry. Desperation drove me to that final, fateful show.

I had been a TV chef for nearly my entire professional life. At the start of my career, it felt like a golden age. The public's capacity for our programs seemed endless. Food preparation was the new ratings-winner, riding high on a wave we thought would never crest. The channels added more cooking shows each year. Then entire networks were launched that showed nothing but cooking. It was glorious! There were game shows and reality shows and competition shows—all about cooking! Viewers also wanted to learn about regional cuisines from around the world, and that was where I carved a niche for myself in the teeming ecosystem. In those heady times, even the native dishes of a small island off the coast of Australia—such as they were—were enough to create considerable interest in the viewing public. At my height, I had my own half-hour program on the Chef Network, made regular guest appearances on the Cooking Channel, was a paid endorser of a major manufacturer of cutlery, and supermarkets around the world were just beginning to stock Chef Dunnally's "Tasmanian Tang" Barbeque Sauce.

And then the bubble burst. . . .

The public's appetite for cooking programs waned, and then waned some more. It seemed that several networks devoted to food might be too many—and that two, or, at most, three, would probably suffice. Whole channels were shuttered. Television chefs were laid off left and right. There was a desperate scrambling for a foothold—a foothold anywhere—as there always is during a downturn. The biggest celebrity chefs would survive, of course. They might have to adjust to living with less, but they would still find new homes somewhere. But for chefs like me—in the second or third tier of fame—it was a mad dash to find any employment at all.

Clearly as if it were yesterday, I can remember being called into the offices of my production company the week we learned *The Tasmanian Chef* had not been renewed. I sat across from the CEO and two other executives at the large, modern conference table, and waited for the ax to fall. Waited for them to tell me that after twelve years of mutually beneficial collaboration, it was time for us to go our separate ways.

Instead, they hit me with a complete surprise.

"As you know, our company produces reality television programs in a variety of genres," the CEO began. "The popularity of these programs fluctuates. That's the nature of the market. Cooking shows, for example, are on the decline right now. But that won't always be the case. In fact, I expect them to be on the way back up sooner than anyone thinks."

I took a deep breath. What was he proposing? A hiatus?

"In the meantime, we need to focus on programs that are on the ascent," the CEO continued. "So let me ask you. . . . How familiar are you with Ghost House Investigations?"

"Um . . . vaguely," I answered.

This was true.

Ghost House Investigations was one of the reality shows produced by the same company that made my show. It aired late at night on a channel aimed at science fiction fans. My general understanding was that it involved a group of awkward men running around dark houses in the middle of the night, screaming and shouting that every mouse-squeak or lens flare was a confirmed manifestation of the supernatural.

Frankly, I wasn't impressed.

"Last year, it brought in three times the audience of *The Tasmanian Chef*," the CEO said. "Networks are adding ghost hunting shows left and right. People can't seem to get enough. And—sweetening the deal for us—ghost shows are cheap to make. These 'ghost experts' work for peanuts."

"Where are you going with this?" I asked, growing uneasy.

The CEO turned the meeting over to one of his lackeys, who was apparently prepared to hit me with the formal pitch.

"If you would be willing to consider a substantial cut in per-episode compensation," the man began, "we believe the market might be right for a new show *combining* the world's most exotic cuisines with inquiries into the supernatural. In fact, I already have soft-confirmation from a network executive that his channel would pick up something like that, sight-unseen."

"Anthony Bourdain travels around the world to weird, interesting places—he does a little cooking, he talks to people, he samples the food—badda bing, badda boom, you got a television show," the CEO chimed in. "You'd be doing all the same stuff . . . except the places would be—"

"Haunted?" I interjected. "You can't be serious."

To show me that they were, one of the executives pressed a button that activated the large flatscreen set into the wall of the conference room. The screen came to life and began to play a 'sizzle reel' of clips from my cooking shows spliced with footage of scary-looking castles, abandoned houses, and dark and stormy skies. An upbeat soundtrack played in the background, punctuated by low moans, rattling chains, and crashes of thunder. After forty seconds, a title card materialized out of a supernatural mist: "Liam Dunnally is . . . Ghost Chef."

The executive pushed the button again, and the television screen went black.

"Ghost Chef?" I asked. "Are you being serious?"

"Liam . . ." the executive began to entreat.

"I am a classically trained French Chef!" I nearly shouted. "I have served princes and kings! Every one of my cookbooks has been an international bestseller! Two years ago, I was voted the most influential living Tasmanian!"

"Look, kid . . ." the CEO interjected before I could list any more of my accomplishments.

He called me "kid," though I was nearly forty. This made me bristle, but I let him continue.

"I hate to tell you, but right now the world is full of chefs with fancy accolades who just got their shows dumped," the CEO said. "You know what the market is. Hell, I'm impressed yours lasted as long as it did! If you've got a better offer coming, I encourage you to take it. But the thing is . . . I don't think you do. If I were you, I would contemplate this opportunity very, very hard before I passed. How well do you think your next cookbook's going to sell when you're not on TV anymore? Huh? How are you gonna be voted the most famous person from Madagascar—or wherever—when you don't even have a show?"

I remained silent. I did not have a good answer for him. Soon, the CEO saw that he had made his point, and his tone turned from stern back to kindly.

"We both know this will be temporary," he continued. "One day, chef shows will be en vogue again. When that happens, you have my word that I'll fight like a damn wolverine to get you a new, high-profile cooking program with a big fat paycheck attached. But until that change happens, we need something to tide you over. Keep you in the public eye until they start green-lighting proper chef shows again. And I think this might be just the ticket."

I walked out of the meeting stunned and silent, but twenty-four hours later I called the production company and said I'd take the job.

Was I acting out of fear? Would a braver, more self-confident chef have chosen to bide his or her time by returning to the kitchen? Possibly. I don't say I was proud of my decision, but when I thought about all of the other TV chefs who would have given an arm and a leg for this chance, it felt like an opportunity I shouldn't pass up. I also had a sneaking suspicion that years of working on *The Tasmanian Chef* had eroded my ability to take orders in any traditional sense. Could I return to a kitchen environment where I was expected to jump at the behest of a stuffy restaurant owner, or even—gasp!—another chef? I wasn't sure I could do that anymore.

For these and other reasons, I agreed to take the job.

The good news was that the production executive had apparently not been bullshitting about network interest. We didn't have to do a pilot or a formal pitch meeting or anything. As soon as I was attached, a network ordered up thirteen episodes for the first season. "Thirteen is a good number for a show about ghosts," the CEO assured me.

The main drawback was that our budget was ridiculously low. Not only would my salary be slight, but so too the production expenses. We would operate with a crew of only three: the camera operator, the sound engineer, and me.

"Even with the editing, won't the audience begin to find a single camera perspective tiresome?" I asked in an early production meeting.

An executive replied that—taking a cue from Ghost House Investigations—I would also be fitted with hidden, infrared cameras for the ghost-hunting sequences of the program. There would even be one in my chef's hat, giving the audience my point of view at all times. I shuddered and tried to remind myself that this was a temporary indignity.

The production company put together a list of supposedly haunted locales that also had regional dishes I could prepare. It was not difficult to find places where food and ghosts dovetailed.

I was initially worried that some of the dishes might be too unusual or difficult for the audience following along at home. When I expressed this concern—in yet another meeting—I was told: "Don't worry about that. Mostly, people will be watching for the ghosts."

Ah, yes, I thought. The ghosts.

I was not an expert in the supernatural. I had never seen a ghost and did not know if I really believed in them.

Further, I was at a loss as to how I should "hunt for ghosts." In the other television programs, the hosts seemed to stake out locations overnight, rely on electronic readouts and special equipment, and even to attempt direct supernatural communication. I wondered if I would be able to do any of that with a straight face— or without dropping my cutlery.

My anxiety fell away, however, when we arrived in Strasbourg, France, to film the first episode. For our location, the producers had secured a chalet that was rumored to be haunted by the ghosts of a pair of lovers—one German, one French—who had committed suicide together when tensions between their respective nations made their romance illegal. We had arranged for representatives from the Strasbourg tourism bureau to join us on camera. They were enthusiastic about presenting their city as a destination for ghost hunting fans, and seemed very familiar with the genre.

I began by preparing a tarte flambé—a dish very like a white pizza, native to Strasbourg—in the small kitchen where the two lovers had taken poison. Once the dish was cooked and sampled, the tourism representatives took me and my crew on a walking tour of the home. We kept the lights low for added effect, but my interests were quickly piqued not by the appearance of an apparition—for we saw nothing—but by what I learned about the history of the city. The tales of how Strasbourg had been traded back and forth between France and Germany over the centuries were fascinating. I came away with a real appreciation for how their unique location had made their food, culture—and even their ghosts—so distinctive. I believed my audience would enjoy this too. When I retired to the hotel that evening to relax, I felt that while I was certainly not doing the caliber of program I once had, I was perhaps not creating something entirely without merit.

I slept well.

From Strasbourg it was on to an abandoned monastery in rural Sardinia. There, in a beautiful outdoor garden,

I prepared heaping bowls of fregula—fleshy balls of semolina dough—and mixed it with local seafood and fresh tomatoes. Afterwards, a representative from the historical society took us on a survey of the monastery grounds and showed us the exact spot where, in the year 1666, the great fire had torn through the building, taking the lives of nearly all the monks within. Again, our cameras detected nothing supernatural, at least that I saw. Yet my crew members—Horst who ran the camera, and Harry the boom-mic and audio—assured me that editors would be able to find shots where the wind had rustled the curtains in the background as I had stirred the fregula. The final edit would zoom in on these rustlings, and an ominous voiceover would call this evidence of undead monks angry with us for disturbing their peace. Horst had worked for two prior seasons on Ghost House Investigations, and seemed to know all the tricks.

Then, of course, came the final, fateful, third show. . . . The show that forever ended my desire to work in television. The show that has passed into lore in the culinary world and the world of ghost hunting alike. So much has been written and said about it, but few know the truth of what actually happened.

What we actually saw . . .

Chef Dunnally stares down into his mixing bowl as though it is a scrying pool, capable of showing him the night in question.

We landed in Glasgow on an overcast, windy morning. The weather seemed appropriately ominous for ghost hunting. We changed planes and boarded a regional aircraft that braved choppy skies to deposit us on a tiny airstrip in one of the Outer, Outer Hebrides to Scotland's extreme northwest. There, not half an hour's drive away, we saw our ultimate destination: MacLaddich Castle.

It was an ancient place, said to trace its history back to the Romans. It nestled precariously at the edge of a rocky cliff overlooking the sea. Its crumbling stone walls had been windblown into a solid, sheer mass. It was on the smaller side as Scottish castles went, with a single stone tower jutting up into the overcast sky. However, I had on authority from my producers that a veritable warren of tunnels extended underneath it, down through dungeons, and eventually out to the Norwegian Sea beyond. It all seemed ripe for exploration, and I was more than a little excited for the evening's work ahead.

We were greeted at the castle gates by a delegation of three locals. Two were from the Outer, Outer Hebrides Visitors Association—a portly fellow named MacDonald and a thin woman named MacTavish. They had been in direct contact with our producers for weeks, and were coordinating the logistics of the shoot. They were scheduled to appear briefly on camera, but neither was my central guest. That honor was reserved for the third person, a very old man named Conkney. He wore a tam and smoked a pipe, and was apparently something of a local expert on the history of the castle. MacDonald and MacTavish welcomed us heartily, and assured us that all preparations had been made. I shook both of their hands, pleased to have friendly, competent people on board.

I had many questions for them about the arrangements regarding the regional cuisine I was to prepare: the MacLaddich Long Sheep. The dish—which I was repeatedly assured bore no relation to the "long pig" of the Polynesians—involved the cooking of a single whole sheep inside a cast-iron cauldron atop an indoor fire. The sheep was slow-cooked and seasoned repeatedly, and the whole process took several hours.

I had not had time to attempt a practice run of the Long Sheep. However, I also knew the One True Secret of the television chef: Namely, that the viewing audience would not be able to taste my finished product. When it came to the success or failure of the dish, the viewers would have to take my word for it.

According to my producer's field notes on Outer, Outer Hebrides tradition, the MacLaddich Long Sheep held a powerful cultural significance. When prepared on the first full moon of autumn, it was thought to serve as a ward against evil spirits. I made a note to ask our hosts about this connection as soon as possible.

Much to my delight, when we entered the castle, I saw that a beautiful ancient cauldron had indeed been requisitioned.

"We found it down in the kitchens!" the large MacDonald cheerfully informed me. "Hadn't been used for centuries, I don't think. Don't worry; we scrubbed it clean for you!"

I thanked the man profusely.

There were also three whole, skinned sheep standing by—I guessed in case I made mistakes with the first two—a chef's station replete with supplies and seasonings, and even a portable handwashing device. And in the expansive but somewhat gloomy great hall, a large bed of coals was already glowing with life.

"We thought we should get them started for you," the diminutive MacTavish added. "Traditionally, long sheep is cooked over coals that have been brought down to a smolder. It used to take them the better part of a day."

I thanked MacTavish for her foresight, and next turned my attention to the creaky old man. His face held a distasteful squint that seemed unrelated to old age. It was clear he disliked being inside the castle, or even felt afraid. A part of me thought me might be "playing it up" for the cameras. I considered informing him that—despite the lenses embedded in our clothing—we were not yet recording.

Instead, I said: "Mister Conkney, I am told that you're the resident historian of this place. I'm so excited you'll be working with us tonight. It's a pleasure to meet you."

Conkney chewed his pipe and considered his words.

"I wouldn't call meself a historian," he said in an almost indecipherably thick accent. "I'm jus' one who knows the tales about this place. And the songs. And the children's rhymes."

As he spoke, Conkney looked up nervously at the vaulted ceilings above. There could be no doubt about it—he seemed genuinely unhappy about being inside the great hall. I wondered how much he was being paid by the Visitors Association.

"Can you tell me a little about the castle before we get started?" I asked. "We'll speak about it on camera while I cook the sheep, of course, but I always like to get some background first. What do you know about the building and the people who lived here?"

Then, as an afterthought, I added: "And, of course, the ghost."

Conkney's ancient eyes grew wide with something like betrayal. He looked hard at MacTavish and MacDonald, who were helping Horst to position his camera tripod.

"Is that what they told you?" Conkney said. "'A ghost?' Because there's no ghost. Never has been."

I felt the pit of my stomach begin to sink. Had the Visitors Association manufactured a "MacLaddich Castle ghost" in some bid for supernatural tourism? I had visions of our racing around to find a replacement location on the fly.

Then my stomach relaxed as Conkney added: "Because it's a demon! It's a demon straight from hell that haunts this place! Everyone knows it!"

The portly MacDonald overheard our conversation and approached.

"The 'Demon of the Dells,' as our spirit is known, falls well within the accepted parameters of ethereal beings suitable for hunting on ghost programs," he said. "Your producers and I were very much aligned upon that point. While the locals like to call it a demon, its predilection for materializing unexpectedly and scaring residents of the castle to death is well-established."

"Scaring people to death?" I said with a chuckle. "That seems rather extreme."

"That's exactly what the thing does!" Conkney insisted. "Ach! You wanted the history of this curst place? Fine! Here it is . . .

The MacLaddich clan came here—to the arse end of Scotland—because no other land would have them! They built their castle on this lonely rock because it was the last place left. The chiefs of the other clans shunned the MacLaddich, excluding them from the landsmeets. At the same time, they took great care not to start confrontations with the MacLaddich—for two important reasons. The first was that life on this accurst rock made them a devilishly tough bunch. Their pleasures were few, and their hard-ships many. The MacLaddich were in a constant war against pirates and raiders from across the sea. Only the strongest survived here. The other clansmen knew it, and so avoided fighting with the MacLaddich. But the other reason is what brings you here today . . .

Back when Robert the Third was on his deathbed at Rothesay, the MacLaddich brought a practitioner of black magic to the castle to perform a horrible rite. The fishing and mining that sustained the clan had fallen off, y'see. Times were at a low. Some even thought that the clan would be dissolved and disappear. But "wee Anne MacLaddich," as she was known—the woman who had governed the clan since her father's descent into mental dotage—believed the words of a strange magician who said he knew a rite that could save her people. He said he could put fish back in their waters and ore back in their soil. The price would be a steep one though, involving many a firstborn son and daughter . . . but the wizard, whoever he was, was correct in his guess that the MacLaddich were bloodthirsty enough to pay it.

To punctuate this, Conkney spat on the stone floor.

Many a trembling lad and lass died on the night of the ritual, and many a parent grieved in the light of dawn and wondered just what they had done. When it was over—aye—there *did* seem to be a few more fish in the nets and a bit more metal in the Earth. But the magician did not tell wee Anne the *full* price the MacLaddich would pay. For the ritual also conjured a demon straight from hell so terrible that—they say—to look upon it would move you to gouge your own eyes in madness or to throw yourself into the sea. The demon began appearing inside the castle, always at night. Usually once or twice a year it showed itself, just as the weather turned cold. That was what the preparation of the Long Sheep was for. The clan thought—I don't know why—that dish could serve as a counter-ritual— as a ward against the demon. To my knowledge, it never worked. The demon still came, year after year. It terrorized brides on their honeymoons and struck strong men down at the peaks of their lives. From newborn babe to doddering crone, nobody was safe.

By the time Queen Anne took the throne of Great Britain in 1707, this wretched place had become an empty shell. Merchants refused to come to trade. In order to do business, the MacLaddich were forced always to travel. Many of those who ventured away found other parts of Scotland more inviting, and there they stayed, often changing their names in hopes of sloughing off the curse. By the start of the First World War, Clan MacLaddich was no more. Few alive today would know they had ever existed, were it not for this empty shell in which we stand."

MacDonald nodded tentatively, to more-or-less second what Conkney had said.

"So, you see?" the portly man added. "It clearly has all the best qualities of a classical haunting."

"Yes," I told him. "I don't think there will be any problem."

I turned back to Conkney and said I had one more question.

"What does the demon look like?" I said.

"Look like?" Conkney said. "What kind of question is that?"

"Well," I said, "in the second half of my program, I'm supposed to search for it. That's what we do. And I need to know what I'm searching for, don't I?"

"They say all who have seen it have died," Conkney replied sternly. "Some were reduced to madness first . . . but all perished. Not a man, woman, or child has lived to tell."

"Ahem . . . actually," MacDonald interjected. "I took the liberty of having a researcher put together a collection of representative illustrations of demons in Scottish folklore. They've already been emailed to your producer. It's just what you'd expect, really. Horns. Wings. Great big mouths with long sharp teeth. I suspect your graphics department will be able to work wonders. Put together some sort of thing with CGI."

"Ah," I said. "I expect you're right. Wonderful!"

We lost no time in preparing for the taping. I set to work readying ingredients for the MacLaddich Long Sheep. I was glad that this required me to be near the fire because the castle was terribly cold. It was only late August, yet the wind howled fiercely and it felt almost chilly enough to snow. I asked MacDonald if this was typical for the region. He shook his head and muttered something about winter coming early and global warming. I wondered if my breath would be visible on-camera.

After readying the opening cooking segment, Horst and Harry lit a second fire in the grand fireplace behind us. This worked wonders in augmenting the severe mood of the castle interior, and also increased our overall warmth. The flames threw flickering shadows across the heavy columns that stretched to the roof of the great hall. The nooks and crannies in the oddly-vaulted ceiling appeared sometimes to shift— or come in and out of existence entirely—in the ever-dancing light. I deemed this quite effective for the mood we wished to set.

"Now it looks like a proper haunted castle," Horst echoed.

"Ach!" spat Conkney. "'Looks like.' Bah!"

The lighting perfected, we deemed it wise to quickly begin filming—especially considering the long cooking time involved in our dish. The schedule called for me to first prepare the sheep while chatting with MacDonald and MacTavish about Scottish cuisine and customs. Then, once the sheep was in the pot, they would "introduce" me to Conkney who would take us on a tour of the castle, during which we would "hunt the demon."

The lighting was given a final tweak, lavaliers were attached to our collars, Horst and Harry took their places, and we were underway.

I smiled and told the viewing audience about this episode's exciting remote location and the unusual dish I would be preparing. MacDonald and MacTavish proved exceedingly garrulous once the camera was running and were happy to speak at length about how Scottish cuisine was 'more than just haggis' with the MacLaddich Long Sheep serving as a fine—if little known—example. As they prattled on about neeps, tatties, and cranashan, I salted our sheep and massaged-in the regional spices. Then I trussed the legs to make it more maneuverable for its trip over to the cauldron.

"I think our little lady is ready to take a dip," I said. "Would the two of you be kind enough to help me lift her?"

I actually did need their help. The sheep must have weighed 130 pounds. I didn't want to have to throw the thing over my shoulder, or—worse yet—lose my grip and send it squirming to the dirty castle floor.

MacDonald and MacTavish hesitated.

"Oh, I don't know if we want to do that," said MacDonald. He gave a little laugh and looked over to MacTavish.

"Oh, right," MacTavish said. "I forgot about that part."

"Forgot about what?" I asked.

MacTavish glanced nervously at her partner before answering.

"Part of the . . . um . . . tradition, I suppose, with MacLaddich Long Sheep, is that those who prepare it are vulnerable to the demon until the sheep is fully cooked."

"Yes," agreed MacDonald. "The idea being that the demon dislikes it when the locals subvert the curse through this ritual. The demon is likely to take it out on the cooks who have touched the sheep."

"Ah," I said carefully. "And that's a great segue to our next guest, right? I understand he will be able to tell us a good deal more about the demon who haunts this place?"

MacDonald and MacTavish both nodded.

"But seriously, help me carry this thing over to the cauldron," I said sternly. "It's slippery and weighs more than you do, Ms. MacTavish."

The pair relented. Working together, we carefully lifted the slippery seasoned sheep from the wooden table at my chef's station and gingerly deposited it into the steaming cauldron. The iron lid was left off, in accordance with tradition, and the scent of cooking meat and spices was allowed to waft throughout the castle. The odor commingled with the raging fire and ever-present breeze from off the sea. The combined fragrances were remarkably pleasing to the nose. I privately decided that—demon or no—cooking this dish on the first cold days of the year must have been a very nice tradition.

This much accomplished, we turned our attention to Conkney. Horst removed the camera from its tripod and we activated the small, infrared ghost-hunting cameras attached to our clothing. It was time to explore.

"Now, we would like to introduce Mr. Conkney," MacTavish said, wiping the sheep from her hands. "He's the unofficial historian of MacLaddich Castle, and knows more about the demon than anybody in the Outer, Outer Hebrides."

Conkney—who had waited patiently to the side as we filmed the cooking segment—thrust his pipe into his mouth and purposefully stalked over.

"Aye," he said uneasily. "I expect I can tell you about this place. Come on."

Conkney headed for the back of the great hall where an unassuming wooden door was set into the wall.

"We'll start in the tower," Cockney called, "then work our way down to the dungeons. May God have mercy on me, but I'll show you the whole thing—top to bottom. The whole blasted thing."

I quickly thanked MacDonald and MacTavish—giving each of them a wet handshake goodbye—and Horst, Harry, and I hurried after the old man. We intercepted him at the door, which Conkney opened with several strong tugs. A landing stood beyond with a winding stone staircase heading up, and a straight staircase heading down. Conkney gestured to the winding one.

"Stairs to the tower," Conkney said. "We'll begin there,"

The circular staircase was very dark. Conkney gripped a plastic fisherman's flashlight. There was also a powerful light on the front of Horst's camera. Yet anywhere these two lights chanced not to shine was bathed in inky blackness.

For a man of advanced age, Conkney did well on the stairs. As he walked, he narrated the history of the demon that he had told me previously. A shunned clan. Hard times in the land. A deal with a dark magician. Unspeakable sacrifices. A demon hell-bent on haunting the castle evermore.

Conkney hit all of the high points and delivered the climax of the tale with an exceeding amount of gusto. It did not appear manufactured. Once again, I had the sense that the old man felt a real trepidation about being in this place. Unlike our guides in prior episodes, Conkney evidently took no pleasure in parading us through the haunted locale. Rather, he seemed to desire that it should be over as quickly as possible.

Conkney finished the castle history just as we arrived at the apex of the tower. Here was a once-stately chamber with high ceilings and large recessed windows that afforded us a beautiful view of the crashing waves below. The floor was covered in a quarter-inch of dust and lichen from off the sea. In one corner was a dingy bed with a moldering straw mattress. A single mouse scuttled past. Horst lingered on it with the camera. Perhaps our editors would imbue it with supernatural meaning when the voiceover was added.

"This was the royal bedchamber of the MacLaddich family," Conkney said. "Many a newlywed spent her first honeymoon here. 'Twas also a very pop'lar place for the demon. In fact, it was from this very window that wee Anne MacLaddich threw herself down—'tis said—when the demon made its inaug'ral showing. She was the first to jump from this tower, aye, but not the last. After some years, they put up a barred grate on the window. You can still see the rivets in the wall. It stopped the clan members choosing that particular option . . . but it did not stop the deaths. A determined person can find other ways to do the job. Twenty years after it went up, they took the bars back down. Each generation wanted to believe the bars were no longer necessary . . . that the demon had come for the last time. That it was done with the MacLaddich. It wasn't."

Horst took shots of the room from several angles, and then leaned his camera out of the large window. Manipulating the lens, he zoomed down towards the waves below, probably duplicating the point-of-view of wee Anne MacLaddich falling to her demise.

Conkney showed us other, smaller rooms at the top of the tower, but none had the majesty of the grand bedchamber. Appearing to be abandoned closets and storage areas, they were filled largely with cobwebs, broken chairs, and more dust. The tower was as silent as a tomb, with the only noise the crashing waves on the cliff below.

Conkney decreed that we would now descend back to the great hall, and from there descend again into the dungeons.

"The places below are what I 'spect your audience will want to see," Conkney said. "Whether or not the demon shows itself, enough tortures and horrors happened there to satisfy the worst kind of curiosity."

Something in me did not want to acknowledge this version of our project, so I merely nodded.

We retraced our steps back along the tightly-spiraling staircase. Halfway down, there was a sudden and piercing scream from below. A woman's voice. All I could think was Ms. MacTavish in the great hall. I hoped she had not somehow injured herself on one of my cooking implements. I did not think we could be sued, but some of these European countries had legal systems that vastly favored plaintiffs. Especially local ones.

I shuddered at the thought.

Being a veteran of ghost hunting programs, Horst instinctively took off with his camera in the direction of the sound. The rest of us followed as quickly as we could. The steps on the staircase were wide, but had been polished into sloping by centuries of use. It was a lucky stroke that we reached the main floor with nobody falling.

Back inside the great hall, we saw MacDonald and MacTavish huddled beside the cauldron where the long sheep still burbled. They looked quite stunned and somewhat disheveled. In a different setting, I would have sworn they were lovers interrupted in the act. But no. This was not the time or the place for that. And a second and third glance showed me something more. Something sinister.

Both held their mouths tightly shut, as if concealing a secret that threatened to physically escape. When MacTavish saw us reappear in the doorway, she bounded over. Before I could understand what was happening, she threw her arms around me.

"I think we just saw it," she whimpered. She held me close and trembled. I looked over at MacDonald for corroboration. Horst's lens lingered on our entwined bodies.

"We certainly . . . certainly . . . saw something," MacDonald said uneasily. He was more introspective than his partner, but his eyes were wide as dinner plates.

"What?" I asked excitedly. "What did you see?"

"Eyes!" MacTavish cried, still hanging from my collar like a loosened necktie. "Horrible, yellow eyes, big as fists! They floated out of the darkness and appeared right in front of us! They had giant, pulsing veins! I swear they looked right at us!"

"It . . . may have been a trick of the fire," MacDonald said thoughtfully. "Twin coals or bits of paper could have floated up and hovered for a moment. Or it could have been steam from the cauldron—a wisp of gas caught aflame. Or ball lightning. We do get that here."

"Are you a fool?!" MacTavish shouted loud enough to hurt my ears. "You saw it! They were giant glowing eyes!"

A beat passed.

I realized everyone was looking at me. It was most disconcerting. I hadn't a clue how to proceed.

Then from behind his camera, Horst gave me a discreet thumbs-up. The man knew good ghost-hunting television when he saw it. Apparently this was it. Cheered by Horst's reassurance, I straightened my spine and declared that we must remain stalwart and continue on to the dungeons below.

"The dungeons!" MacTavish cried, releasing her grip as though I had turned to ice. "I wouldn't go down there! No, not at all!"

Another thumbs up from Horst. Very good television.

Perhaps too good.

I thought again of the upswing in ghost hunting shows across all channels and networks, and then of the ignored and dying tourist towns that might pin a desperate hope on a new breed of visitor looking for a glimpse of the supernatural. How convenient that MacTavish and MacDonald had seen these 'giant glowing eyes' in the few moments when our cameras had been out of the room.

I was not ready to put all of my money on a ruse . . . but no part of me was concerned that we would actually encounter a demon if we ventured below.

"Yes, to the dungeons we must go," I said with a resolution I hoped would look brave on camera. "If the demon could be down there, we can't risk missing it."

I struck a pose that felt intrepid.

MacTavish rejoined MacDonald over beside the burbling cauldron where the sheep still cooked.

"You can come, if you like," I told them. "Maybe there's safety in numbers?"

MacTavish shuddered and shook her head no.

"The dungeons are damnably dark," said MacDonald. "I've been down there once. That was enough for me. You go on ahead. We'll stay here by the fire."

Our hosts thus unmovable, I signaled for Conkney to lead Horst, Harry, and myself down to the dungeons. Conkney grimly plodded to the straight stairs leading down into the darkness. We left the smell of cooking sheep and burning firewood and traded it for a slimy limestone passageway that reeked of overgrowth.

"The old castles never had proper plumbing," Conkney explained as we descended. "You'd think they would have learned it from the Romans, but—ach!—apparently not. Anything anybody ever pissed or shat went down and stayed down."

"Lovely," I said sarcastically. Behind his camera, Horst cracked a smile.

The stone staircase beneath our feet continued its descent, but the tight, suffocating passage around us soon opened into a large, high-ceilinged room filled by what appeared to be a small subterranean lake. It was overgrown with moss or lichen, and the water was very still.

"There," Conkney said, pointing to the watery pit. "I tell you about the plumbing to prepare you for this. Everything the MacLaddich ever wanted gone, they threw into that foul brine."

It smelled bad, but not as foul as I thought it should following Conkney's explanation. Perhaps the passage of time had mitigated the odor.

"When wee Anne made her dark bargain—and the 'uman sacrifices happened—all the bodies went there," Conkney continued as we reached a landing near the watery. "They were cast out, as if they were nothing, those wee lads and lasses. As if they were shite. But they weren't. They were people."

Horst, quite an athletic chap, leapt to the edge of the pit and let his camera creep across the surface of the dark water. His lens probed the membranous layer of organic growth. It looked like a bacterial sample that a giant had sneezed onto an even gianter petri dish.

On the far side of the landing was an ominous iron door with large metal clasps. Conkney shined his flashlight across it. I saw that the clasps had already been unfastened.

"There," Conkney said. "That's the way to the torture rooms. I've been beyond that door, but not far. If you ask me—"

Conkney stopped talking as a bloodcurdling scream resounded from the corridor above. I jumped an inch in my shoes. Horst—despite his experience—staggered wildly, and I was momentarily afraid he would drop the camera in the ancient dung-pool.

It sounded like MacTavish again. Perhaps she and MacDonald had been revisited by the great, glowing eyes. Or perhaps, I thought cynically, they were creating more sound-effects in case our tour of the dungeon should prove less supernatural than hoped. Horst shone his camera light back toward the stairs.

Moments later, MacTavish and MacDonald came running into view.

"Hello there," I said mischievously. "Did you have another visit?"

MacDonald nodded his head yes. His expression said they clearly did not intend to wait around for a third. MacTavish looked too frightened to respond, and merely shuffled past me until she stood beside Conkney.

"Well then," I said. "It looks as though we'll be together after all. Mr. Conkney, if you are ready, please proceed with the tour."

Conkney gave MacTavish and MacDonald a long look to say that this was all very strange. Then he pried open the iron door—it was small and hatefully wrought—and took us down the coal-black tunnel that sloped beyond. There were sconces every few feet, but no torches. After what seemed like thirty or forty yards, we came upon the first of the cells—low and tiny with unevenly-spaced iron bars. I was not filled with any supernatural dread, but to see this place firsthand put a sorrow in my heart for anyone who had ended his days in such a wretched, uncomfortable locale. We continued down the passage-way and passed several more just like it.

"These were where the prisoners were kept between interrogations," Conkney said. He began to advance more slowly. Again, I had the sense that he genuinely dreaded whatever lay inside these vaults.

"Of course, the MacLaddich were only ever attacked by raiders from overseas," Cockney continued. "Far overseas, usually. I don't think the MacLaddich and their foes spoke enough words in common to learn a damn thing from the people they tortured. But that didn't stop the MacLaddich from trying."

The tunnel began to level off. Soon, I discerned another iron door just ahead.

"We now step into the torture chamber," Conkney said. "This is as far as ever I've been. And as far as I hope ever to go."

This door was still latched, and we all waited for Conkney to undo the ancient iron clasps that held it shut. One clasp had been tied with metal twine. It was clear that it would take our guide several tense moments to unravel it. Horst used this pause in the action to train his camera on our faces, one-by-one. He included Harry— our boom mic operator—and then his own face, turning his camera around and assuming an expression of great trepidation.

A minute later, the twine was unfastened, and Conkney drew open the door. It had not been greased for centuries, and we jumped at the horrible grate of metal-on-metal. Conkney's hand was now shaking, and this was reflected in the beam of his flashlight as he shone it across the dingy, low-ceilinged chamber just beyond. The room was circular, with a stone floor and rough rock walls. Everything had been stained black with soot. We followed Conkney inside.

Within the room were piles of broken furniture and small mounds of scrap iron. It made me think of the ruins of an ancient garage or machine shop. Nothing in the twists of metal on the floor gave me a clue as to exactly which implements of torture had been used here. In a way, not knowing was worse. I looked at the wreckage and imagined unspeakably horrible machines of pain, and the faces of those who spent their last moments upon or inside of them.

Horst stood in the center of the room and panned in a slow circle. I leaned close to each pile of wood and metal, allowing the camera on my chef's hat to capture everything I was seeing.

I reflected on Conkney's claim that he had been no deeper than this. At first, I wondered how it would be possible to go any lower. Then I spied a small, craggy opening on the far side of the chamber. It looked just large enough for a person to traverse. Had people not been physically smaller hundreds of years ago, owing to poor nutrition and such? Perhaps it was just the right size for a MacLaddich of five hundred years before. I again recalled the tales of the "rabbit warren" of passages that ran underneath and down to the sea.

No sooner had I noticed this dark passageway than MacTavish and MacDonald began acting strangely. They wordlessly brushed past the rest of us, traversed the length of the torture chamber as if uninterested by its wrecked contents, and filed into this craggy passage on the opposite side of the room.

"Ach!" Conkney said, clearly baffled. "Stop! Wait! What're ye—? Don't go down there!"

MacTavish and MacDonald seemed not to hear. Though moments before they had given the appearance of being most terrified, now they marched forward as if possessed by supernatural courage. Soon they had disappeared entirely into the blackness of the craggy opening.

"Fools!" Conkney shouted into the passageway after them. "That way has not been traversed in a hundred year!' Tis not safe!"

Apparently unmoved, MacDonald and MacTavish did not reply . . . or return.

Horst, ever intrepid, attempted to follow them into the passageway, but quickly found he could not fit his camera rig inside. He looked me up and down, his eyes indicating that I should give it a go. I am a larger man, but I thought I might just fit.

"You mustn't follow them," Conkney cautioned, seeing my intentions. "They've gone mad, those two. It isn't safe down below. The floors are crumbling. There's holes you can fall through, and who knows what else!"

For not the first time that evening, I had the feeling this was all a little too perfect. Though Conkney's concern indeed felt real, I imagined more and more that MacDonald and MacTavish might be manipulating him for the cameras—goading a feeble old man, already known to be superstitious, into doing the acting for them. I felt less in the grip of a haunted locale and more under the manipulation of a master puppeteer. I did not enjoy the sensation.

"Here," I said to Horst. "I can just fit. I'll follow them and use the camera in my hat. Mr. Conkney, may I please have your flashlight?"

I took the heavy flashlight from him and shone its white-blue beam down the passage. The way ahead curved almost immediately, and there was no sign of the twin representatives from the visitor's bureau. I ducked, pulled in my shoulders, and set off down the craggy tunnel.

The rocky floor beneath my feet began to slope, and the tunnel curved and twisted many times.

"Ms. MacTavish!" I called. "Mr. MacDonald! Are you there?"

There was no sign of them. Wary of Conkney's warning about holes in the floor, I was loath to quicken my pace. Yet it soon became clear that MacTavish and MacDonald were walking or running at a good clip, for I did not seem able to catch up with them no matter how fast I went. Soon, despite my trepidation, I was jogging.

After two or three very confusing minutes, the tunnel ahead elongated into a straight shot. It was then that—finally!—I spied MacDonald and MacTavish up ahead. They seemed to walk at a normal pace, but had somehow made a very fast go of it. I trudged after them, calling their names. They moved like zombies or sleepwalkers, drawn forward by an unseen force that commanded the entirety of their attention.

Moments later, I saw that the passageway terminated into a large, cavernous room with a high natural ceiling. I detected a low light source also, yet it was difficult to understand exactly what it could be. The floor of the room was filled with a shallow layer of dark water, only a fraction of an inch thick. MacDonald and MacTavish ventured out across it.

When I reached the edge of the room, I confronted an astounding sight that stopped me cold. Two great, circular orbs—big as bowling balls and incandescent—floated in the air ten feet above the water. They were yellow and had identical black centers very like pupils.

I hesitated. What could this be? Luminous gas from the sewers was my first guess. And MacDonald had remarked that ball lightning was a possibility.

I hesitated to follow my hosts, who continued to walk in the direction of the orbs. It was like they were drawn to them. I paused at the edge of the water and thought. What possessed them? Why would they not respond to my calls? I was suddenly less sure that this was a contrived event.

Perhaps they were entranced, and must physically be shaken from a stupor. For this reason, I approached the diminutive MacTavish—who was right ahead of me—and attempted to grasp her shoulder. *My hand went right through her frame.*

For a second time I froze. I felt dizzy and sick to my stomach.

MacDonald and MacTavish—*or else forms representing them*—continued their march across the shallow water toward the glowing orbs. Then another realization struck home. As I looked at it more closely, I saw that the water beneath them was not shallow at all. It was—in fact—very, very deep and went down hundreds of feet. Possibly, it connected with the ocean below. The forms of MacDonald and MacTavish were not walking atop a shallow pool. They were floating unnaturally on the surface of the water.

Then the thing that drove me half mad and sent me running in the direction from whence I had come . . .

After probing the waterline in astonishment with my flashlight beam, I looked up again at the two orbs. They were adjusting themselves; the black centers were looking at me. They were now clearly eyes, and they were aware. All of this was apparent to me in one horrible instant.

Then the black lake below—upon which MacDonald and MacTavish now floated—seemed to change shape subtly so that it gaped like one enormous mouth. Hungry. Waiting for me to fall inside. To become its meal. To change from preparer of food to food myself. I have never seen so perfect an expression of deep gustatory anticipation . . . and I am a chef.

I turned and fled in madness, retreating down the passageway with all the speed I could muster. I hit my head and scraped my arms along the narrow walls. I was not thinking logically. It was a primal, animal response. It was a fear I hope never to feel again.

Within moments, I saw the torture chamber looming ahead. Horst, Harry, and Conkney looked on curiously as

I blew right past them, heading back up toward the great hall. I was also, apparently, screaming. I have no memory of this, but the recordings from our cameras place the matter beyond doubt.

I fled past the underground sewage pit and bounded up the steps, taking them two at a time. I was breathing hard. My pulse was in my ears. My heart was in my throat.

Ahead of me, I saw the firelight from the great hall and smelled the MacLaddich Long Sheep cooking in its pot. The odor was stronger now, and apparently the seasonings had a time-release property. What assailed my nostrils as I neared the great hall—while still certainly holding a bass note of boiled sheep—seemed now infused with a new flavor, entirely unknown to my palate.

I burst through the doorway at the top of the staircase. The cooking fire still blazed, and the filming lights still cast their powerful if unforgiving glow. To my great relief, I was now able to see beyond the limitation of my flashlight beam. Behind me, I heard the crew and old Conkney racing to catch up, shouting confused questions as they went.

I steadied myself against the nearest stone pillar and took several deep breaths, trying to forget what I had seen. The lake that was a mouth. The horrible, sentient eyes of fire.

Then I saw that I was not alone in the hall. A human figure lay prone on the floor beside my chef's station. A pool of deep crimson surrounded it on all sides. Steeling myself for another terror, I crept over. It was Ms. MacTavish. A large kitchen knife was beside her on the floor, also stained red. Her throat had been cut, and so had both of her wrists.

At that moment Horst and the others burst through the door and shared in my discovery.

"What the hell is happening!?" Horst cried in alarm. The veteran ghost-hunter swagger had left him entirely. When he saw the corpse on the floor, he went white as a sheet. The camera shook in his grip.

"But . . . she was just downstairs with us!" Harry said, lowering his boom mic. "How did she get back up here so fast? Who would have killed her?"

"It looks very much like she killed herself," I said, preparing to dial for the authorities.

"Slit her own throat?" Horst said doubtfully. "Is that even possible to do?"

"Maybe it was MacDonald, that fat man?" Harry tried. "Maybe he did it."

"Ach!" Conkney spat. "If 'twas he, we won't ever know why."

"How's that?" I asked, turning to face the old man.

Conkney merely pointed to the burbling cauldron. There, two men's loafers on the ends of stout legs jutted forth just above the waterline. MacDonald had plunged—or had *been* plunged—head first inside the roiling water. From the look and smell of it, he had been cooking for some time.

Horst, Harry, and I all shook our heads. Our mouths hung agape. We couldn't think of any explanation.

"The demon," observed old Conkney. "It hasn't lost its touch."

And that was all he would say.

Despite the impediments inherent in servicing a rural locale, the Outer, Outer Hebrides emergency services arrived quickly and worked with exceeding efficiency. Conkney, my crew, and myself were questioned by the police. The entire castle was turned into a crime scene. At least the parts aboveground. The police, like Conkney, seemed hesitant to venture below.

All of my cooking implements were confiscated for forensic analysis. Our footage, too, was taken into custody. The Ghost Chef shooting schedule had us leaving the following morning for a tour of Ohio's most haunted colleges—and corresponding regional fare, such as it was. But when it was clear that we would be detained indefinitely, the show was suspended and all future shoots were put on hold. By the time we were cleared of wrongdoing and released, I received word that Ghost Chef had been officially cancelled. On the phone, a producer told me that word was already spreading about what had happened at MacLaddich Castle. The network was hesitant to associate itself with something so upsetting. Inquiries into the supernatural were one thing, but actual murder was—apparently—another.

I still don't know what became of my cooking equipment that was confiscated for analysis. I certainly never asked for it back. The thought of slicing a celery or ham hock with a knife that might have been used to take the life of Ms. MacTavish was too much for me. I did not inquire, either, as to the state of our footage, though weeks later some of it was mysteriously leaked onto the Internet. I believe that the footage backs up my version of events. The footage from my chef's hat camera does seem to contain some curious omissions toward the end, especially in the shot where my hand passes through the ghostly form of MacTavish. It is very difficult to discern her figure at all in the grainy, internet footage. Likewise, the appearance of the giant glowing eyes seems noticeably diminished in the online version, the orbs rather appearing to be circular lens flare.

I do not apologize for any of our actions that evening. I believe we behaved correctly and reasonably at every turn. Of course, when the basic details of this mishap emerged, the news outlets ran wild with exaggerations of the facts. Bloggers especially claimed to have on good authority that MacDonald's body had been cooked intentionally by me to appease the ghost, and that I had served it to the local peasants in the countryside around MacLaddich Castle.

But the Internet is the Internet, and there will always be exaggerations.

Chef Dunnally takes up his mixing bowl and spoon and begins to stir the batter once more. We listen for a moment to the repetitive, almost hypnotic *clack* this produces. It comes again and again and again.

"That's sad," one of the visitors whispers.

"Such a tragedy," says another.

"I don't care if there was a murder on the set of his show," another opines in a tone that says she is determined to remain positive. "This man's a genius, and I have all his books. His recipe for white truffle flan ought to be in the Smithsonian."

Dunnally smiles from above his bowl to acknowledge the compliment.

The visitors have finished their dinner rolls. I'm well aware that if I do not move them along, they may ask for seconds or even thirds. And Dunnally, kind chap that he is, will happily oblige them. However, a prolonged detour does not serve my current purposes.

"Thank you, Chef Dunnally," I announce. "What a rare treat! A behind-the-scenes look into the high-stakes world of culinary television programming."

Most of the guests understand I wish for them to move along, but a pair of admirers indicate that they would like to remain behind. They say that they desire to have their photos taken with Chef Dunnally and then to speak with him in more detail about specific cooking techniques.

"I'm such a fan," one woman tells me. "Getting to meet him in person. . . . This really is an unexpected pleasure!"

"Of course," I tell her. "Yet the tour must continue."

Chef Dunnally interjects to say that he would be more than happy to show the pair out afterwards.

"Ooh, wonderful!" the other of the fans quips. "Can we please?"

"Well then," I say to them both. "I suppose there is nothing wrong with that. It has been a pleasure having you along. I hope we see you again soon."

Years of practice allow me to avoid laughing outright.

"If you will all kindly follow me . . ." I announce to the rest. "We will next climb the second set of stairs at the end of the hall. Though I know it's difficult to leave these wonderful sights and smells behind, our next stop will provide sustenance for your souls. Something, I'm told, that can be almost as pleasurable."

I point across the kitchens to an alcove where a pair of marble staircases stretch away. Both display exceedingly exquisite—if disparate—ornamentation. One features decorative flourishes that hold a forestry theme—fauns, ducks, and rabbits decorate the handrails and balusters. The other can be said to confer feelings that are insectoid if they are anything. Antennae, body segments, and spindly legs are all invoked by the strange forms that wrap themselves around the handrails. It is difficult for me to declare for certain which one I prefer.

"That chef was really something, Vick," the red-haired girl says with a smile.

For the moment I elect to ignore her impudence.

"Isn't he," I respond evenly. "Those dinner rolls are divine."

"I didn't see you take any," the girl observes.

Eagle-eyed, this one.

"I . . . ate before," I respond truthfully.

"I never saw his show, *The Tasmanian Chef*," says the red-haired girl.

"It probably went off the air before you were born," I tell her. "Just between you and me, it never ranked with the finest in the genre."

I take one last look at the pair of guests who have chosen to remain behind. One mugs for photos with Dunnally while the other peppers him with questions about his favored cooking implements.

"Another two down," I say.

"What?" asks the red-haired girl.

"Oh, nothing," I tell her.

The other visitors have crossed the kitchen and now begin to ascend the second marble staircase, looking warily at the spider-like extensions framing the rails.

"Should we follow them?" the girl asks.

I shrug as if I could go either way.

"I suppose," I tell her. "But first, a question."

"Of course," the girl says brightly.

I frown at the speed of her reply. Confidence is one thing, but overconfidence kills.

"Chef Dunnally's tale is haunted," I tell her. "It is haunted in many different ways. The end, in particular, I find exceptional. Exceptionally disturbing, perhaps, I ought to say. The commingling of sheep and human in the cauldron. . . . A nasty business, no?"

"Is that the question?" the red-haired girl asks. "Because, yes, it is nasty."

"I'm curious," I tell her. "What if you were to eat some of the sheep from the cauldron in the story? Chef Dunnally swears that no one did, but that is beside the point. What if you ate some of the sheep, and were unable to detect the presence of the . . . unfortunate Scotsman who had boiled with it?"

The red-haired girl wrinkles her nose. I can tell she dislikes the direction this is going. Thus, I proceed.

"What if you couldn't tell?" I ask her. "What if you were eating food that was, to some small degree, human in nature . . . but weren't able to detect it?"

The red-haired girl opens her mouth in exasperation.

"Ugh," she says.

"Well . . ." I continue. "Where would be that harm in it?'

The girl looks away and rolls her eyes.

"That's your question?"

"Indeed," I say.

"You can't eat people!" she says. "Everybody knows that. Cannibalism is wrong."

"Even just a teensy little bit?" I press.

"Yes," she says as if it should be obvious.

"Have you ever bit a fingernail, or sucked on a bleeding finger after you cut it?" I ask.

"Of course, but that's different."

"A mother feeds her baby with milk from her own body," I say. "Men and women exchange vital essences in the physical act of love. None of this is called cannibalism."

"But . . ." she wavers, then stands firm again. "No. It's wrong. Eating someone who was in a pot is different."

"Why?" I ask her.

"It just is," she says. "And I don't care if you think that's the wrong answer; it's the one I'm giving you because it's true!"

She is breathing hard, exasperated. It is clear this question has strained her beyond all others.

"Who said anything about it being the wrong answer?" I tell her, heading toward the staircase.

"Oh," she says, following after me. "Okay then."

"One thing, incidentally. If you call me 'Vick' again, I will scatter your essential parts to the four corners of the world and eat your soul. Or else dismiss you from the tour. I'm not sure which is worse. Do you understand?"

The red-haired girl is silent for a moment. Unbowed . . . but certainly aware that I am not kidding.

"What should I call you then?" she asks as we start up the insectoid stair. I climb ahead of her—taking the steps two at a time—to avoid providing an answer.

Signora Regina

The tour group has gathered in a semi-circle around the pair of heavy walnut doors at the top of the stair. I have been told that the architect of the Grand Hotel intended that these doors should be entirely soundproof—and, indeed, that they once were . . . at least for the hotel's first hundred years—but time has a way of wearing down even the most ingenious marvels of engineering. The felts that line the doors have rotted off and never been replaced. The rubber stoppers that once made an airtight seal have disappeared. (It is possible that they wore away over time, but I have a hunch that they were intentionally removed.)

By the time the red-haired girl and I arrive on the landing, the visitors have sufficiently "shushed" one another to allow the honeyed noise coming from within to seep through the openings in the walnut. It is the sound of a bow across strings. It is deep, golden, perfect. The player steers her instrument slowly and passionately through its paces; without rush yet without rest. A few in the group are hard of hearing and lean in close with their ears cupped. Others soon become annoyed with this practice, as it tends to block the sound for the rest of them.

I stand quietly, watching them listen for the better part of a minute. It is always more gratifying to break the spell when the audience is completely under its sway.

"Signora Regina will be wrapping up her practice session shortly!" I cry, looking down at my watch. Several members of the group jump. Several others face me with expressions of the deepest annoyance. I savor them for as long as I can.

"Ahh," I say, checking my watch a second time. "In point of fact, she has already lingered beyond her allotted hours. The Grand Hotel is not insensitive to an artist's desire for a late-night practice session—the muse strikes when it strikes, no?—but the Signora's relationship with our residents directly above the recital hall can become strained when she goes overlong."

"A recital hall?" one of the guests asks.

"That's correct," I reply. "It is not a large space, and we have never advertised the performances held within. However—especially in the hotel's earliest days—we found that many guests were desirous of a private salon in which they could perform for one another. Come . . ."

And with that, I knock three times on the dark walnut. The doors have a remarkably percussive quality. We listen as three identical notes thunder into the room beyond. A moment later, the stringed instrument stops completely.

Some of the crowd begins to edge forward, but I lift my arm to stay them.

"Let us delay ourselves just one moment," I whisper.

Experience has taught me that musicians and singers—or, really, artists of any kind—do not react well to being surprised in the midst of their work. It is prudent to give them a moment to collect themselves before receiving outsiders. Otherwise, the results can be downright unpredictable.

When I have finished counting to fifteen inside my head, I carefully push open the walnut portal and allow the visitors to peer within. Beyond the doors they see a small theater with seating for barely more than thirty persons. A small stage is raised perhaps two feet from the rest of the floor. It has an ancient lectern to one side, carved to resemble a walnut tree. In the center of the stage is a wooden chair with a thick red cushion. A music stand rests nearby. Standing beside that is Signora Regina.

A striking, tall woman, her age is largely indeterminate (much like mine). Yet if there is a single grey hair amid her fine dark locks, I have never seen it. Her eyes are nearly black and her lips are a fiery crimson. Her dress this evening is tight, yes, but not overly revealing. She almost always wears red.

As I step into the salon, she lowers her viola and begins to return it to the velvet-lined case at her feet.

"Signora," I call to the stage (for I have learned that she will answer to nothing else). "Do forgive my interruption of your rehearsal . . . which I see has extended somewhat past our agreed-upon hours."

She rolls her eyes at me, then grins, revealing beautiful straight teeth. I linger on the sight, probably a beat too long.

"I have a group of visitors who are enjoying a tour of the Grand Hotel," I say as they slowly begin to enter the salon. The chairs are arrayed in short rows. We approach Signora Regina by walking down a center aisle between them.

"Vick," she says, placing her delicate bow on the lip of the music stand. "It's a surprise to find you in this part of the building. Is anything wrong?"

"Hardly," I say, my smile unwavering. "In fact, things are very, very right."

I feel the red-haired girl tugging at my sleeve.

"How come she gets to call you—"

I wave the question away.

"We have just come from the kitchens," I continue. "The group was quite taken with Chef Dunnally's cuisine. A few even stayed behind to chat."

Signora Regina opens her mouth to say something, but is rather rudely cut off by one of the visitors.

"We heard you through the doors!" the guest cries, smiling, overloud, bristling with excitement. "You play the violin so beautifully!"

"A viola, actually," I clarify.

Signora Regina merely smiles.

"Do you perform with an orchestra?" another visitor asks.

"Ooh, yes," says yet another. "Are you rehearsing for a show? A concert in a big amphitheater, I expect?"

The Signora smiles in embarrassment and looks away. I do not like to see her uncomfortable.

"Signora Regina has performed on several globe-spanning tours with a variety of musical acts," I explain. "Classical, popular, baroque, jazz, even punk rock, if I'm not mistaken. There have been articles written about her playing and she's graced the covers of publications, though usually as a member of a larger group. Signora Regina is the very picture of modesty when it comes to her talents. I, however, do not hesitate to sing her praises. We are incredibly fortunate to have her as one of the Grand Hotel's permanent residents."

"Do you . . . does she . . . play concerts for the guests?" one of the visitors asks, uncertain which one of us to address.

Signora Regina crosses her arms, looks down at me from the stage, and smiles expectantly from ear to ear. (However I respond will doubtless be an amusement to her.) I do reply, but not for a moment. Her smile is captivating and I cannot stop myself from pausing to bask in it a few instants longer.

"The Signora is . . . a born entertainer," I explain. (My response indeed has its intended effect, for she nearly guffaws. [This expression is only attractive in the most striking of women. Luckily for me, the Signora falls squarely within that category.])

"At present, however, I expect she is tired of playing—her rehearsal having stretched beyond its allotted time limit."

I drink in the disappointment and alarm in the visitors' eyes. It's like a tall lemonade after a long evening's hot work. Delicious. Even the fair Signora cannot compete.

"Your guide is correct," the Signora says. "But I know better than to be rude. If he will consent to it, I can play an abbreviated passage. Perhaps from an original composition."

There is agreement all around that this is a fine idea. The visitors quickly file into the wooden seats in front of the stage. One says: "Ooh, the folks who stayed down in the kitchen haven't a clue what they're missing."

I choose to remain standing, aloof, off to the side. (The red-haired girl lingers next to me for a moment, unsure what to do. I indicate that while she may be favored, she is still a member of the tour group. She nods and takes a seat with all the rest.)

The Signora retrieves the large viola from her case, places it in the crook of her neck, and takes up her bow. Then she looks hard at her music stand and inhales, quietly but very deeply. Ahh, that lovely moment of silence—of anticipation—before she actually begins to play. How I enjoy the total, utter disconnect between what the visitors are expecting to hear, and what I know they will experience as she begins to move the bow across the strings.

Except tonight, it seems, the joke is on me.

Instead of her usual onrush of mad, mechanical fiddling—so wild it reliably raises the hair on the back of my neck—Signora Regina plays a slow, gentle tune, almost childishly simple. A few bars in she gives me a wink over the top of her viol. I cannot help but laugh. After all these years, she still finds ways to surprise me.

For a time, the tune sounds vaguely Hungarian or Romanian, though those distinctions have less and less meaning for me as time passes. Then the opening theme returns, and we are once again in the land of lullabies.

All at once it strikes me.

Treachery! Sedition!

Annoyed with me for despoiling her practice, she contrives to use her art to lull my visitors into a state of insensibility, spoiling my project entirely. With mounting anxiety, I hazard a glance at the red-haired girl. Her eyelids have already begun to droop. As have those of the guests surrounding her. This cannot stand.

I wait for a quiet ritardando during which the Signora's touch becomes especially delicate, then begin applauding as loudly as I possibly can.

"Bravissima!" I cry. "Huzzah! My dear Signora, you have not lost a step."

The visitors shake awake. Trained since birth like monkeys, they follow my lead and a powerful applause soon mounts. You would be surprised by the noise that a modest but determined audience can muster.

The Signora understands that I have detected her poisoned dagger and employed my own counterstroke. She continues to play for a few moments more, her expression indicating that she is not finished. Yet I have rallied my troops. Armed with wave after wave of applause, we have soon broken her sleeping spell.

She puts down her viola and gives me an annoyed glance. The visitors begin to rise from their seats, already anticipating a journey to the next stop on our tour. I raise my hand to stay them.

"Signora Regina," I call. "That was a beautiful—if somewhat muted—demonstration of your talents. I wonder, perhaps the visitors would also enjoy hearing the story of how you came to be our guest at the hotel? It is such an interesting and personal tale. . . . And the effect would be notably less soporific, if you'll pardon my saying so. You may elect to tell it to them, certainly . . . or I could always step in and do the honors."

Her annoyed glances quickly consolidate into a frightful scowl.

It is still remarkably alluring.

"That story is mine to tell," she cries. "Mine alone!"

"Well then . . . " I say, and gesture to the audience.

The Signora moves the music stand so that the tour group can see her face. Then she lifts her neck. (It is an unconscious imitation of the moment when she readies her instrument. These things become ingrained. Ventriloquists follow you with their hands, even when Punch and Judy have been placed back inside their cases. The military man stands at attention even when a noncommissioned person of importance enters the room.)

The Signora hesitates for another tantalizing, nearly ineffable moment. She looks over at me. Does my face betray my breathless expectation? My own deep, abiding pleasure? No, I have trained myself well. I appear unmoved as a subterranean stone a thousand feet beneath the Earth's crust. Something in the Signora's red lips says that she sees through my bluff. Yet this may be only a bluff of her own. . . .

Moments later—mere instants by the tick of a clock, but eons in the theater of the mind—the Signora begins to speak.

My story is about love. You have to understand that before anything else will make sense.

My first love was music. I was born in a small village in Italy, into a very musical family. My father was an instrument-maker by trade, and my mother and sisters were singers. I cannot remember a time before I made music. In our house, it was as natural as breathing.

Neither do I have a strong sense of when I first began to play the viol. In my father's workshop, I was playing *with* instruments before I was playing them in any proper sense. Precisely where and when one activity transitioned into the other I do not know. Yet I must have been quite young. I remember playing a violin in my father's shop the morning before I started school.

Throughout my life, music has been a passion. It has also been a source of great love, great friendships, and even great romances.

Does the Signora's eye flit in my direction for the smallest fraction of a second? No. My imagination, almost certainly . . .

Only once has it been the source of anything other than goodness and light. That single instance is the story I must relate. The story of how I came to be a resident in . . . this place.

I do not speak immodestly—only accurately—to say that my father was a master of his art. He oversaw every aspect of his craft and personally made excursions into the forests to select the right trees from which to create his remarkable instruments. I can clearly recall him, ax in hand, taking me along on these trips when I was no more than nine or ten. I remember the coarse bark against my hands as we hauled a cut tree back to his workshop, then watching as he chipped away the bark and began to work the wood.

My father told us that he had learned the art of selecting trees from his own father, who had learned it from his. And once—I remember it was during the holidays, and he had had more to drink than usual—he told me that our forest grew a special kind of wood, called heartwood. It was a hybrid created by our ancestors, and I would not find it in any book. It made a finished product that looked like oak or maple, but in truth was something else entirely. This wood, unknown to the larger world, was what gave his instruments their celebrated beauty and quality.

It was apparent from a young age that I wished to pursue a musical vocation. My family did not, generally, attempt to dissuade me. However, there were certain types of which my father clearly approved, and certain types which he did not. When the urge toward rebellion hit in my teenage years, I knew that that which was closest to my father's heart would be the greatest help in breaking it. Yes, I smoked cigarettes and spent time with the wrong crowd—as, of course, one does—but I also began to play the wrong kind of music. The knockout punch came when I foreswore my classical training altogether, stole one of my father's finest creations—an exquisite viola upon which he had been working off-and-on for many years— and ran away with a group of gypsy musicians.

A bold move for a young girl, you may say. And it was. Yet I knew what my skills were, and I knew that musical groups of all types were always looking to update their rosters with fresh, new talent. I bet that if my role with the gypsies did not "work out," there would be others, and others still. In this assumption, I was completely correct.

After two years of touring with the gypsies, I left when an opportunity with an orchestra presented itself. That, I quit almost immediately, when unwanted advances from the snare drummer did not subside.

From there it was on to an ironic alternative country and western act. Then, when my acumen in that style of music became established, to a non-ironic one. Soon, my permanent membership in any musical group became rather fluid. When tours happened, and I was available, I took the work. Soon I had accumulated enough wealth to live well and independently, and to select only the gigs that I liked best.

The stories from my touring days could fill volumes, my dears. But, then again, they would not be the story of how I came to the Grand Hotel . . .

That story begins on a rainy night in Chicago inside a music club called The Abbey. I was playing there with a touring act loosely described as "folk rockers." Their name is not important. What *is* important is that it was onstage with them that I first noticed the woman in the green dress. She also wore black glasses and had long, dark hair flowing over her shoulders. Her eyes were bright and piercing and her mouth was curled into a smile as if she were in possession of a wonderful secret. My description does her no justice; she was really quite stunning.

It was the last of three consecutive shows at this venue. When I first looked out into the audience and glimpsed her, I thought immediately that I had seen her somewhere before.

Now I will tell you a musician's secret: Many traveling acts have groups—or even legions—of followers who come to their concerts regularly. This is a good thing, and musicians appreciate it. Without people buying tickets, we wouldn't have jobs! Yet within this category of appreciative fan, you must now imagine the most-appreciative one percent: The dedicated admirers. The ones who attend concerts night after night and travel from city to city to view their favorite musical acts.

The secret is that there is usually something wrong with these people. They are like bar patrons who stay and drink all day and night. Like gamblers who never leave the casino. Something is broken inside of them. What are they looking for? Why do they hope to find it at our concerts? Does our music simply numb the pain of their existence?"

That was what blindsided me about the woman in the green dress. I was suddenly aware I'd seen her before, perhaps repeatedly. This was not her first time as a member of our audience. But even if she were one of these broken souls who came night after night, I decided then and there that I still had to have her. I was not a typical romantic, given to falling in love impulsively. Yet I would pursue this one with all my might.

To be more precise about the circumstances, it was during the end of our first set that she came to my attention. In those days we played three sets a night and sometimes also an encore. The mystery woman hovered off to one side, right at the foot of the stage. I couldn't tell if she was there with friends or had come alone. She did not fix her eyes on me, but rather let her gaze linger across the entire band. Even so, when she did glance my way, it was as if I could feel the weight of her attention physically resting on my shoulders. It was wonderful.

She was so beautiful, so exotic—and, yes—so familiar.

The band had pulled into Chicago directly after a series of gigs along the Eastern seaboard. Could it be that I knew her from New York, or Boston, or Washington D.C.? Audiences had a way of blurring together in my memory.

A few members of our band were always keen to sleep with enthusiastic fans, but I usually did not indulge—preferring instead to meet the men and women who shared my bed in other, private circumstances. I had, however, watched my amorous colleagues in action, and there did not seem to be much trick to it. As I looked down from the stage at the mysterious woman, I tried to recall their best techniques for flirting.

After our first set, I excused myself and headed out to the crowded floor of the concert hall. Attempting to appear casual, I walked to the line at the bar—already three deep—and ordered myself a cocktail. I stirred the drink idly, accepted kudos from a few appreciative fans, and searched for the woman in the green dress.

She looked younger than I do now, but only just. This did not concern me. I had often found the embrace of an older woman quite to my liking. I hoped that she would be interested in me. The thought made me more and more excited.

And yet I could not find her.

My point of view from the bar was not what it was up on the stage, but as I made a slow circuit of the busy venue she was simply nowhere to be found. Had she gone outside to have a smoke, or gotten in line for the ladies room? I climbed to the balcony level and kept an eye on the doors. Still nothing. No woman in the green dress. Soon our break was over and I was forced to return to the stage.

We began the second set, and I saw her again almost immediately. It did not take her long to push her way back to the front row and linger there, right beneath me. She could have reached out and touched me. I grew bold and allowed myself to make eyes at her.

She seemed to return the expression in a playful, if noncommittal way. I privately vowed that after the second set, I would make her mine.

Pleased to know the object of my affection had not departed from the music hall, I became once again lost in my playing. That night we were—as they say— "on fire." It was one of those special concerts when the mix is perfect, the crowd is full of energy, and you find yourselves playing flawlessly. My viola took on a life of its own.

Was I overplaying, with the goal of impressing my would-be beau? I have no recollection, but probably.

By the end of our second set I was out of breath and my forehead was slick with sweat. Yet one look out into the eyes of the woman in the green dress was enough to make me forget my exhaustion. As the audience applauded and we prepared to take our final break, I signaled for her to wait where she was.

We walked offstage and I quickly ducked through the side door and out into the audience. And yet again she was gone!

I walked to the spot where she had stood just a moment before. I began to feel a vertigo that had nothing to do with exhaustion or cocktails. It seemed logistically impossible for her to have passed so quickly out of sight.

I slowly turned in a circle, surveying the entire venue floor. What was happening? Had I scared her away? Was she too shy to be approached? I was at a loss.

In mounting frustration, I asked the nearby audience members if they had seen a lady in a green dress. They shook their heads. This was also unnerving. She was so striking. So unusual. So lovely. It felt unlikely that anybody would fail to notice a woman like that.

Confused and sullen, I went back onstage for our final set. Again the woman in green reappeared! Utterly baffled, I gazed down into her eyes. Somehow, she looked even more alluring than before. Perhaps she had spent the last break in the washroom touching up her face. Yes, that must be it, I decided. She wanted to look her best for me, here, now, at the end of the evening.

We played long into the night. The crowd did not taper off, even when it passed into the early morning hours. When our final encore was complete, they stamped their feet and cried for more.

As usual, I stepped off of the stage in something of a daze, like an athlete after a long game. Still, my focus was on finding the woman in green. In my mind she hovered like a shining emerald amid the darkness of the concert hall.

Several fans were waiting to meet the band, but the woman in green wasn't among them. My mind raced anew. Would she meet me outside? I followed the audience filing out of The Abbey and searched the sidewalk. Nothing. I jogged back to where our tour van was parked behind the building. Two people were smoking beside it, but neither was the woman in green. I searched the ladies room, the band lounge in the basement, and the contiguous bar. Nothing. Nothing. Nothing. Just like that . . . she was gone.

I hung my head in defeat, crippled by a longing like I had never known.

That night in the hotel, I could not sleep a wink. I thought again and again of how I might have reached down and touched her, and how that chance was lost. Of course I had left my number with the bartenders and manager, with instructions to give it to anyone even vaguely fitting the description of the woman. But no message ever came. The next morning we left for a show in Indianapolis. I sulked for days.

Yet this is a story about the kind of people who follow a musical band, is it not? So I think you can guess what happened next . . .

To be precise, it was one month later—near the end of our tour, at a venue in Los Angeles—when I saw her again. Or thought I saw her. This time she was standing off to the side of the capacity crowd we had brought to the Viper Room. Her appearance had changed. Her hair was no longer flowing, but short and bobbed. Her eyeglasses had been shed entirely. She wore shiny metallic earrings and had piercings in all parts of her face. Instead of a flowing green dress, she wore tight, black leather.

Yet it was the same woman!

As we played, I stared dumbfounded as the truth of this dawned on me. It was her. Differently attired and halfway across the country, but still her. I was so awestruck that I missed several cues during our first song.

I smiled at her cautiously. She smiled back.

I knew that I must have her! She had not left my thoughts in the four weeks since Chicago. I silently vowed not to let her creep away without at least learning her name.

When our first set came to a close, I did not allow myself even to remove my eyes from the mysterious woman. I did not go backstage. Still clutching my viola and bow, I leapt straight down into the audience until I stood next to her. The woman did not budge or try to run from her spot on the venue floor. It seemed finally that she would be mine.

"Hello there, my dear!" I cried brightly.

She only smiled.

"Am I going crazy, or did I see you at our show in Chicago?"

Here, a nod. And then a smile. A beautiful, enchanting smile.

"It's nice to see you again. Can I get you something from the bar?"

She seemed to indicate that this would be acceptable.

"Great," I said. "Why don't you come with me?"

The woman agreed, and we pushed our way to the nearest bartender. I ordered two drinks and paid for them with our band's vouchers. But when I turned back around . . . she had vanished once again.

And that was where I began to sense that something was really wrong.

I set down the drinks and returned to the stage for our second set. Part of me knew that the mysterious woman would reappear when we began to play, but now this knowledge was tinged with uneasiness. With wrongness. When, indeed, she did appear, her face wore no expression of contrition.

No glutton for punishment, I tried not to allow myself to think about her beautiful smile or how enticing her body looked in all of that leather. I cleared my mind and thought only about the music.

When I remembered to look for her at the end of the night, she was gone.

In the weeks and months that followed, flashes of this mystery woman became a regular feature of my life. At some shows, she appeared for a second or two. I might get a fleeting glimpse of her face up high in a second-tier balcony, for example. Other times she would linger in her familiar position at the foot of the stage and dance tantalizingly close all night.

I began to wonder how long she had been doing this—how long she had been appearing and disappearing at our shows. The rainy night at The Abbey was the first time I'd really noticed her, but I might have scanned her face in the midst of a throng a hundred times before that. Or a thousand.

Her appearance changed from show to show. Her hair grew longer or shorter. Her clothes went in or out of fashion. Her makeup came and went to varying degrees. Yet it was always the same woman. Still bewitching. Still enticing. Still impossible to capture. I felt like a hunter chasing a mysterious white stag that he is not completely sure exists.

Most of the time I tried to hide my fixation with her. Not least, because I was not sure that other people could see her. One night after a show in Stockholm, I asked our accordion player what he thought of the temptress in the miniskirt and leggings who had swayed back and forth in the second row. He was very interested in women and never one to forget a fetching beauty.

"What are you talking about?" he asked, wrinkling his nose. "The second row was nothing but chinless blue-bloods and duggardly monsters. You should get your eyes checked, Signora! Now, the seventh row, on the other hand. . . . stunners one and all. Mwah!"

He kissed his tented fingertips on one hand.

I let the matter drop and muttered something about being overdue for an eye exam.

I made a few other queries with different band members, but this result was typical. The other members were either unwilling or unable to notice her. Soon I stopped asking.

The mystery woman also did not seem to appear in photographs. I reviewed frame after frame of media from our concerts on my laptop and could never quite find an angle that showed her.

Before long, I considered psychotherapy. Alas, the peripatetic nature of a musician's life meant I would be unable to see the same mental health professional regularly. I was always on tour.

In desperation, I reached out to my few friends who were not musicians. When I hinted that I thought I might be seeing things, they worried that I had fallen in with the drug-using crowd. I insisted that I eschewed anything stronger than a vodka and tonic, but they remained concerned and disapproving. Because of this, I ceased sharing the phenomenon entirely.

Then something remarkable happened.

It was about eight months after the first sighting in Chicago. I had transferred to an entirely different tour, backing up a French electro-pop singer. Our tour had wended its way back to my home country. On the night in question, we were playing a large nightclub in a suburb of Florence.

I had not seen the mystery woman for a few gigs, but this was not uncommon. She came and she went. This night, however, she was out in full force; dressed in an exquisite high-fashion gown with a plunging neckline and even a small bustle. Her face had been painted with glitter and she literally reflected the lights from the stage.

I regarded her cautiously, as I always did, like a dieter passing a cake shop. I wanted her in every understanding of that word . . . yet knew that it could never be.

The electro-pop singer had fans who liked to throw roses. Just before the first encore, I watched as my mystery woman produced a rose of her own and flung it toward the stage. The crimson flower arced through the colored lights and flashing lasers . . . and softly struck my cheek.

I froze. You could have knocked me over with a feather. This strange spirit . . . she had finally touched me! Technically her rose had, but this was certainly a start. I looked down and saw the flower resting on the stage with all the others. I prodded it with my shoe. It was real.

I looked back into the audience. The woman was smiling and nodding. My heart raced! Was tonight different from all other nights? Would we finally make contact?

As it turned out, the answer was no. When the concert concluded, I strolled out to the venue floor. As usual, I found nothing. But when I returned to my dressing room, one of the backup dancers handed me a bouquet with an envelope attached.

"Some lady left this for you," she said.

On the outside of the envelope was written my name. On the inside was a card with one word in a careful calligraphy: Napoli.

We were due to play Naples two days later.

This was a revelation. The mystery woman had not only been seen by someone other than me, she had hand-delivered flowers. And a note. Many times I brought it to my nose and breathed deep, detecting a lingering perfume, the scent of the rose, and . . . something else. An under-note that was as troubling as it was hard to place.

I did not truly sleep for the next forty-eight hours.

At the show in Florence, I was almost too nervous to hold my bow. I had paid more attention to my appearance than usual. Despite our history together—or lack of it—my hopes were high. I dared to dream that tonight something special would occur.

We walked onstage, and there she was, front row center, wearing a white linen dress with a yellow sash. This is hard to articulate, but somehow she looked more "real" than she had previously. The idea that she could ever have been a figment of my imagination suddenly seemed ridiculous.

Usually, when the band is smoking and the crowd is responsive, performances seem to fly by. You look down at your watch and—poof!—it's already midnight. But not this evening. Every song was another barrier between us. Each extended solo further delayed the moment when we would finally embrace.

For her part, the mystery woman seemed as enraptured in the music as ever. If she felt the same impatience, it did not show. She swayed her hips ever so slightly and seductively. I began to feel sick to my stomach from the sheer desire of it.

Finally, blessedly, the concert came to a close. When the lights went up, I saw that the mystery woman was gone. Yet something told me not to despair.

I raced backstage and found her waiting for me at the entrance to the dressing rooms. In her hand she held a strange bouquet of flowers and small sticks. She saw me and raised the bouquet.

I approached slowly, as though she were a forest animal that might dart at any moment. I drew closer. Then closer still. I could smell her perfume. She smiled, and looked directly into my eyes. I did not speak. Soon, I stood with my face only inches from hers. I breathed her breath.

Then she moved her hand forward and it touched mine. I finally felt the warmth of her skin against my own. After a wait of so many months, it was electric. If she had proposed making love then and there, I might well have consented.

So when she leaned in to my ear and whispered—softly, breathily—"Come along with me," I was all but powerless to resist.

Barely stopping to grab my coat, I followed the mystery woman through the corridors at the back of the venue. She navigated them easily, and soon we were through a back door and standing in an alley where an idling Alfa Romeo waited. It was black with tinted windows, and a uniformed driver sat behind the wheel.

"Where are we going? What is your name?" I asked as I followed her into the back seat. She only smiled and winked at me. The car pulled away. The driver conducted us swiftly through the city streets.

The mysterious woman relaxed beside me and draped her arm around my shoulder. All at once, I was like a teenager on a first date. I nuzzled into her, intoxicated by her presence. I was really here! With her! After all these months, it was finally happening!

I had fantasies of our tryst happening in a luxury hotel room, but the Alfa Romeo took us out of the city and into the farms and fields. Whenever I craned my neck to look out the window, the mysterious woman pulled me in close. I felt weak with lust and wanting all anew.

The minutes flew by, and soon we turned off of the highway. Then we left the asphalt and concrete, heading down a dirt road that stretched deep into a forest. Now my brain began to conjure visions of a quaint cottage that might become our love-nest for the next twelve hours.

As it turned out, I was not far off.

The trees soon gave way and we found ourselves in front of a large lawn. Across it, set back against the forest, was a somewhat dilapidated manse. Its exterior was covered in so much ivy that it was often difficult to tell where its walls terminated and the surrounding forest began. I looked over at my mystery woman. Was this her home? She grinned like she knew a secret. The driver depressed a button and the garage door on the ancient manor creaked open.

The car pulled inside and we got out. My mistress dismissed the driver with a single motion, and then led me from the garage into a tastefully appointed sitting room with elegant divans and chairs with soft cushions spread over them. The walls, somewhat curiously, were filled with objects from the forest—tree stumps mounted as though they were artwork, pastiches made from seeds and seed pods, pressed leaves and flowers stuck together on canvases.

Candles burned on almost every surface.

The mystery woman sat at a stately beech table, and I joined her. I was about to lean over for a kiss when we were interrupted by the return of the valet. He carried a silver tray upon which sat two alkaline-glazed stoneware mugs. I could not tell what they contained, but it was warm and steaming.

The valet set the mugs in front of us, then showed himself out. I wondered how he'd had time to heat anything since exiting the car moments before.

The mystery woman took a drink from her mug and motioned for me to do the same. I did. It was some kind of tea, thick and unfiltered. My tongue found bits of bark and flowers in the watery mixture. When I set the mug back down, mud and leaves burbled up to the surface. That much said, the taste was not unpleasant and the immediate effect was quite calming.

For some moments we sat quietly, sipping our beverages. When I could take it no longer, I rose from my seat, stepped over to the woman, and bent forward to kiss her on the neck.

She shrank back and shook her head no.

I cast an expression that said: What have I misunderstood? You brought me all this way . . .

She pointed to my viola case. I had set it on a side table.

"Play first . . ." she whispered.

I was befuddled—and, yes, romantically frustrated—but decided that if a private concert were the final hurdle, I was game to jump it. What was one more performance in the grand scheme of things? I lifted the viola to my chin and began to draw my bow across.

I did not play any specific song. Instead, I created a new composition there in the moment. It was sad and powerful and full of longing. I channeled into it the confusion and frustration of seeing my ephemeral mistress vanish at the end of each performance. Then I expressed my deep longing for her. The craving. The confusion. The sadness. All of it was there in the music.

The woman's expression showed that she was indeed moved by what she heard. Her gazed fixed on me and her eyes sparkled with the first glistening of tears. More than once, her lips tightened as if to show empathy. She lifted her delicate brown nose and breathed heavily, as if fighting back a sob.

It was also during this period that I realized the ingredients in the tea were not entirely inert.

After five minutes of playing, my head began to swim. I felt a thick, narcotic glow rising in my stomach. I was drunk on something more than proximity to the object of my affection.

Before long, the intoxication began to impact my ability to play. I had to stop, and lowered my bow. There was now a ringing in my ears and I felt lightheaded. The darkness in the corners of the room where the candles did not shine seemed to flinch and twitch of its own accord. The walls of the room, very subtly, began to ripple.

Whatever I had ingested, it was hallucinogenic. What I saw next leaves no room for doubt on that point, as I think you will agree.

Now the mysterious woman rose from her chair and approached me. Despite the sway of the tea, I still felt a powerful, drunken craving for her. She reached me and I threw my arms around her and nuzzled close. Ahh, ecstasy! All at once, the wonderful smell of her was in my lungs again. Her body was taut and hard, almost as if she wore a ribbed undergarment. Did my mistress use a corset to create her fetching curves? No matter. I kissed her cheek and ran my fingers through her hair. It was smooth like flax, smelled of harvest time, and was decorated throughout with very small flowers—blue and yellow. I leaned in and put my lips to hers.

All this time, she was likewise moving her hands across my body. Yet suddenly, I had the stark realization that this was not to reciprocate my love-making. Puzzled, I pulled back and saw that she was stroking my viola. I still clutched it absentmindedly against my shoulder. The mystery woman's eyes were drawn to it. They wandered across the ancient instrument, lingering on the tuning pegs, slowly tracing the length of the fingerboard, then taking in the voluptuous curves of the instrument's body.

Confused, I held out the instrument, offering it to her. The woman took it from me with the most complete and utter look of gratitude I have ever seen. Then she resumed moving her hands along its body. As she did this, I began to disrobe her.

Though staggering under the effects of the tea, I succeeded in removing her cloak with relative ease. Next, I began to feel for a zipper or button on the back of her dress. Again I was struck by how strong and unyielding the sides of her body seemed to be, as if she wore a girdle of whalebone. As I carefully explored her, the mysterious woman held my viola to her bosom as though cradling a baby. While it was certainly important to be careful when holding rare instruments, this felt a bit excessive.

The powerful effects of the tea struck again. The shadows in the corners lurched forward. Then they spread upward, stretching to the ceiling like branches in a forest. The ceiling was soon covered in a strange canopy.

The effect was disorienting. I lost my balance and began falling backwards. I reached for something, anything to steady myself. In my flailing, I gripped hard at the collar of the mystery woman's dress. To my surprise, it yielded easily, and I fell to the floor still clutching the white cloth in my hand.

On my back, I saw the strange dark shadows spreading evermore against the ceiling. How did they move so? A trick of the light combined with the power of the tea?

I stared over at the mysterious woman. She continued to cradle my viola, whispering to it, as if it were indeed a child. She did not seem to notice the strange, contorting shadows all around us, or even that her dress had been ripped away.

I beheld her naked torso. On her back were twin tattoos of "f-holes" as one sees on the bodies of stringed instruments. Yet as I looked closer, it seemed they were not tattoos at all. For I could see candlelight flickering *through* them from the other side of the room.

My mind raced to explain it. Was this some new trend in body modification? But no. It seemed impossible any living thing could survive a procedure of that nature.

The mystery woman stared down at the instrument in her arms. She looked like a mother who has just rescued her child from great peril. Her face bespoke a deep, enduring love. It also held a powerful fortitude that said, no, we would never again be separated. Not ever.

Now the room began to spin. All at once I realized that I had *never* been the object of this woman's affection. That all those nights she had been watching my viola, and not me. I was suddenly sure of this and only this. It is the last thing I remember with any clarity. The rest, even to myself, is mostly conjecture.

My eyes closed and I fell into a series strangely vivid dreams. In the first, I was a young girl, accompanying my father into the forest on a beautiful spring morning. We hiked deep into the trees. Suddenly, my father stopped in front of a mossy mound where a human woman grew out of the ground. She was nude and her body hair was bright green. Instead of fingers, her hands terminated in long flowering shoots. I looked away as my father laid into her with an ax.

Later in the dream, I stood in my family's house, peering down the long hallway that led to my father's workshop. At the end of the hall I could see my father standing over a table with a green woman strapped to it. He held sharp metal tools like a surgeon. Moments later, I began to hear her horrible screams. My father worked away, seeming to hear nothing. I thrust my fingers into my ears, yet still came the ear-splitting cries. Interminable minutes later, the workshop fell silent. I crept to the doorway and saw that it was not a woman on my father's table, but a long green log. Emerald ichor spilled out of it and pooled on the floor. The center of the log had been removed. At a lathe to the side of the room, my father sat shaping the wood. The dream dissembled just as I realized my father was molding it into the shape of a human heart.

In the final part of the dream I saw my great-grandfather, but in his youth. He stood in the middle of a dense forest, and beside him stood a nymph or elf. It had delicate, pale wings and pointed ears like the tips of knives. The creature—which could have been no more than two feet high—allowed my great-grandfather to follow it through a myriad of pathways that led deep into the wood. They stooped under fallen trunks and waded through beds of flotsam until they reached a strange clearing in the heart of the dense forest. The clearing was perfectly circular, and its floor of short green grass was totally clear of debris. In the direct center of this clearing was a heartwood tree. It was roughly human-sized. The bark seemed to sparkle in the sun as if freshly lacquered. In a trice, I realized this effect stemmed from an abundance of sap. The tree was fit to burst with it. No sooner had I seen this much, than I watched in horror as my great-grandfather seized the elf-nymph by the back of the skull and bashed its head against side of the heartwood tree. After several hard smacks, the nymph's tiny wings ceased their fluttering. My great-grandfather tossed it to the ground without a second thought. Then he removed a hand ax from his pocket and raised it high above his head.

As the ax connected with the tree, I jarred awake.

It was dawn, and I was somewhere outside. I could hear the song of birds and feel sunshine on my face. Yet when I opened my eyes, I saw that I was still within the sitting room. But it was utterly changed. The rustic estate was in ruins. I could feel the sun on my face because there were large holes in the roof. The furniture around me was moldy and broken.

I rose to my feet. There was no sign of the mysterious woman, her valet, or my viola. I did find the case, but it

was empty. My horsehair bow was also gone. Upon exiting the manse, I saw that its derelict state was even more
pronounced on the exterior. It was difficult to imagine
that I could have failed to notice such deterioration
and neglect the night before. Had the house appeared
differently, or had I been so distracted by venery that
I had simply failed to notice? Both felt eerily . . . and
concurrently . . . possible.

I knew I must return to Florence before I was missed.
I set off down the rough road leading away from the
ruined mansion, trying to retrace our route from the
previous night. I wandered for the better part of an hour
before I came to a paved street and finally encountered
other people. From them, I learned my location, which
turned out to be remarkably close to the town in which I
had grown up. How the surrounding community had
changed since I had departed those many years before!

Wary of being recognized by one of the locals,
I paid a farm lad a handsome sum to drive me into
Florence. There, I caught a cab back to the hotel. My
absence had not even been noted. We were due to
leave that evening for the next stop on the tour, and
I soon became completely preoccupied with procur-
ing a replacement viola. I called the police and told
them I had gone home with a woman who had robbed
me, which was technically true. I gave them a rough
description of her, leaving out the more fantastic elements. This resulted in an official report which would

be enough for our insurance to reimburse me for the instrument.

In time, I procured a permanent new viola of the blackest African ebony. Though it did not allow the subtleties possible with my father's heartwood, it carried a new range of tonalities that I quickly came to appreciate. The strange woman never again appeared at any of my concerts, but I did begin to see a new figure with some regularity. He was a tall, broad shouldered man who often wore a bright dashiki and many pieces of gold jewelry. His appearance uncannily resembled images I had once seen of a Senegalese king. Usually he stalked the periphery of the audience, or only flickered into view for a moment or two. Yet as our tour wound its way closer to the coast of North Africa, he became a fixture at the front and center of our shows. Often, he seemed be making eyes at me, but when I looked more closely, I thought perhaps he was actually focusing on the instrument in the crook of my neck.

Shortly thereafter, I retired from touring completely and resolved to take up a private life. I have found the Grand Hotel most suitable for this purpose."

The Signora relaxes in her seat and throws her shoulders back like a great soloist who has finished a dazzling performance. The expression quite suits her; I could probably gaze at it for hours.

The visitors are not unmoved by the language of the Signora's body, and a few of them burst forth into applause. (Who am I to say that her voice is not music?) I happily join them. The Signora nods in bashful appreciation.

"Signora Regina, it is a pleasure as always," I say when the clapping has died away. "Now if everyone would please follow me, we have another important stop on the tour just ahead. While it is not the Signora—but what is?—you will almost certainly find it pleasing to the ear."

Several of the visitors rise from their seats to follow me, but several others do not.

"'Ere . . . we just got here," protests the large woman in an ornate hat with feathers. "I want to listen to more of the young lady's music. Can't we do that?"

"Ooh yes, please?" cries another.

A man who clearly wishes only to continue to bask in the beautiful expressions of the Signora—for which, I can hardly blame him—he has waited to speak. Now he is emboldened to add his two cents.

"I say, quite," he manages from below a mustache heavy with a lecher's perspiration. "If I have any free choice in the matter, I elect to stay and listen a bit longer. I do have free choice, don't I?"

The man stares at me hard, daring me to suggest anything to the contrary.

I sense a mutiny on the wind. The Signora glances at me from her seat, evidently bemused.

"Very well," I announce. "Perhaps we should, as they say, 'split up.' Those who wish to stay behind with the Signora may do so. I am inclined to believe that she would be happy to help anybody making that decision to set his or her affairs in order . . . by which—of course—I mean that she would happily return them to the lobby of the hotel afterwards. Signora?"

I look up at her for verification and grin. (Mostly, I am just pleased to have another excuse to look up at her.)

"Of course, Vick," she tells me.

Then, almost absently, she shrugs and her hair spills down over her shoulders. It rather causes one to consider and reconsider the entirety of her figure, at least above the waist. I fight the impulse to go noticeably weak in the knees.

"Yes, then," I say, collecting myself. "If you would all be so kind as to sort yourselves, please have at it. Make your choice, make your choice. No time like the present for a bold decision."

I clap my hands to urge them along. With a modicum of mumbled discussion, the group separates into two camps like an organism dividing on a microscope slide.

"There, now," I tell them. "Was that so hard?"

They seem to agree that it was not.

"Signora," I say. "I realize that you have already rehearsed tonight. Thank you for agreeing to perform again for this audience. You really do go above and beyond."

"It's nothing," she says with a devilish grin, and raises her viola to her chin.

"Ahh ahh ahh," I say, signaling that she should wait until my half of the tour group has exited.

I cast an expression to indicate that I could not possibly compete with her for their attention. In truth, I know that her music has the uncanny power to lull them into virtually any state she sees fit. I have often wondered if she could incite an audience to the act of murder, if she so desired. One day I will probably find this information out . . . but it will not be this evening.

As my group exits the recital hall, a few cast glances back at the lovely Signora. They wonder if they have made a choice they will regret. (Of course they have . . . just not in the way they think.) One or two raise a finger or open their mouths to say they would like to reconsider. I pay this no mind and rather forcefully put my hands on their shoulders, ushering them into the hallway beyond.

"I say, it's frightfully late!" a guest suddenly observes. He has only now thought to look at his watch.

"Is it?" I say, closing the walnut doors behind us.

"But of course, you'd be used to it . . . as the night clerk," the man clarifies. "I hope your tours don't bother guests who are trying to sleep. I know I hate it when my rest is disturbed."

"A fair point," I say, turning down the corridor. "But I know a guest who welcomes visitors at all hours. He rather considers it part of his duties to be on-call around the clock. I've assured him countless times that this conscientious devotion is entirely unnecessary, but he simply will not be moved on the point. Actually, he would be disappointed if he learned you were here and I did *not* bring you by . . . even at such a late hour."

"Oh, who is he?" asks a mature woman with grey hair.

"I think it will be more interesting if you find out for yourselves," I tell her. "But let it suffice to say that he accepts all comers."

The guests open their mouths to pose more questions, but I make it clear that I will answer none.

I conduct them through a twisting hallway with regularly spaced windows and flowerboxes set just beneath them. Curtains hang from the walls and the hotel's rich red carpet resumes underfoot. I allow the guests to outpace me, offering encouraging expressions and telling them that they are all headed in the right direction.

I locate the red-haired girl and encourage her to hang back with me. The rest of the group takes a turn in the corridor and we lose them. I stop walking. So does she.

"I don't think heartwood is real," the red-haired girl says before I can open my mouth. "But I also don't think it matters to the story. The Signora-lady thinks it's real. She thinks it's all connected. Whether or not heartwood is real doesn't really change anything."

"Who are you?" I ask her.

I have been at the Grand Hotel for a long time. Over the years, I have met youngsters more precocious than this ginger haired sprite. I have also met wizened sages, overflowing with wisdom; powerful executives at the top of their games; and young Turks next in line to helm the empire. I have met savants—often impaired somehow physically, but tremendously endowed in other areas. I have also met visitors who were entirely unreadable by me at the start of the tour . . . but who could not help but divulge a little more about themselves with each answer they gave. And something about what they divulged invariably told me that their next answer—or perhaps the one after it—would be dead wrong.

Yet, now, as I think back, I find it beyond my ability to recall a candidate about whom I knew absolutely nothing. Who had betrayed not a thing about themselves by this point in the game.

Certainly, I can recall no candidate who gave me the answer to a question before I had asked it.

"Who are you?" I say again.

The red-haired girl does not immediately respond. I cross my arms and lean against the wall of the corridor, indicating that there can be no further progress until she capitulates.

"I didn't mean to do anything wrong," she replies. She seems ready to object that my tone is unwarranted.

"I didn't say that you'd done anything wrong," I clarify, the scowl upon my face growing. "I asked you who you were."

"My name is—"

I wave my hand back and forth in the air.

"Your name doesn't matter any more than mine," I tell her. "I want to know who you are. What's your story? What do you want?"

My questions make her uneasy. She looks back and forth along the passageway, and takes a step away from me.

Perhaps I have said too much, too soon.

But no. It is she who has been impudent, I remind myself. I must press the attack.

"Though you are a child, I do not see that you are accompanied by any adults," I tell her. "The ones whom I thought might be your parents have now been left behind."

"I am on my own," she admits.

"But not in a larger sense," I tell her. "That would not . . . make sense."

She shakes her head.

"I snuck out of the hotel downtown where my family is staying," she admits. "They think I'm asleep in my room right now. I wanted to explore the city. I've never been here before. I walked along the river and looked at all the shops. Then I found the tour group in the city square, and I just kind of fell in with them. We ended up here. They went inside, so I did too."

"Do you believe in coincidences?" I ask her. "That is to say, do you believe that some meetings can be fated to occur?"

"I don't know," she says, as if the question is trivial. "What does that have to do with-"

"I see," I tell her. "I am now going to make several statements about you. You will stop me if any of them are incorrect. Do you understand?"

The red-haired girl looks a bit distempered, but nods.

"Your father or your mother—or someone else in your family line—is very powerful. They may have been part of an empire that's been wealthy and established for hundreds of years, or their fortune and status might be new. The important thing is that you are likely next in line for the . . . shall we say . . . throne."

The red-haired girl opens her mouth. Then something occurs to her and she closes it again. She stares up into my eyes suspiciously.

"And how do you feel about that?" I ask her.

She only shakes her head.

"Wanting is important, young lady. You must decide. Do you want the life—the responsibility—that the world has in store for you, or do you want something else? Do you even know? I don't think you do."

She hesitates a moment.

"It's not that easy. It's not a thing you can want or not want. There are a thousand different ways my future could unfold. There are a thousand things that could happen when I take over for my mother—if I do that at all. I don't know if I'll want them or not. Don't you think I understand that already? Don't you think I think about it every day, all the time?"

Red-faced, she flees down the corridor, away from me.

I watch her go. Her footfalls disappear into the crimson carpeting. At the end of the hallway she turns the corner and moves out of sight. I am completely alone. The bulb above me flickers once.

I take a deep breath and remind myself that the young have not yet learned to think abstractly and control their more powerful emotions.

Very slowly, a decorative sconce set into the side of the corridor—shaped like a hand that clutches a bouquet of porcelain flowers—extends out from the wall behind me. It moves on an arm of plaster, stretching ever longer, like a telescoping appendage, until the decorative hand rests reassuringly on my shoulder.

But I am in no mood to be consoled, not least by the Grand Hotel.

Besides, I think it is far too early to eliminate the red-haired girl's candidacy.

Everything wants. Everybody wants.

But not everybody understands that they want.

That is the secret.

Some humans characterize want as a failing, or even as a vice. As if they did not grasp that it alone separates us from inert matter. From the false. From the fake. From things like mannequins and artificial intelligence computers and androids that can appear to be so very human—but are somehow not. That "somehow" is want. Wanting things is not just a fact of life. It is life. The red-haired girl may not wish to admit this, but that does not mean she hasn't gained some sense of its fundamental, underlying truth.

I shrug my shoulder like a lover indicating that—tonight at least—I am not "in the mood." The prehensile hallway molding seems to understand, and silently retracts to its original position.

Assuming a casual gait, I follow after the red-haired girl.

Father Cyning

The sight that awaits me when I round the bend is rather comical. The hallway ahead terminates in pair of large doors with religious iconography emblazoned across them. To either side of the corridor stand the remaining members of the tour group. (Are there so few left now? Egad!) In the center of the corridor is the red-haired girl, and she is weeping softly. Comforting her is the stout figure of Father Cyning. He looks down at her in tender concern, thereby displaying his balding pate. (It looks uncannily like a monk's tonsure, but he assures me the hairstyle is naturally occurring.) His heavy brown robes, collar, and serious expression all instill a feeling of authority. I am not surprised that the red-haired girl has—on sight—enveloped him in a hug.

"'Say, what did you do to her?" one of the visitors barks at me.

"You've got this little one bawling her eyes out, you do," agrees another, giving me a very judgmental look.

"Is someone here her guardian?" asks a third, looking around. "Did she get separated from mommy or daddy?"

Cyning looks up and shakes his head to say he is disappointed in me.

It is, of course, risible. But for the moment I play along.

"I see you have all met Father Cyning," I announce with a sigh (noting privately, for perhaps the thousandth time, the pleasant coincidence of his name rhyming perfectly with sinning, despite starting with a hard 'K'). "But I wonder if he has forgotten to introduce himself?"

Cyning ignores me.

"My dear girl," he says softly, betraying an English accent. "Whatever is the matter?"

The red-haired girl collects herself quickly. (Almost suspiciously so.) After a few seconds, she has stopped sobbing. In half a minute, she appears almost fully recomposed.

"I . . . no . . . I'm fine . . .thank you . . ." she says, backing away from Cyning. She wipes away her tears with her palms and manages a smile.

"Are you quite sure?" Cyning asks in a gentle, avuncular tone.

"Yes," the red-haired girl says, sniffling as she nods.

Cyning gives me another harsh look and flaps his robes like an enormous bird adjusting itself on a cold day.

"Father Cyning oversees the interfaith chapel here at the Grand Hotel," I announce to our diminished group. "He is something of an ecclesiastical scholar. How many degrees is it now, Cyning? Five?"

He waves away my flattery.

"His knowledge and abilities are remarkably ecumenical," I continue. "Though he answers to 'Father,' his duties are not exclusive to any faith or subset. In its time, the Grand Hotel has seen followers of Jesus, Moses, and Mohammed, of course. But also of Zoroaster and Buddha and Odin and Ra. And Father Cyning proved able to provide something for each of them—if not a full religious service, then at least a few learned words on the subject."

Now Cyning brightens in a way that is genuine. If he has a sin, it is pride—though it may be warranted. Cyning's ability to connect with people of all backgrounds really is unmatched.

"This group is enjoying a tour of the premises," I inform Cyning.

"In that case, I would be happy show you the Grand Hotel's interfaith chapel," Cyning tells them. "You are, of course, free to use it at any time during your visit."

Here I roll my eyes, for I have never understood this phrase in regards to the chapel. "Use it." For what? How?

"Now I wonder . . ." Cyning continues, beginning to sound an awful lot like a British schoolmaster. "Do we have followers of any faith traditions with us today?"

After a moment the group realizes they are being addressed. I open my mouth to encourage them to share—if they feel comfortable, obviously—but the religious officiant cuts me off quite completely.

"We don't need to hear from *you*," Cyning says with a stern look in my direction. "Your positions on the matter are already well known."

I frown and close my mouth, amused as ever.

With the excruciating labor of pulling teeth, the remaining members of the tour slowly volunteer their own religious leanings. Some are orthodox-this or reform-that. Some name a make and model, but then quickly qualify that they have made their own modifications to the vehicle. Others are willing to admit that they were *raised* within a certain faith, but are hesitant to divulge how this upbringing may have impacted their current worldview. A few say they have no religious views at all, yet even these souls find a way to categorize and brand their particular variety of unbelief.

I notice, after the rounds have been made, that the red-haired girl has said nothing. Cyning begins to prattle about his familiarity with the faith traditions they have named. But he has to have noticed her silence. Why has he said nothing about it?

It becomes excruciating.

I look at the red-haired girl. The remains of dried tears are still visible on her cheeks. She seems to be following Cyning's words, but as my gaze lingers on her, a smile sneaks its way to the corners of her mouth. A smile—I would bet my kingdom—that has nothing to do with the religious man's lecture. Her eyes flicker over and meet mine, quickly and intentionally. Then they turn back to Cyning.

My hopes remain high.

Cyning continues. His words wind now from honeyed to positively saccharine as he speaks of the strong commonalities that join all world religions. Most, anyway. (I do my best to keep a straight face. Even the guests begin to find his monologue tiresome after a while. There is an audible yawn, and more than a few silent ones.)

"Father Cyning, perhaps our guests would enjoy seeing the interior of your . . . facility."

"Ah," he says. "That's right. A fine idea. If you will be kind enough to follow me . . ."

Cyning turns and makes his way to the large doors of the interfaith chapel. As he opens them, the guests have just a moment to peruse the religious runes. And to note that something about the familiar iconography is a little bit . . . off. The rugged cross is crooked in a way that might suggest a variation imposed by some esoteric sect. The crescent moon has either waxed or waned a little too extremely (which one, I can never tell). The tips of the six pointed star are ever-so-slightly tilted in strange directions. The Dharmachakra's spokes are crooked, and one is broken in half.

A couple of the visitors notice these corruptions and are momentarily flummoxed, but most are not even paying attention.

Cyning swings the doors wide and our view of the warped symbols is suddenly removed. We now confront the interior of the interfaith chapel. It has several rows of wooden pews and a lone altar on a slightly raised stage. In point of fact, it looks not entirely dissimilar from the recital hall, where we only just were.

The lighting has been carefully designed to replicate the feeling of a cathedral. One might forgive a visitor for feeling that the ceiling of the place must extend high above us in the artificial gloom (when in reality it terminates after just fifteen feet). A censer has recently perfumed the air, adding to the mysterious feel. The walls have been adorned with tastefully bland stained glass; the frowning, bearded men holding staffs could be from any faith tradition. Or from none at all.

"'Ere, that one looks like you," observes a guest beside me. I see that she has gestured to a particular window. The tall, dark man depicted in the corner does bear something of a passing resemblance.

"Do you really think so?" I ask enthusiastically.

I hasten over to the glass and pose next to it.

"What do you say?" I ask the group.

"Naw," the guest says. "Now I don't see it at all. Never mind."

"Oh, drat," I say, my tone indicating deep disappointment. "I had so hoped to be immortalized."

"Ahem."

We look over. Father Cyning is evidently not pleased with my antics. His glare says that while this might not be the Vatican, there are those who still regard it as a place requiring a degree of solemnity.

I pretend to be cowed and step away from the glass.

"Father Cyning?" someone says in a quiet, high voice. It is the red-haired girl. She stands near the altar.

"Yes?" he says.

"This is an interfaith chapel . . . but I take it that your initial qualifications are in the Christian church?"

It's a fair question. Cyning allows as much.

"That's right," he says, nodding. "C of E. I started as a parish priest in a village in the English countryside. A wonderful place. Wonderful people."

"Did you always know you wanted to be a priest?" the red-haired girl presses.

This is an impressive display. I am largely unnecessary . . . at least so far.

"I think so," Cyning says. "I always knew I had some sort of calling."

"And how did you acquire your knowledge of world religions?" she asks. "I would think your responsibilities in rural England would be rather . . . specific to that part of the world."

"They were, generally," Cyning responds evasively.

"Generally?" I say with a laugh, stalking up to Cyning's position near the altar. "But you're being modest, Father. I do recall that you once told me of a particular inciting event that sent your career careening in entirely new directions."

"I suppose it did," Cyning allows.

"When you came aboard here at the hotel, we discussed it in your interview," I remind him. "I do not mean to say that your hiring was contingent on it exactly, but . . ."

"Yes, yes," Cyning replies. "One says all kinds of things in job interviews, you know. More importantly, I believe I told you that I felt called to this work here at the hotel. I still think that calling was true.

"You might be surprised by the needs of a hotel's guests. Some of the long-term residents can't attend services elsewhere in the city, due to advanced age or bad mobility. And travelers just passing through—for business, pleasure, or even as tourists such as yourselves—can find a sudden yet tremendous need to confer with a qualified person regarding matters of the soul. I provide that service."

"Back to your qualifications . . ." I say casually. "Was there not something about a particular—what is the appropriate word?—*case* that you handled? Something that caused you to undertake your survey of the faiths of the world?"

"No," responds Cyning, growing cross with me. "You make it sound like it caused me to doubt my faith. That was never the case. I only sought to increase my own knowledge of . . . of . . . the many ways of expressing spirituality."

I nod and smile to signal that he has surely hit upon it. I am finished with my questioning.

Though now, of course, the cat is out of the bag.

"Your 'case?'" the red-haired girl wants to know. "Were you like a detective?"

"No. Well. . . .Yes, actually. I suppose I was, just a bit."

The red-haired girl puts her hand on her hip and wrinkles her nose.

"Sometimes country priests are called upon in special capacities," Cyning explains. "We can console people in need of solace. We can provide a compassionate ear when someone needs to vent their troubles. When necessary, we can refer a member of our flock to someone more qualified, like a professional counselor. We are problem solvers. I was led to undertake my survey of world religious after a particularly interesting problem was brought to my doorstep."

"Which was?" the red-haired girl asks.

Her style is a little blunt, but it gets the job done.

As I said, many years ago I was a country priest. My parish was outside Kirkby Overblow, not terribly far from Leeds. I took my vocation seriously and did my best to make myself approachable to everyone in the community. And not just on Sundays! Those who sat in my pews knew the hours when they could count on finding me in my office at the back of the church, ready to lend a supportive ear. And find me they did. In my time at the parish I saw community members through all manner of tragedies, joys, and challenges. I helped husbands and wives to reconcile, or at least try to. I did my best to assist those who'd crawled into a bottle—or a syringe—to crawl back out again.

I don't know if I was the best priest the parish ever had, but I didn't entertain any delusions about being able to do everything singlehandedly. I asked for help whenever I needed it. I referred parishioners to qualified experts if I saw that their problems would be better handled by a therapist, doctor, or by law enforcement. And I prayed hard on a case whenever something about it seemed strange or wrong.

But nothing felt strange or wrong about Ms. Margaret Worthridge. She was a vibrant, cultured woman in late middle age—and quite sopping wet on that cool afternoon in March when she knocked on the heavy wooden door to my office in the midst of a rainstorm. Her thick curls had been disarranged by water and wind, and her floral-print dress was quite soaked through. At first, I assumed she had made herself my guest merely in the course of seeking shelter from the downpour.

I was wrong.

As I found a spare towel and let the poor woman dry herself, it soon became apparent that something specific had brought her to my door—something that she hemmed and hawed about for quite some time. I was beginning to recognize this sort of hesitation.

"My dear Ms. Worthridge," I said when she was dry enough to settle into the chair opposite me. "I have helped members of our community with all manner of situations—some of them very, very delicate. I quite assure you, there's nothing I haven't heard before."

"This matter concerns a ghost," my guest said.

A beat passed.

"The holy ghost?" I asked, hoping I had not been made a liar.

"I suppose that it might be involved . . ." she said after a moment.

Content to have uttered only a half-truth, I soldiered on.

"Then please tell me all about your ghost," I said.

"Are you familiar with Radish Manor?" she asked, blotting at her face with the towel.

Of course I was, and nodded to confirm it.

Radish Manor was the former family home of Lord Radish, an English nobleman of some renown. Yet as with many British manor houses—and, indeed, with many British nobles—the Radishes had fallen on hard times. The changing economy and the dispersal of inherited lands over the generations had taken their toll on the proud family. Though it had been a political and economic powerhouse for most of the nineteenth century, the Radishes had found their power, privilege, and—above all—finances slowly draining throughout the twentieth. By its end, they lacked the means even to pay for the upkeep of their estate and grounds.

Faced with these dire straits, the diminished family chose a solution frequently selected by formerly wealthy families not wishing to give up their ancestral homes. The manor was opened to the public as a tourist attraction, specifically as an example of early eighteenth-century architecture and décor. Visitors paid an admission charge and enjoyed a guided tour of the house and grounds. The resulting funds were then used to support the continued operations of the manor. The remaining members of the Radish family retired to a small set of apartments at the very top of the house which were not included on the tour. There they stayed between the hours of ten and four, as looky-loos from across the world plodded through what had formerly been their private home, photographing furniture and fixtures and pronouncing on which amenities were or were not to their liking.

This transition had taken place at Radish Manor a few years before I found myself assigned to the parsonage of Kirkby Overblow. Despite their situation, the Radishes remained fixtures of the community. Lady Olivia Radish herself had come to greet me personally when I first arrived in the village. A charming widow with grown children, she had been exceedingly kind and welcoming toward me. I immediately came to hold her in the highest esteem. She did not become a regular at my Sunday services, but I could rely on her to turn up on Easter and Christmas.

"I am a longtime family acquaintance of the Radishes," Ms. Worthridge explained, now transferring the towel to her shoulders. "Olivia and I attended school together and we have always been close friends. Though I married and moved away, we stayed in contact through correspondence and regular phone calls. A year ago, when my husband passed away in an auto accident, I joined her family at Radish Manor. I have been allowed to take up permanent residence in one of the outbuildings at the back of the property. I hardly need to say it aloud, but I will: Olivia's kindness and compassion toward me have been the central factor in my ability to find happiness again after the passing of my dear husband."

"Having met Lady Radish, I can say that this account of her kindness is no surprise," I stated. "They are a truly exceptional family. If only half the stories of their generosity are true, they cannot be praised too highly."

"It is so," Ms. Worthridge said, yet now a shadow seemed to fall across her face. "Which makes the current difficulties all the more tragic."

"Difficulties?" I asked carefully.

"Indeed," Ms. Worthridge said with a solemn nod. "Olivia is most distraught. This problem. . . . It threatens to endanger what remains of their livelihood. In fact, it concerns her to such a degree that she has recently taken the extreme measure of calling in an expert. A 'so-called' expert, I should say. And, Vicar, I am not at all convinced that this woman is completely on the level."

I could take no more mystery.

"What is the problem—if I may be so bold—and who is this 'expert' that Lady Radish has called upon?" I asked. "Tell me plainly."

Ms. Worthridge averted her eyes for a moment. Her pupils probed the modest walls of my study as she looked for any sign of reprieve or escape from the situation—any mitigation that would require her to speak no further. But after a suitably thorough survey of my books, award statuettes, and mental health bureau pamphlets, she seemed to surrender to the task at hand.

"Radish Manor is haunted," my guest confided. "A ghost stalks the halls . . . and not only in the night. It has been seen by day. Several times, it has frightened tourists as they passed through the home. Most take it well enough—a few even claim to enjoy the sighting—but enough have reacted badly that word is beginning to spread. Sensitive people have run away from the manor, screaming their lungs out. Old folks have fainted. One young lady had an asthma attack and had to be taken away in an ambulance."

"What exactly do the visitors see?" I asked, my curiosity mounting.

"Well . . . I have not seen it myself, of course . . ." Ms. Worthridge qualified. "And the accounts vary. But there are undeniable . . . commonalities."

"Such as?" I pressed.

"The visitors claim to see a man in a mask," she continued. "A metal mask. Some have said it's made of iron. Others say bronze. It has a nose that pokes forward out from the front, and there are large circles around its eyes. Some guests say it wears spectacles. Other than the mask, it wears black from head to toe—a cloak or perhaps robes and smallclothes. Black shoes. Black gloves."

"There is no possibility that this specter is . . . a person *wearing* a mask?" I had to ask.

My guest gave me a look as though I had proposed an indiscretion.

"Certainly not, Vicar!" she responded.

"But how do you know?" I said, feeling skeptical.

I received another look, this one usually reserved for children who have asked 'why' one too many times.

"It appears and disappears at will! One moment it is there, and the next is has vanished. And it has molested Olivia! One night as she turned off the lamp to go to sleep, she saw it hovering above her. It sat down on the foot of her bed. She felt its weight. Yet the moment she turned on the light, it was gone."

"And this has been happening for some time?" I asked.

"For several months, I think," Ms. Worthridge answered. "Olivia has not been entirely forthcoming with me, I fear. I gather what I can from her. Poor woman. I believe she sought to hide the problem initially, hoping that it would go away on its own. But it didn't. It got worse. So that then—a couple of weeks ago—she was forced to bring in the . . . expert."

I rather fancied *myself* something of an expert when it came to life after death. I wondered whom Lady Radish might have called in in my stead. I also tried not to take it personally.

"It's a young woman from London," Ms. Worthridge confided, suddenly taking on a confidential tone. "She. . . . She concerns me, Vicar, if I may speak frankly. I have not been able to determine exactly how Olivia found her; if she was referred by friends or some such. Initially I wondered if you might have been responsible for her."

"What is the woman's name?" I asked.

"Samantha," Ms. Worthridge intoned. "And she is a *young* woman. She seems far too young."

"To be an expert on ghosts?" I asked.

"To be an expert on anything," Ms. Worthridge replied. "She's hardly out of university if she's a day."

I could tell that something about this interlocutor upset Ms. Worthridge above and beyond her age.

"What is the problem with this Samantha, if you had to put it simply?" I asked.

Ms. Worthridge pursed her lips and thought seriously for a moment.

"She is encouraging to Lady Olivia in quite the wrong way," Ms. Worthridge said. "I do not know how Lady Olivia is paying her, but it may be by the hour. Correspondingly, the young lady shows no urgency to solve the problem or to rid Radish Manor of its ghost. And what she has to say only appears to feed poor Olivia's anxiety. To make it worse!"

"What can I do to help?" I asked,

"Please . . ." Ms. Worthridge asked desperately, almost begging. "Call upon Olivia and see what you can learn. You may have abilities in these matters where a charlatan from London does not! In fact, I pray that you do. Lady Olivia will no longer listen to me. Perhaps she will listen to you."

I ran my fingers through my hair and thought.

"I suppose I could pay a friendly call on the manor," I said.

"Yes, oh would you? It would mean so very much. Things cannot continue as they have. If they take Radish Manor off the tour bus routes, the loss of revenue will be disastrous. A proud family already so diminished . . ."

My guest trailed off.

"I'll see what I can do," I said.

"And please," Ms. Worthridge continued, "do not tell Olivia that you have come at my prompting. She has already heard enough from me. You, however, would add an outsider's perspective on these events."

I assured her that she could count on my discretion. When I popped by the Radish estate, it would be as nothing more than a country priest making a routine check upon a member of his flock.

"You can say that you have . . . 'heard things' . . . indeed, perhaps you should . . . just not from me," Ms. Worthridge clarified. "And, Vicar Cyning, I urge you not to delay in this matter. Each day, it seems, the problem grows worse. The specter finds some new way to trouble us."

The storm had abated. I gave Ms. Worthridge one of my old umbrellas and sent her back into the elements.

Three days later, the skies were clear and the weather uncommonly temperate. I resolved to use the occasion to fulfill my promise and took my bicycle on a ride to Radish Manor. It was not far from my house and I timed the journey in hopes of catching the Radishes just as the last of the tour groups were departing.

I made my way out of the village and into the woods surrounding the manor. The grounds of the estate held an enormous playground for the local children, with rope-nets, climbing frames, and myriad other diversions. Usually, you could count on seeing at least two or three local lads and lasses cavorting among these structures. Today however—despite the fine, invigorating weather—they were abandoned. The swings creaked sadly in the warm spring wind. The climbing frames threw long, spider's web shadows.

I pedaled deeper and soon the manicured lawns of Radish Manor came into view . . . except they were not very manicured at all. The topiary had been allowed to lapse and the grass was a bit longer than it should have been for this point in the year. I pulled my bicycle into the gravel parking area in front of the public entrance to the manor.

Walking to the entrance, I loudly knocked on the stately wooden door. The sound of my blows reverberated down the long stone hallways on the other side. A few moments later, I was greeted by Doris, the weekday docent.

"We're about to close for the—" she got as far as saying before recognizing me.

"Oh!" she tried again. "I didn't know who you were without your collar!"

"Hello, Doris," I said cheerily. "Haven't seen you at services in a while."

"Ah, no," she said softly. Then she looked at the floor and her lower lip trembled as if she might cry.

"What is it, child?" I asked.

"It's just . . . been a hard few weeks around the estate," Doris managed. She nervously smoothed her long skirt, though it did not appear to be wrinkled. I could not tell if she hoped that I would depart or if instead she wished me to press her for the true reason behind her disconsolate appearance.

Remembering my mission, I did neither.

"I wanted to have just a few words with Lady Olivia this afternoon, if possible," I said, hoping my request sounded modest.

"I don't know if she is receiving anyone," Doris said, collecting herself. "But she would be in her rooms. Shall I call?"

"Would you?" I asked.

Doris took up the telephone from the welcome center desk just inside the entrance and used it to inform Lady Radish of my presence. It seemed to me that there were many awkward, halting pauses in their conversation, but the upshot was that Lady Radish would be down shortly to receive me. Doris suggested I have a seat on one of the wooden benches near the entryway—usually reserved for queuing tour groups—and allow her to bring me a cup of hot tea. I found this suggestion exceedingly agreeable, and took my place on the long wooden bench. As Doris departed for the kitchenette, I let my eyes wander around the stately hallways of the manse.

Like the external grounds, the interior appeared somehow lessened. It was difficult to say precisely what had changed. The tapestries still hung in their places. The immaculate oil portraits still frowned along the walls. The period furniture had been polished or vacuumed, as was warranted. And yet an almost tangible gloom seemed to have settled over everything. There was a dimness that even the brilliant late-afternoon sun streaming through the windows could not dispel.

A few minutes later, Doris returned with my tea. Lipton in a Styrofoam cup. She took her seat behind the welcome center desk and shut down her computer, preparing to leave for the day. Moments later, we heard the approaching footfalls of Lady Olivia Radish.

I set down my tea and stood just as she rounded the corner and came into view. She was dressed casually, in a long sweater, blue jeans, and fuzzy pink slippers. I imagined her ancestors who lined the walls wincing at a lady receiving guests in such dishabille. She smiled at me. It was a warm, genuine smile, but I could tell that her delicate features were under some great strain. The circles under her eyes made her look ten years older than she actually was. Even her gait was reduced; she had literally 'lost a step.'

I had seen this kind of transformation before in the bereaved, and was shocked to see that it now enshrouded Lady Radish.

Still, she put on a brave face for me as we shook hands.

"How wonderful to see you again, Vicar," she told me. "Were you in the neighborhood?"

I could tell from her tone that she was glad to see a friendly face.

"I was," I told her. "Out having a ride, and—wouldn't you know—it took me straight to your doorstep. And I thought, 'It's been far too long since I popped round to the manor.'"

Another smile.

"We were just about done with tours for the day," Lady Radish explained. "I'm surprised to see Doris still here. Doris, you should head home, my dear."

Doris gathered her things and departed. On her way out, she pressed a button that turned off or significantly dimmed the lights in the manor. No doubt this was done to conserve electricity. Lady Radish and I were now alone in the enormous—and darkened—front hall.

For a few minutes we discussed idle matters—the unpleasant weather that had only recently abated, an accounting scandal at a local firm, whether the new midfielder for Leeds United would have any impact on the team's chances—but I have always been a direct person. I withstood these niceties for as long as I could, but as soon as there was a pause in our conversation I cut to the chase.

"So a little bird tells me that there is a new guest here at the manor," I said.

A look of dismay crossed her face.

"A woman from London, if I'm not mistaken," I continued.

"Yes, that's true," Lady Radish replied. "She is an expert in . . . let's say . . . eliminating disturbances that disrupt historical tours."

She smiled at me again, but I could see it crumbling around the edges of her face. I knew that this was very far from the complete truth. She wished to conceal her feelings, but there were already cracks in the wall that held them back.

"Because I am concerned for your health—and the health of all my parishioners—I must say that you do not look well, Olivia," I said abruptly, seeking to fully sunder her defenses and arrive at the heart of the matter. "Are you sleeping? Are you eating? What is wrong?"

A moment of brave hesitation, then the floodgates opened.

Lady Radish looked away, nodding, trying not to weep.

"Please, my child," I said. "I am here to be a resource, but first you must tell me about it."

Lady Radish looked up at the paintings surrounding us, the suit of armor near the entrance, and the lenses of the small, circular security cameras mounted above the door.

"Perhaps we could talk outside?" she said.

I agreed to this immediately, and we stepped back out into the late afternoon sunshine.

"It began several months ago," Lady Radish said as we commenced to stroll together along a pebble path running around the east side of the house. "I started to hear noises at night. Not up in our private rooms—not at first—but in the lower parts. I thought it must be burglars or local kids having a lark. Nothing was ever taken, and our security tapes showed nothing. But soon it became clear that things were being . . . disturbed. Small objects would occasionally be transported from their original places. The house staff began to accuse one another of having moved things. The senior staff blamed the lesser staff. Such is the way of the world."

"To be clear," I interrupted. "The estate has several employees by day, but at night . . . ?"

"At night I am entirely alone," Lady Radish clarified. "As you know, I have had no husband for some time. Lord Radish passed many years ago, and I never remarried. Our boys—Robert and Benjamin—are at Oxford and Cambridge respectively. When they are home, they have their own rooms near mine up in the family quarters. But when they are away at school . . . I am quite alone."

"Not so much as a dog?" I asked.

Lady Radish shook her head.

I did not wish to reveal my source, and so tread carefully with my next comment.

"I hear that your friend Margaret Worthridge has lately taken up residence on part of the estate grounds. A remarkable act of kindness on your part, if I may say so. Perhaps her presence brings you some comfort?"

Lady Radish smiled.

"That's true, but still . . . I am alone at night inside the main house. Anyhow, it hardly matters. For it was right after these initial movements that we started seeing the man in the mask, and now it looks like he will never leave."

"The man in the mask?" I said, doing my best to appear uninformed.

"I believe I was the one who saw him first, in the smoking room," she said. "He exited through an opposite doorway as soon as I entered. He wore flowing black robes and a metallic mask. I was not particularly alarmed. It was just after open hours, so I wondered if a lost tourist had simply wandered off. But when I pursued him into the next room, there was nothing there. Neither did he seem to appear in any of the security footage. But people saw him. Again and again, they saw him and their descriptions were always the same. At first the staff, and then the tourists. There is no telling when he will materialize. He does not molest us, but neither does he explain himself. He looks at us with giant, round, metal eyes . . . then fades from view. It is this fading that has proved problematic with our visitors. When he simply walks past, we can often convince them that he is a staff member attired for some obscure local celebration, or even a historical re-enactor. But when he walks into the hallway in front of the group and simply fades into nothingness like frost on a windowpane. . . . Well, there is little to be done. And lately . . ."

Here she sniffled a moment, and I placed a comforting hand on her shoulder. At first she resisted, then allowed me to touch her. Not soon after she gripped me in a full-on hug and pulled me close.

"Lately he has started visiting me at night inside my bedroom," she whispered. "I will rise after midnight to use the loo, and he will be sitting on the toilet. Or in the kitchens if I head down for a sandwich. Or standing beside the medicine cabinet if I have to take a pill."

"First of all," I said as she released me. "You should not be alone at a time like this. Surely, there is someone you can contact who . . ."

"But I have," Lady Radish insisted. "And since you already know what is happening and wish to be of help, perhaps it is time that you met her."

Lady Radish led me through the spacious manor floor and up the back staircase to the family's private rooms. I had never been on the second level of the house.

"I gave her Robert's room," Lady Radish explained, pausing to knock at the heavy door in the middle of the hall.

"Samantha?" she called. "Are you awake? It's Olivia."

Then aside, softly, to me: "She stays up most of the night looking for the ghost."

A moment later we heard a latch being undone and the door creaked open to reveal a striking young woman. She was in her early twenties, had beautiful skin, long brown hair, and piercing azure eyes. The room behind her was filled with odd equipment. There were several suitcases spread around, and also plastic equipment cases with rollers. Every surface seemed to be covered with paper files. On a massive table at the center of the room was a computer with three monitors that showed feeds from security cameras throughout the house. The bed looked recently slept in. There was also a small, circular end table with candles burning atop it, and another piled high with very old books. On the floor next to the bed was a pile of dirty laundry that I tried not to look at. In addition to candle wax, the room smelled like coffee; there was a fresh pot brewing by an outlet near the dresser.

"Hello!" the young woman said enthusiastically. I noticed a bright silver pendant around her neck. It terminated in an occult symbol, the meaning of which I had once known but now could not place.

"Hello Samantha," Lady Radish replied. Her tone was measured, rather as if she were addressing a hyperactive child. She introduced me to the young woman and we shook hands.

"You must be the famous expert," I said in a way I hoped sounded kindly.

"Samantha is here to see if something can be done about our unwanted visitor," Lady Radish explained. "She comes highly recommended in these matters—has a PhD in this business—and has had two confirmed successes down in London."

"Olivia is very kind," Samantha explained, opening the door wider and kicking some papers and cases out of the way so that we might enter. "I'm a researcher; that's all. But I suppose it's true that in a couple of instances my inquiries have resulted in the . . . dissipation . . . of the phenomenon in question."

"That's right," Lady Radish said with a smile. "Study it all you like, as long as it goes away in the end. Our poor family has been through enough, Lord knows. If anyone deserves to have this matter resolved, it's us."

Lady Radish put the back of her hand to her fore-head, a little too dramatically, I thought.

"I was just waking up and reviewing tapes," the young researcher explained. "Would you like to have a look?"

"You have footage of the ... thing?" I asked, genuinely surprised.

Samantha nodded in the affirmative, but her eyes probed Lady Radish's face. I realized she was asking if I could be trusted.

"This gentleman has proven himself a friend to our community," Lady Radish said. "You may feel free to con-fide in him. Furthermore, he already seems to have got wind of the ghost. In my experience, there is very little that can be kept from a country priest. And who knows? He might even have a suggestion about how to clear this matter up."

Samantha looked at me doubtfully, but pursed her lips to say that anything was possible.

"Did it come again last night?" asked Lady Radish.

"Yes," Samantha said, stalking over to her computer. "In the kitchen, and only briefly. I was in the wine cellar at the time. As usual. Missed it entirely."

"The wine cellar?" I asked.

"Samantha has a theory that something may have happened down in our cellars," explained Lady Radish.

"Have you seen the thing personally, with your own eyes?" I asked Samantha as she began to pull up videos on her computer.

"Once, yes," she said, clicking away. "A few weeks ago, when I first arrived at the estate. It walked past me in the study. I thought it was someone in costume."

A thought occurred to me.

"Lady Radish, the house has had security cameras for years. Do they show nothing of the ghost?"

"No," Samantha answered for her. "But they're the wrong kind. Mine pick up changes in heat and electro-magnetic variations in the atmosphere. There, look . . ."

And I looked at the trio of monitors in front of us. In one of them, I saw what appeared to be black and white footage of an empty kitchen. There was a counter with a block of knives, and a row of pots and pans hanging from the ceiling. Suddenly movement flickered into the frame. A glowing, incandescent figure walked past for a fraction of a second.

"Here," Samantha said, adjusting the media player. "I'll slow it down so you can see."

The slowed version of the video showed a fuzzy humanoid figure striding through the kitchen, swing-ing his arms casually as he walked. He looked as though he were searching for something. I would have said he was wearing some sort of costume—his cloth-ing somehow unusual—but it was difficult to discern more.

Samantha played the video once again, even more slowly, and stopped it just as the form came into view. Now I could indeed discern a smiling metal mask on the front of the figure's face. The back of the head was obscured by a night-black hood.

"Is there any way you can zoom in, or bring it more into focus?" I asked, squinting hard to try to discover additional details. "It's so difficult to see like this."

"No," Samantha answered, "but there are others."

With that, she clicked an icon and all the three screens were flooded with video captures of the masked man. Though black and white and usually grainy, he had been photographed from nearly every angle in different places throughout the manse. It was clear the mask did indeed have a protruding nose and great, circular eyes. In some of the images, it also appeared to have small horns sprouting from its forehead.

"My goodness," I said quietly.

"As you can see, the damn thing goes everywhere," Lady Radish observed disdainfully.

"It does seem to disperse itself evenly throughout the house," Samantha said. "But I feel I am on the cusp of detecting a pattern to its actions."

She motioned to a stack of blueprints of the manor on which the ghost's wanderings had been plotted.

There was then an unexpected and loud buzzing near us, and I must admit I jumped a little. Realizing just how agitated these ghost images had made me, I laughed when it was revealed to be Lady Radish's mobile.

"Excuse me, but I simply must take this," she said. "The new gardener. A true incompetent. He costs less, but—my word!—the other prices you pay!"

Lady Radish stepped into the hallway and began to berate the person on the other end of the telephone. I stayed were I was, staring at the masked figure on the computer screens.

"Tell me, Vicar, are they already talking about me in the village?" Samantha asked, pouring herself a fresh cup of coffee. "Olivia is worried that if the gossip gets too bad, they will take Radish Manor off the tourist routes. Then she will lose everything. She wants me to solve her problem—and I don't even know if I can—but if people learn that she has called me here, it will be tantamount to acknowledging that the rumors are true."

I shook my head and frowned to show it was definitely a conundrum.

"I don't believe that it's general knowledge yet," I said to her. "I myself only just found out."

"But someone did tell you that I was here?" Samantha pressed, sipping her drink.

I could tell that this young lady was very, very bright. Experience had taught me that there little is to be gained from attempting to conceal the truth from the very intelligent. They always learn it eventually, and then you feel like a fool for having thought you could mislead them in the first place. I decided there could be little harm in divulging my source.

"Between you and me . . . it was Margaret Worthridge," I said. "She paid me a visit at my offices. But I believe she only knew because she lives on the estate grounds. I don't think your presence is known yet among the general populace. I'll do my best to keep it that way, if it helps Lady Radish."

Samantha set down her ceramic coffee mug and put her hand on her chin. Something seemed to have occurred to her.

"What are your plans this evening, Vicar?" she asked.

It was a rather forward query, but I replied—honestly—that I had nothing that could not be postponed or cancelled.

"As you are probably aware, spirits and apparitions can sometimes have strong responses to the presence of a person of the cloth," Samantha said. "I've checked the guest logs and reviewed the security footage. With the exception of an Italian nun who was in a wheelchair and almost completely blind, you are the first clergy to visit since the start of the problem."

I smiled and looked around nervously, as if the ghost might choose to appear this very moment in the room with us.

It did not.

"I wonder if you would consider joining me for part of my observations tonight," Samantha said. "I would not ask you to remain until dawn. You doubtless have commitments tomorrow requiring at least a little rest beforehand. But if you wanted to watch with me from, say, a little past ten to a little past midnight, I believe we might be rewarded."

I had never received such an invitation. I felt some trepidation, yes, but part of me was exhilarated by the idea. With the exception of working with subjects who spoke to their departed relatives in the course of grief therapy, I had never been in the presence of direct communication with the deceased.

At least I didn't think I had.

One night back in seminary, the pages on one of my books seemed to have moved by themselves for a moment. Another time, as a boy, I heard a strange voice singing out in a barn where I knew nobody was. But these things, odd as they were, had somehow never quite felt definitive. If a man in a metal mask appeared and disappeared right in front of me, that would be a whole other kettle of fish.

After a moment's consideration along these lines, I agreed.

"Very good," said Samantha, just as Lady Radish came back into the room. "I will meet you downstairs a little after ten. Please wear your collar. I think the ghost we are dealing with is a bit theatrical. Costumes are important. He may respond well to a priest in uniform."

We quickly explained our plan to Lady Radish, and she agreed without hesitation. Frankly, I believe she would have agreed to *anything* that she thought would bring her household an inch closer to ridding itself of whatever walked through its walls.

"I shall already be in bed when you return," Lady Radish informed me as we retraced our path to the lonely parking lot in front of the estate. "I do not say 'asleep,' for these days I sleep very little—and when I do, it is only in small snatches that do not permit me to dream. However, Samantha will let you in. After visitors' hours, she gets the run of the place. You may knock when you arrive, or depress the bell, but Samantha will probably see you on her video cameras. In any case, she will admit you."

We stood now at the entrance to the manor. As I turned to retrieve my bicycle and depart, Lady Radish put a hand on my shoulder to stay me. She had something more to say.

"Thank you for agreeing to help Samantha," she said from underneath eyes unused to rest. "And thank you for keeping this matter a secret. I dream of the day when the ghost will depart. Though my family's fortunes may never be restored to their former glory, with the income from the tourists we find a way of life that is at least manageable. I tell you, Vicar. . . . When we were forced to turn our home into an attraction, I was horrified. I wanted to die that we had been brought so low. But there are lower places. Now, I would give anything just to ensure our current arrangement continues."

I shook Lady Radish's hand and told her that I would keep her secret and, moreover, do everything in my power to rid her home of the tormenting spirit.

I returned home. Despite my vigorous cycling, I found I was not in the mood for my evening repast and ate almost no dinner. There is something peculiarly distracting about knowing one may soon encounter an agent of the numinous. It tends to turn off the parts of the brain that might otherwise want leftover veal paprikash and claret.

I had no precise idea how to prepare for an evening of ghost hunting. I wore my collar as directed, but was torn between making the rest of my outfit even more vestment-oriented or instead dressing practically. I pictured myself running through the halls of Radish Manor and tripping over my robes as the suits of armor came to life, the pots and pans in the kitchen shook, and masked phantoms chased us hither and thither. A fantasy, yes, but I did not really know what to expect.

In the end I decided upon a plain black coat and trousers, and well-worn athletic shoes.

At half past nine in the evening, I got into my car and drove to Radish Manor. The night was warm and still. There was no traffic to speak of and I arrived quite a bit early. I pulled into the parking lot and found mine was the only vehicle in sight. I looked at my watch and considered using the extra time to pay a visit to Ms. Worthridge. However, the lights in the small outbuildings behind the manor were already extinguished. Furthermore, I didn't even know which one was hers.

As I stood beside my automobile, looking out across the darkened estate, I heard the front door to Radish Manor unlatch and open with a creak. I looked up and saw Samantha waiting for me in the doorway. She was attired differently than she had been earlier. Now she wore something like a black jumpsuit and a headband with a complicated-looking earpiece and phone receiver attached. A large, glowing tablet computer was strapped to her forearm, almost like a buckler shield. She looked me up and down. Her eyes lit on my collar, and her face formed an expression of general approval.

"Hello there, Vicar," she said as I jogged over. "Glad you could make it."

I apologized for being early.

"It's no problem," she said. "I've just finished setting up."

"What do you 'set up,' exactly?" I asked as we ventured into the darkened manse. The place had a strange new smell at night. A pervading mustiness, yes, but also something else. Something less definable that spoke of age and wood and a somehow familiar floral perfume.

"I keep a sort of base camp in the wine cellar," Samantha said as I followed her down the corridor. It was hard to keep up, as I had to concentrate on the light from her glowing tablet computer just to make note of where we were.

"Are the ghost's bones buried there?" I asked.

Samantha opened the cellar door and began to creep down the creaking steps.

"As Olivia may have mentioned, I have been 'successful' in dispersing the presence of the undead on two occasions only," she said as I followed her. "Neither of them involved my learning where someone's bones were buried."

The young lady's tone was almost jocular, so I responded a bit jocularly myself.

"Oh no? What did it, then? A sprinkling of holy water? A Voodoo ritual? I hope a full-on exorcism was not required. You'll remember that I am C of E, and yelling loudly at Satan is rather more the provenance of the Roman Catholics."

Samantha did not respond, though in the glow from her tablet I saw a grin cross her face.

We reached the bottom of the staircase. The cellar was massive. Bottles of wine were stacked upon shelves that extended back into the darkness farther than my eyes could see. In the near corner of the room, Samantha had another computer and three more monitors set on an ancient wooden table, the arrangement seeming similar to the one in her bedroom. On the stone floor, five candles burned inside a white circle.

"When the souls of the departed walk among us, it is not without reason," the young woman said, taking a seat in front of the monitors. "Not every ghost knows why it returns, but that doesn't matter. The ghost doesn't need to know. It only needs to want. That is the key . . . or at least it is the first step. All ghosts want something. Some of them even want blood. But there is always the wanting."

A small twitch from the red-haired girl. Miniscule, really, but enough for my trained eye to detect.

"Do you know what this ghost wants?" I asked. Samantha pulled up a display on her monitor and scrolled through a series of security camera readouts.

"It knows what it's doing, I think," she said matter-of-factly. "It's interrupting the tourist trade. It's bothering Lady Radish. But why—why it wants to do those things?—that, I am still searching to discover."

"Have you learned anything else?" I asked.

"The mask it wears is ancient," Samantha said, still looking to her computer screens. "Iron age or bronze age. One of my first actions in this investigation was to research the Radish family. Trace their line back to its beginnings. I got to the 1300s before the genealogy got too murky to follow. The Radishes made their share of enemies over the years, but mostly they fought over trifling things. Over marriages and over insults people made when they were drunk. Nothing that should have cursed subsequent generations. And nothing that I see connects to this masked figure."

"Interesting," I told her.

"It may also be that I simply cannot go back far enough," she continued. "That mask may well predate the Romans."

I nodded thoughtfully. For a few silent moments, Samantha continued to review her computer screens, completely immersed in her pointing and clicking.

"So . . . how exactly does this work?" I asked, beginning to feel a bit useless.

"On most nights, I sit here and review the camera footage," she said. "Sometimes I will introduce a factor that I think might incite the ghost to appear, but so far this has not usually worked. Generally, I have better luck if I begin my efforts here in the cellar. If I see something—the ghost, or just movement, curtains rustling or so on—I go to wherever it is and investigate. I take the portable computer along. It has a camera too."

"Ahh," I said. "Very sensible."

"But I think you might change things tonight," she said rather cryptically.

"I might?"

"Yes," she said. "You may be my . . . bait . . . for the ghost."

I swallowed.

"Bait?"

"Yes," she said. "And for that reason, I think we should start in the southwest sitting room. It tends to get the most action this time of night."

"Will I be there alone?" I inquired.

"No, I'll come up there with you . . . at least at first," Samantha said, with a smile that told me how quaint she found my trepidation. "But if the fish aren't biting, I might ask you to try sitting by yourself. It's not as bad as all that. You may even find it meditative. I know I often do."

I wondered if this could possibly be correct, but resolved to give her the benefit of the doubt.

"There," Samantha said, making a final click on her computer. "We're all set. Shall we?"

I nodded absently. This was all happening so fast.

Allowing my companion to lead the way, we climbed back out of the cellar. Following the light on Samantha's computer, we wended our way to a sitting room. I had not taken the Radish Estate walking tour, but I quickly surmised that this must be one of its high points. It was an expansive room, with large windows that looked out on the rear lawns. Large chandeliers hung above us, silent and magnificent in the darkness. An almost comically enormous fireplace was set into the southernmost wall, with a huge portrait of a Radish ancestor in a high collar directly above it. I did my best not to look the oil-rendered figure in the eyes.

Samantha perched on one of several exquisite chairs. They had black and white striped cushions and gold leaf adorned the armrests. The Radish family crest had been carefully embroidered into the seats.

I moved to take a chair near hers, but she said: "No. Please sit in front of the fireplace. I think it will make you more conspicuous. Anyone entering the room will have their eye naturally drawn to your position."

I looked around and decided she was right.

I walked over and sat in the designated chair. True to the form of most ancient, priceless furniture, it proved much more pleasing to the eye than to the backside. I squirmed a bit and tried to find a comfortable position. Then Samantha pressed a button on her tablet computer and we were plunged into darkness. The sky outside had intermittent patches of clouds, but at that moment the moon was not obscured and it sent powerful rays through the tall, clear windows.

A long moment passed. Soon, I could no longer make out Samantha's features. I stared over to where she was silhouetted in the moonlight.

"From where do you think the ghost will emerge?" I asked, looking around at the possible entrances. I found my voice had fallen to a whisper.

I saw Samantha's outline shrug.

"It's hard to say," she said quietly. "I have seen it enter and exit through both of the open doorways. I have also seen it simply materialize in the center of the room."

"So it might appear right in my lap?" I said with a laugh. "How exciting."

"That is a possibility," Samantha said. Her tone did not mirror my own. I realized that she was deadly serious.

"But will we be able to see it in this darkness?" I asked.

"Yes," Samantha replied. "It is faintly incandescent. I thought that was clear."

"Ahh," I said, my trepidation growing. "Ought I to announce myself? Utter a prayer?"

I watched Samantha's shadow shake its head no.

"And what if the ghost appears?" I asked.

Suddenly, the tablet computer was reactivated. In the resulting glow, I saw an expression on Samantha's face that said I was being silly.

"If that happens, leave everything to me."

I nodded. Her expression asked if I had any additional questions. I assured her that I did not, and she once again returned us to darkness.

We sat. And sat. I became acutely aware of the smallest sounds. The ticking of a grandfather clock in the next room. The wind across the lawns outside. Our own breathing.

I watched alertly for the ghost. It was somewhat colder than it had been during the day. I had read that abrupt drops in temperature often signaled the approach of the supernatural. This drop, however, had been very gradual. I decided it probably meant nothing.

I remained alert and interested for about half an hour, after which my attention began to drift, despite the circumstances. I found myself looking out the window at the semi-manicured grounds, or simply staring at the crescent moon. During one of these periods of distraction, I seemed to glimpse a shadow that slowly moved toward the manse. No sooner had I dismissed it as a trick of the moonlight than it came again, stronger and more clearly than before.

"I say, I think I see something," I announced into the stifling quiet.

"Where?" Samantha whispered in a voice so muted and low it was almost sensual. Her head turned as she scanned the room.

"Not here," I said, rising to my feet. "Something's moving outside on the lawn. Could it be a burglar?"

My tone was not one of serious concern, only bemusement. It was nice to have something to notice after such a long period of boredom.

"I highly doubt . . ." Samantha began, turning to look out the window.

"I do believe it's Ms. Worthridge!" I announced, cutting her off. For indeed, a familiar shape was now approaching our position from across the lawn.

Samantha wrinkled her nose and activated her tablet computer. In the resulting glow, I waved through the window at the approaching entity. And indeed, the form of Ms. Worthridge soon came gradually into view. She was eerily backlit by the moon, but I could see a cheery—and somewhat mischievous—expression on her face. She smiled and returned my wave. Despite the chill, she was wearing slippers, a housecoat, and had a towel around her head as if she were just out of the shower.

There was a small side-window in the sitting room, more-or-less level with one's face. Ms. Worthridge did not move to enter the manor, but rather motioned that I should undo the latch on this particular window. I did, and she spoke to us through the opening.

"Ms. Worthridge!" I called, now speaking at a regular volume. "This is an unexpected pleasure."

"Why hello!" she called. "What are you doing here?"

There was a wink and a nod in her tone of voice.

"I've offered to sit with our resident researcher as she undergoes her ghost hunting," I said. "Rum luck so far. The ghosts aren't biting . . . or whatever they do. Are you out for a walk? It seems a bit late for that sort of thing, no?"

"Oh Vicar, when one ages, one's legs can get frightfully restless at night," she said. "It comes from my mother's side of the family. When I was a girl, my mother would pace through the neighborhood at all hours, trying to get her legs to tire out. I find that one lap around the borders of the estate usually does it for me. I start with a hot bath, then have a cocoa with heavy cream, then do my lap. But you don't need to hear all that. I should leave you to your duties."

"Thank you," I called through the window. "It was nice to see you. And do be careful, Ms. Worthridge. You haven't even got a flashlight."

"Oh Vicar, I couldn't be safer," she said dismissively, and began her trek back across the lawn.

I returned to my chair.

"That was a nice distraction," I said to Samantha. "Ms. Worthridge is such a kindly old soul."

"Yes . . ." Samantha said with a neutrality that seemed out of place.

I wondered if the younger woman found the older one futzy or unpleasant. A 'relic' of a prior generation, perhaps. The young are always so quick to dismiss those who have come before them.

"Does she visit the main house often?" I asked.

"Not that I have seen," Samantha whispered. "Then again, I am usually asleep during the day."

I said nothing more. Samantha turned off her tablet and once again we sat in silent darkness. Now and then I scanned for further signs of Ms. Worthridge making her circuit of the grounds, but she must have kept to the shadows along the edge of the woods, for I saw nothing.

The moon moved slowly in the sky. The regular noises of the house settled over us. I felt bored, then positively sleepy. I worried I would soon begin to doze. Being an inveterate snorer, even in sitting positions, it would probably be difficult to hide a soporific lapse from my neighbor. The ghost continued to avoid us. I began to wonder if, rather than an attractant, the presence of a man of the cloth might repel the undead.

"Samantha?" I whispered in the gloom.

"Yes?" she whispered back.

"How are we coming on, then? I'm getting rather tired."

I hoped she would respond that I was no longer necessary and should call it a night. Instead, she said: "I have been monitoring the cameras throughout the house—I can do so with my screen dimmed very low, you see—and there is particular activity in the cellar tonight, where we began. The spirit has appeared at least twice that I am sure of."

"Oh?" I said. "Then why aren't we down there? What are we still doing in this dusty old sitting room?"

Samantha activated the bright light on her computer. In the resulting glow, I saw her, for the first time, appear unsure of herself. She slowly rose to her feet. Her face held an odd expression.

"I guess we can go take a look in the cellar," she said, "Nothing's happening there now. But maybe the ghost will make a third visit before the night is through."

"That sounds fine," I said with a smile. If I couldn't doze, at least I would get to stretch my legs.

"But one thing Vicar, if you don't mind . . ." Samantha continued.

She approached me, stretched out an arm, and poked me—there is no other word for it—hard on the shoulder, pressing down for a good three seconds. Then her strange expression left, and she was herself once more.

"Okay," she said. "To the cellars. Follow me, Vicar, and mind the ottoman."

She began to carry our only light-source out of the room.

"I say . . ." I cried as I hastened to follow her. "What was that all about? I'll have you know that as an important official in this community, I am not accustomed to being . . . jabbed and prodded by just anybody."

Clearly my words had done harm. Samantha froze in her tracks, as suddenly as if she had seen a ghost. But no, we were still alone.

"Do you know why I asked you to accompany me on my observations tonight?" she whispered. "It is not because you are a priest. There is no correlation between supernatural manifestations and the presence of clergy. Every serious researcher knows that."

"Then why?" I asked.

"Because Margaret Worthridge is dead," she whispered into the darkness.

For a moment, I took this as a threat on the matron's life. But that made no sense at all. So then . . .

"What are you talking about?" I asked. "We've just spoken to her. She's the whole reason why I am here."

"Margaret Worthridge died a year ago—it may be one year to this day—in an auto accident in Wales," Samantha said. "She was on vacation with her husband. He was driving. They went off an embankment and the car went into the sea. The autopsy said her husband, Thomas, died from impact, but that she died of drowning."

"No, no," I said. "It must be some other Margaret Worthridge. This is a coincidence. The one who invited me here—who is friends with Lady Radish—lives in one of the small outbuildings behind the manor house. She's the lady we just talked to. This afternoon I mentioned her to Lady Radish."

"Olivia likely mistook your meaning," Samantha said quietly. "Margaret Worthridge is here, in the sense that she is buried in the small graveyard in the back of the estate. Just *behind* those outbuildings."

"What?" I began to object. "You cannot possibly . . ."

But then Samantha turned her tablet computer toward me. And I wish that she never had.

The images on the screen were of photographs and news headlines about the accident. Samantha scrolled through them. There were articles from the local papers. Then obituaries. Then a photoset from the funeral, both caskets side by side.

"This can't be . . ." I said.

"Maybe you just didn't hear about it," Samantha said. "The funeral was private, held several towns over at the behest of a relative. She was buried out back, however, because everyone knew that Olivia would want her friend nearby for eternity. Olivia plans to be buried there herself one day."

"But . . ." I stammered. "I have seen her at services! I have spoken to her!"

"Have you ever touched her?"

"I've handed things to her," I replied.

"Many ghosts can manipulate matter for a moment," Samantha said. "But I mean, have you actually touched her?"

I strained to recall. I found that I could not be sure.

"Come with me to the basement," Samantha said. "There's something else you should see."

At once befuddled and astonished, I followed the young woman through the darkened house. We descended the cellar staircase and stood once again before the rows of wine, the burning candles, and the table of computer monitors. All of this, Samantha ignored. She reached underneath the table and came out with a leather-backed artist's pad. She opened it and began to flip through pages. They were filled with charcoal sketchings.

"When I said that I had only once seen the masked ghost who haunts these halls, I was not being entirely forthcoming," Samantha said.

"Oh no?" I replied.

"No," she said. "In the weeks since I first arrived here, he has been coming to me in my dreams. When I awaken, I try to jot down whatever I can recall of him."

Here she proffered the sketchbook.

On its pages I saw various renderings of the same man. It was the masked ghost, yet in the images from Samantha's dreams he had removed the mask—sometimes it dangled from his fingertips, other times it was beside him on the ground. The face behind the mask was a rather plain looking gentleman in perhaps his middle fifties. He had a receding hairline, long nose, and a black mustache. And he was sad-looking. Very, very sad-looking. Anguished, in fact. In some of the renderings, he was down on one knee, seemingly overcome with grief. In others, he appeared to be loudly weeping. There were often tears running along his cheeks.

I recognized him. Not from life, but from the images Samantha had just shown me.

"It's her husband, Thomas Worthridge!" I exclaimed a little too loudly. My voice echoed down the rows of wine.

Samantha nodded.

"He is sad. He is sorry for something he has done. He tries to tell me, but always he is unable. He opens his mouth to say it, but cannot speak."

"Sorry for what?" I wondered aloud. "For crashing his car? Why would he feel bad about that? It was an accident. They happen."

"Yes . . ." said Samantha, putting down the computer to tent her fingers like a master detective. "That was my confusion as well. But I think this evening another clue has emerged. Namely, that the spirit of his wife Margaret is largely unaware. Or wants to be unaware. The departed can delude themselves just like the living."

"I'll tell you one thing," I said. "The ghost shouldn't be sorry it crashed its car. It should be sorry for ruining the livelihood of poor Lady Radish! The woman has been through enough. If you see this ghostly interloper in your dreams tonight, you must tell him to knock it off."

Samantha continued to tent her fingers. She stayed very still, her eyes unfocused. And when she spoke, it was as if a voice borne on a distant wind.

"I told you before that sometimes a ghost wants blood," she said. "That was a lie. In my experience, a ghost always wants it. The only question is whose?"

"There is nobody here at this time of the year except for poor Lady Radish," I said.

"Exactly," Samantha returned. "What I have been trying to understand is why does the ghost of her dead friend's husband want to destroy her?"

"Perhaps there is something wrong with the burial arrangement?" I offered.

Samantha smiled and shook her head no.

I was still having trouble believing that the same Margaret Worthridge, whom I had regularly seen in my pews, was a phantom.

"May I see where they are buried?" I asked. "That is, can we go out to the graveyard? Surely your computer will still be able to receive its signals across the lawn."

Samantha seemed lost in thought, but replied: "Yes, we could do that . . . briefly."

"Perhaps we'll run into Margaret again," I said. "In which case, I'll see if I can shake her hand. I still feel that this must all be a mistake. That she is still alive."

We climbed out of the dark cellar, walked through the house, and let ourselves out via the side door. Samantha switched off her tablet computer. Outside there was plenty of moonlight by which to navigate. We did not follow the gravel or dirt paths that crisscrossed the estate, but walked directly across the dewy lawn. Sooner than later, we arrived at the crumbling, ancient outbuildings.

"No one lives here," Samantha said. "They used to house servants back in the nineteenth century, but now they're storage sheds or garages. It's possible that some of the staff that work the grounds might occasionally sleep in one of them, but these are no one's permanent residence."

I looked closely at the crumbling brick-and-stone structures. They were covered with moss and cobwebs, and the windows were crusted with dust. Once, their exterior walls had been painted white, but that had peeled off almost entirely. From a distance—like from the mansion interior—this caused them to look positively quaint. Up close, it was rather depressing.

"Are these the only other structures on the grounds?" I asked. "Is there any place else that Margaret Worthridge could live?"

"I'll show you where she is," Samantha replied. We circumvented the outbuildings. Behind them, just a few paces off and partially obscured by a row of trees, was a small burying ground. Most of the headstones looked like they dated to the original construction of the mansion. A few of them, however, were conspicuously contemporary. Samantha paraded us along until we stood in front of two vaguely Egyptian-styled obelisks that bore the names of Margaret and Thomas Worthridge.

"I was right!" Samantha declaimed. "Look at the date of their passing. One year ago tonight, exactly."

"Yes," I said quietly.

I was befuddled. Here was the evidence staring me in the face, yet some part of me still refused to believe that the Margaret Worthridge with whom I'd chatted moments before could be a spirit from the other side. I turned away from the monuments and cast my gaze along the edges of the property. Margaret had said she went once around the mansion before returning to her slumbers. I wondered if I would see her walking along. Would she return here to the graveyard?

Yet nothing. No sign. We stood there waiting for several minutes. There was only the wind in the trees and the slow shifting of the clouds overhead.

"Vicar, are you still feeling tired?" Samantha asked.

"I don't know how I feel just now," I answered honestly. "This has been a most confusing evening."

"I ask because I think there may be one more thing you can do to help my research," she said. "How would you feel about sleeping here at Radish Manor tonight? There are several beds to choose from. You could even sleep in one of the period beds along the tour route . . . as long as you made it again before the tourists came."

"Sleep here?" I said. "Does this have to do with your own dreams of Thomas Worthridge?"

"Yes," Samantha said. "You—for a reason I have not been able to detect—are particularly receptive to visitors from beyond. Experience has taught me to take advantage of receptive people whenever I can. All I would ask is that you sleep until dawn, and then let me know if you remember any dreams. That's all. You will be quite safe, I assure you. I'll be watching over you."

Here, she indicated her tablet computer.

I sighed and wondered what to do. I did feel tired, and allowed that it was not such a bad suggestion. I had bit of trepidation about being visited in my dreams, but seeing ghosts in the dreamworld felt preferable to spectral encounters during my waking hours.

Within ten minutes, Samantha had me bedded down in a guest room on the second floor of the house, down the same hall from where Lady Radish slumbered. There was a small, circular camera on the nightstand trained directly at my head. Samantha left me and presumably returned to her command center below.

I anticipated great difficulty falling to sleep under these conditions. I had once undergone a medical sleep study, where the combination of a strange bed and the knowledge that a camera was trained on me made drifting off almost impossible. Thus it was with considerable surprise that I found myself transported to the land of dreams almost directly upon closing my eyes.

I woke up screaming.

Or so Samantha told me—and so the footage shows. It was a blur to me, and I have no firm recollection. My first real waking memory is of being shaken awake by Lady Radish.

"My dear Vicar, what's wrong?" she cried.

Moments later, Samantha burst into the room, half out of breath.

"Forgive us, Olivia," Samantha said. "The Vicar grew tired, so I suggested he sleep here in the guest room. He's obviously just had an unpleasant dream. Don't let us bother you any further. By all means, please, return to your own bed."

Lady Radish looked my way, as if wishing me to verify what Samantha was saying.

I nodded bashfully, and managed a: "Yes . . . a bad dream."

Lady Radish offered to bring me tea, warm milk, or even a sleeping pill, but I declined all three.

Looking only semi-convinced that I had experienced a run-of-the-mill nightmare, Lady Radish nonetheless agreed to return to her own bedroom. She soon departed, and Samantha closed the door behind her. I looked at my watch and saw that I had been asleep for over three hours. It was nearly dawn.

"What did you see?" Samantha asked seriously.

"The spirit," I said. "Thomas Worthridge. I saw him. Good God! He was so much more terrifying than I expected."

"Yes," said Samantha. "Seeing him has the same effect on me."

"Why didn't you warn me?" I asked somewhat angrily.

"I hoped he might somehow spare you," she answered sheepishly.

"Well he damn-well didn't!" I barked.

"What exactly did you see?" Samantha asked. "Tell me every detail."

She reached into her pocket and produced a metal flask, offering it to me. I took a healthy slug of the bourbon inside, then began to speak.

"We were at my old school, St. Crispin's. Me and some of the other boys. We were in the dining hall. We were joking around and throwing food. Everybody was about twelve years old. Then this thing just walked into the dream. A tall man in a metal mask and flowing black robes. He entirely disrupted the dream. It fell away. Collapsed around him until it was only he and I looking at one another. Even the dining hall went blurry when he got there. That was the frightening part, the power this spirit had to interrupt every projection of my own mind; every part of the experience that came from me.

"The figure approached, and very slowly—so slowly it was awful to behold—removed its mask. I expected a monster, but the face underneath was a plain, dumpy man. His face showed the most sincere contrition I think I've ever seen. He got down on one knee. He was crying. It seemed, in the dream, that I could hear each tear with crystalline clarity as it dropped against the floor. He looked up into my face with giant eyes, slick with tears. And then he said something. I don't remember precisely *how* he said it, but I remember what he said. 'King's Crossing.' Then the flesh seemed to fall from his face and soon he was only a moldering, burned skeleton inside those black robes. And that was when I started screaming."

Samantha looked up at the corners of the ceiling, as if an explanation would there be found.

"You're sure that's what he said?" Samantha asked. "'King's Crossing?' This is entirely new information."

I nodded yes.

"What does it mean?"

"I will need to find out," Samantha said. "Vicar, I believe that you have served your purpose tonight. Thank you for your participation. If you leave now, you can probably be in your bed before the sun is up."

"Yes," I said somewhat absently. The idea of my own bed in familiar surroundings suddenly sounded very good indeed.

"You're certain there's nothing else I can do this evening?" I asked.

Samantha said that there was not. I remade the bed in which I had slept, and then followed Samantha down to the first floor and back to the front doors. We stepped outside into the cool, fresh air. I could already smell morning on the wind and the smallest hint of blue was on the horizon.

"Thank you," Samantha said. "I'll be in touch."

She closed the doors behind me. I stood there, looking at my car in the parking lot. It was a strange sensation. Out of the uncanny and back to the familiar. I drove home and fell into my bed just as dawn was breaking. I did not dream of the sad ghost in the mask . . . or of anything at all.

In the days that followed, a strange depression overtook me, almost like a sickness. I stayed inside as much as possible and did only the minimum of errands and housework. When friends called for drinks at the pub, I begged off.

When it came time for the next Sunday's services, I gave an old sermon that I knew by rote. All morning I kept an eye out for any sign of Margaret Worthridge, but she did not appear. Neither did she show for Sunday school or the afternoon coffee klatch. Then, in the late afternoon, as even the most enthusiastic adherents were having trouble finding a reason not to leave the church, I looked out through the front door and saw a figure that looked similar to Ms. Worthridge standing on the hill some distance away. I excused myself from the conversation that had entrapped me and headed closer to the church door. The figure stood very still. After a few moments, it—she?—turned and walked out of sight. I knew better than to pursue.

Three weeks passed, and I received a message from Samantha asking if I was available to meet for lunch the next day. I had appointments, but something in her tone said that this would be very important. I cleared my entire afternoon and showed up early at the restaurant.

Samantha was already there.

We took a table and she got right down to business. The youthful energy that had pervaded her character in our previous interaction had drained considerably. She looked like she had been awake for an extended period of time . . . very like Lady Radish had.

"Two days ago I found out what King's Crossing means and I haven't slept since," she said, as if reading my thoughts.

"What?" I asked. "What does it mean?"

"It's Thomas Worthridge's email password," Samantha answered coolly.

"You hacked into a dead man's email?" I asked.

Samantha gave me a look that said we were far past the point of compunction in such matters.

"Yes," she said. "And I believe that what I found there explains everything."

"What did you find?"

Samantha took a deep breath.

"Lady Olivia Radish was having an affair with Thomas Worthridge. It appears to have started as a purely physical entanglement, but soon became more. Each had something the other wanted.

"Lady Radish had a title, but no money. Thomas Worthridge had lots and lots of money, but no title. Combined, they would be unstoppable . . . or so they thought. I have read enough of their correspondence to understand that it did not take them particularly long to hatch a plan to do away with Margaret and make their union a legal one. It had to look like an accident, of course. Thomas was a skilled driver, and believed that he would be able to convince Margaret to lean out of the window of their car and then kick her. If he did this while they drove over a precipitous drop, this would surely result in her death. It was to have occurred down in Wales last year. The emails leave little doubt. It was premeditated murder.

"Of course, things did not go to plan. I have no correspondence relating to it obviously, but I think I can make a good guess. Margaret was a strong woman. A college rower who did aerobics every day. And how she was built! Those strong, wide shoulders. Anyway, I think that something went wrong when Thomas tried to force her out of the car. I think Margaret realized what was happening and fought back. Either she tried to stop him and the car accidentally crashed, or she intentionally forced the car down the embankment and into the water; killing both of them."

"My God!" I exclaimed. It was hard to imagine a paragon of our community colluding to murder her best

friend and steal her husband. Then I thought of how
upset and unsettled Lady Radish had been. How angry
at being reduced to turning her ancestral manor into a
tourist attraction. If something would once again make
her home her own, make her money problems vanish,
and restore a legion of attendants and servants to her
beck and call—as they had attended to the Radishes for
some two hundred years before—would she do it? Even
if it meant murder? I began to think the answer might
be yes.

"So this is why Radish Manor is haunted?" I asked.

Samantha stared straight ahead for a moment.

"I believe the ghost of Thomas Radish is genuinely
sorry for his crime," she said, not directly answering my
question. "In some way, he wishes to express this to
Margaret. And though her ghost walks the grounds as
well, it is not possible for him to do this. Not on his own."

"What can be done?" I asked. "Should we go to the
authorities? Show them the emails?"

"I was hoping you would have that answer,"
Samantha said. "I've already removed my equipment
from Radish Manor and told Olivia that I won't be able to
provide any further assistance. She took the news better
than I thought she would. I think she suspects I may have
learned about the murder, but has said nothing. Still, she
has to know it's connected to the ghost on some level."

Our food arrived. We began to eat and I tried to
decide what to do next.

"If word gets out about what happened—if people know Lady Radish was involved in a plot to kill her friend—will the ghosts be at peace?" I asked.

"Probably, yes," Samantha said.

"Probably?" I asked.

"Vicar, I work in a field that most scientists do not even acknowledge as existing. If I had the resources of an endowed university chair behind me, I might be able to provide a more definitive answer. As it stands, I am one person working alone with limited resources. So my answer is 'probably.'"

"Do we have a choice other than showing these emails to the authorities?" I asked.

Samantha shifted uncomfortably.

"Despite her situation, Olivia still has powerful friends and good lawyers," Samantha said. "It would be hard to prove we had not doctored these emails in an attempt to slander her. And what would we say about how we gotten into the account in the first place?"

I imagined sitting in court, testifying that Thomas Worthridge's email password had come to me in a dream. It made me wince just to think about it.

"But there are other options," Samantha continued. "We could go to the press. Give them the emails and let them take it from there."

"That would . . . destroy Lady Radish," I said, furrowing my brow.

Samantha dropped her fork and it clinked loudly on her plate.

"What do you think can happen now, Vicar?" she asked in raised tones; several other patrons looked in our direction. "There are only bad options left! A ghost wants blood. It has made us into its sword and now we must draw that blood . . . one way or another."

I put my head in my hands and took a deep breath.

"I must pray on this," I told her.

"We need to make a decision *soon*," Samantha insisted. "I'm going back to London as soon as I can."

"I can have an answer for you tomorrow," I told her. "Give me at least until then. I can't decide right now."

So . . .

I suppose there is no reason to draw out the rest of the tale.

Samantha said she would give me twenty-four hours to ruminate on the matter in whatever way I saw fit. I retired to my office and began to think about what to do. I prayed seriously and fervently for over an hour. A thunderstorm raged and roiled outside as I knelt with my hands clasped and my eyes closed. While it might have reflected the torment in my soul, the storm did nothing to indicate the best way forward. I received no divine guidance that I could discern. Uneasy and depressed, I spent the rest of that day and night online, researching everything I could find about the admissibility of emails in murder conviction cases. Samantha called a little after dawn. I was still awake.

"What have you decided, Vicar?" she asked, getting straight to the point.

"We must go to Lady Radish personally and ask her to do the right thing," I told Samantha. "I have not been able to think of a more appropriate course of action."

There was a very long pause.

"And what? Force her to confess? I won't do that. I'm done with her. I'm done with this place. Haven't you thought of anything better?"

"No," I said, growing cross. "Now look, young lady, I'll talk to her myself if you won't do it, but I still have faith that she can be convinced to take responsibility. We *must* have faith."

Samantha hung up the phone. It was the last time I ever spoke with her.

I planned to confront Lady Radish on my own later that day. However, a wave of exhaustion overtook me. Staying up all night had been nothing in my university days, but now in early middle age I found I was not quite as resilient. I bedded down to take a nap and ended up sleeping all day. When I awoke, it was already the next morning. Somewhat disoriented, I got in my car and set off for Radish Manor, determined to confront Lady Radish as soon as possible. I was acutely aware that I had seen none of the incriminating emails personally. While I had no reason to doubt Samantha, all the same I wished to hear what Lady Radish would have to say for herself.

I pulled into the parking lot of Radish Manor to find two busloads of tourists looking bewildered and confused. There were also five or six emergency vehicles with their lights flashing. I recognized one of the policemen as a member of my congregation and approached him.

"Hello Vicar," he said solemnly. "If you're here to talk down Lady Radish, I'm afraid you've come too late."

"'Talk her down?'" I asked. "Whatever do you mean?"

"Haven't you seen all the news in the past—oh—twelve hours?" he asked. "It's been all over the telly and the websites."

"No," I confessed. "I was asleep."

"Story leaked that the old bird tried to kill her friend and marry the husband," the policeman informed me. "Can you believe it? It was for money. Guess she wasn't as rich as people thought. I knew the Radishes were on hard times—relatively speaking—but you never know how hard, do you?"

I absently shook my head no.

"One of the tour guides found her inside about an hour ago, hanging by her neck," the constable continued. "That doesn't mean the accusations are true, of course. But for her sake, I hope they are. It'd be a double shame for a lady to take her life out of plain embarrassment."

I agreed that it would.

At that very moment the doors to Radish Manor opened and a pair of emergency workers wheeled out a cart. Atop it sat a black bag trimmed with yellow reflective coating containing the final remains of Lady Olivia Radish. An audible gasp went up from the tourists. The body was wheeled into an ambulance. Doris, the mansion attendant, stood in the doorway bawling her eyes out. The tour coordinators began hurriedly loading the visitors back onto the buses.

After comforting Doris and giving her my cell phone number, I drove back to my office. By then the entire village seemed to be talking about it. My inbox was full of emails—from friends, colleagues, and even from the press—asking about my relationship with Lady Radish. A few had heard a rumor that I was working with a 'ghost hunter' to determine the source of a haunting at the estate. Was there any truth it?

I deleted every message and did not answer calls.

A few weeks later, I officiated at the ceremony in which Lady Olivia Radish was laid to rest. It was a mostly private affair, held on the grounds of the estate. According to family tradition, Lady Radish was buried in the family cemetery, in a grave not terribly far from the final resting places of Thomas and Margaret Worthridge.

The service was sparsely attended. There seemed to be only the most distant and tangential relatives present to help support Lady Radish's sons—Robert and Benjamin—who now stood to inherit the mansion and grounds. Toward the end of the service, I noticed to my great surprise that Samantha had also chosen to attend. She had taken a seat in the very back pew and I did not initially recognize her. Her funereal habiliment was so different from her customary jeans and sweatshirt that it almost constituted a disguise.

I could not decide if I thought her presence was appropriate. She had acted rashly in sending the email exchanges to the press, true. Yet she was also still young, and youth act rashly. In her way, she likely thought she had done the right thing. I decided not to confront her, at least not on the day of the funeral.

It was after the solemn but well-catered reception inside the manor, right after the saying of goodbyes, that I saw Samantha for the final time. As I made my way out across the parking lot to my car, I chanced to look back at the manor. I felt strange and wistful. The entire affair had been such an odd experience. I had that uncanny sensation one sometimes has that an important chapter of one's life has just come to a definitive close. I also felt inverately sure that—no matter what—I would never set foot inside Radish Manor again.

It was during this last, emotional gander that my eyes chanced to light on the large bay window just to the side of the mansion entrance. Through it, I could see the remaining guests who still dawdled. They were down to a handful, but among them was Robert, the eldest son. Next to him was Samantha, again, near to unrecognizable in her formal black dress. Something about the way they stood struck me as odd, and so my gaze lingered.

It was in this second moment, I think, that I realized they were actually holding hands.

Silence.

I have always found a deep, personal satisfaction in stating bluntly and inelegantly that which others have floated with discretion and tact. In addition, I dislike it when speakers allow a rest to linger longer than it should.

"So. . . . And stop me if I've heard wrong. . . . Might it be that your young friend Samantha could have been in league with the elder Worthridge boy?"

A few of the visitors turn in my direction and deliver withering glares. I soak them up like the first sunshine of spring.

"It's possible," Cyning says. "Do I believe that Lady Radish saw something, and that I saw something . . . at least in my dreams? Yes. I have no doubt that a creature walked within those walls. But what's one to do with that information? How should the fallout of Lady Radish's suicide have been handled? That becomes a more difficult question."

"Did the ghost go away after Lady Radish died?" one of the visitors asks. "You said you never went back in."

"Yes, I believe that it departed after the events described," Cyning answers. "Not long afterwards I resigned my position and took up a more generalized study of world religions. The incident at Radish Manor had that kind of effect on me. I had to learn more, and see more of the world. It was the start of my research into other faiths."

Now the red-haired girl speaks up.

"What did you learn from studying other religions? Did anything convince you you'd made the right decision at Radish Manor? Or the wrong one?"

Father Cyning searches the cathedral-like ceiling for a moment.

"My child . . . I do not believe my survey is yet concluded."

The red-haired girl narrows her eyes, as if concerned that Cyning is having a joke at her expense.

Suddenly an unseen bell chimes, deep and sonorous. Only Cyning seems to be expecting it. He looks at his watch.

"How the hour gets away from us," he observes drolly. "It is almost time for the next service."

Indeed, no sooner are these words out of his mouth than the doors behind us open, and several shadowy figures begin to shuffle in. They are hotel guests who have been waiting patiently outside during the officiant's story. They stick to the dark corners of the chapel and take the seats closest to the walls. They have a way of remaining indistinct.

"I'm certain you must be moving along," declares Father Cyning. "And though I have taken up more than enough of your time already, providence compels me to note that your visitors would be welcome to attend the upcoming service . . . if any so desired."

"A fine idea," I allow. "At this point, there is not very much left on the hotel tour. I cannot, in fact, think of anything on our remaining itinerary that could compete with what can be found within these four walls."

The red-haired girl looks at me with an annoyed purse of the lips, but her eyes are bright.

"I wouldn't mind sticking around for a nice prayer service," says one of the visitors. "Goodness knows, after the things I've seen tonight, I could stand to talk things over with the Lord."

"I'll join you," agrees another. "I've had enough of surprises and weird stories for one evening."

A few others make similar declamations and brush past me to take seats in the open pews. Thus, our group bifurcates once again. The guests who remain standing next to me—presumably indicating that they wish to continue along the tour—I can count on one hand. The red-haired girl is, of course, among them.

"Very well," I indicate to Father Cyning. "We shall leave you to your important [don't laugh don't laugh don't laugh] work."

"Thank you," he says with a bow of his head. And to the other guests departing with me: "You are always welcome here."

I exit the chapel and allow what remains of my followers to file out after me. I close the door just as Cyning dons the apron and raises the ceremonial knife. The cries of confusion from the guests who have remained inside are almost entirely obscured by the bleating of the goat which Cyning's cowled assistant leads onto the altar.

Almost entirely.

★ ★ ★

I direct the remains of our party even deeper into the massive building. The way before us looks very similar to places we have already been. The visitors, however, seem to accept on faith that each step takes them closer to something new. (I once conducted a tour along a circular route as an experiment, to see if they would notice that they were passing the same doors and staircases again and again. It was not amusing for very long, and I quickly discontinued the project. Not a soul realized what I was doing. They are so very trusting.)

"So what's left for us to see?" the red-haired girl chirps. "Anything good? We're near the end, right?"

"Oh," I say with a sigh. "I suppose we might have a look at the library before we call it a night. One or two of you might find something to appreciate inside."

"Oh good!" the red-haired girl says. "I like libraries."

Her tone indicates that she is rested, refreshed, and ready for the next challenge. I wonder if this is a bluff.

"I can ask you a question about Father Cyning's story now," I inform her. "But . . . I mean . . . you're not going to start weeping or anything, are you?"

I frown down to indicate my disappointment with her prior behavior.

"That depends entirely on the question," she responds. "No promises."

She is stone cold, like a warrior, and refuses to be needled into indiscretion. Or, apparently, to be ashamed at all. It is fascinating.

"I think Father Cyning genuinely wanted to help the members of his flock at Kirkby Overblow," I say, training my gaze ahead of us. The tread of our footfalls is rhythmic and pleasant. The red-haired girl nods in agreement.

"He helped people with all sort of problems before the incident at the manor," I continue. "And when he heard about the haunting there, his only desire was to be of assistance. But I wonder. . . . Out of all the persons in his story, which one did he help the most?"

For several moments, we walk in silence. Then the girl speaks.

"I think the real winners in that situation—maybe the only winners—were the tourists who came to visit the manor."

"Why?" I ask sternly.

Will she cry once again? No. Her eyes remain calm and clear. Have I lost the ability to squeeze even a drop?

"They weren't really involved," she says. "It wasn't about them. I mean . . . it was. The ghost in the mask wanted to hurt Lady Radish by frightening away her paying customers. But the tourists didn't do anything to deserve being scared like that. They were innocent bystanders who kept getting hurt. So it was good that the priest stopped that from happening."

"You say they did not 'deserve' to be scared," I say. "Are you saying that people should get what they deserve?"

"I don't know," she says. "That's a different question, right?"

She quickens her pace, moving ahead of me down the hallway.

The sheer arrogance! She doesn't even know where she is going. I would be tempted to stop walking entirely . . . if I were not so completely astonished by the utter correctness of her reply.

"It's the gold door on the right at the end of the hall!" I shout absently after her, bewildered, flustered. "The library! You can't miss it!"

Ms. Ou

I take my time. We are near the end of the tour. I am not—by habit or temperament—a superstitious man, yet to have come this far and to still have a viable candidate is rather remarkable. Something deep within me says that to acknowledge this fact would be to hex the undertaking. One knows better than to mention that a no-hitter is eminent until at least the seventh inning. But we are so much further along than that. It is nearly the bottom of the ninth. Perhaps there is no harm in it.

At the end of the hallway, beside the library entrance, hangs the portrait of Dorothy Ranislee. She was the first—and to my knowledge, only—curator of the library. Though she had a lengthy tenure in the position, her final days at the Grand Hotel still predate my own arrival by several years. In her portrait, she is posed as the ur-librarian. The arch-librarian. Her grey locks are done up in a bun. Her eyeglasses dangle near the tip of her nose. She looks out from above the frames with the gaze of one who has seen your secrets—or at least seen you passing notes.

Yet there was obviously so much more to this mysterious figure. I have long wondered if the artist has left some clue to her character hidden around the edges of the canvass or woven into the fabric of her clothing. But these clues, if they exist, have so far eluded me.

Most frustratingly, Ms. Ranislee left behind no written record of the thought process directing her acquisition strategy, and there are no remaining residents here who knew her in life. Of course it is the library itself that is the true testament—and clue—to her character. Each time I borrow a volume, I believe that I discover something new about her.

Still . . .

The idea that the dark canvas in the hallway might hold some hidden indicator is almost irresistible. As I pass the sizable portrait, I lovingly blow the dust away from the brass nameplate at the base of the frame. Then I turn back and see the remains of the tour group—including the red-haired girl, of course—standing in front of the ten foot high burnished gold doors that open into the library.

The guests look back and forth between me and the golden handles.

"We thought we should wait for you," one of them says.

"Yes," agrees another. "Is it okay for us to open the doors? This place looks important."

I shake my head in disappointment.

"It couldn't be commoner," I tell them. "The world is full of libraries. There are thousands of them. Thousands upon thousands."

"Oh come on," the red-haired girl says. "You don't build doors like this for a normal library."

She has me there.

"I never heard of a hotel with a library before," another guest offers.

I nod as though this is a reasonable observation.

"Once, the convenience of access to a library of great books was an attraction for guests of the hotel. An amenity they wanted and appreciated. Now, I'm afraid, they tend to look elsewhere for entertainment. The world has so many diversions these days. Still, you may find something of interest. By all means, open the doors."

They do.

We walk inside, into a darkened room with very high ceilings, similar to a ballroom. The odor of ancient parchment confronts us in a heady wave; nearly overwhelming. In front of us are rows and rows of enormous stacks of books, each nearly eight feet high. In the dim, one becomes vaguely aware that the walls are also almost entirely lined with books.

"Here," I say, feeling for a switch. "This should help somewhat."

With a flick of my finger, the fixtures hanging from the library ceiling come to life. The entire library is bathed in light. The resulting impression is that of a bright golden explosion, as though the stacks of books have supernaturally caught fire. One of the remaining guests actually shields her eyes.

For a while they are stunned into silence.

The red-haired girl recovers the fastest, however, and is the first to speak.

"The books . . ." she says, gazing transfixed into the shelves in front of us. "They're made of gold! You didn't say that they were made of gold!"

"Technically, they're not made of gold," I explain. "Only the dust jackets are."

"Gold dust jackets!?" cries a guest. "For every book? Astounding!"

"And there must be millions of them!" another guest cries.

"An effect of the glare . . . and of the coiling architecture of the library itself," I tell him. "In truth, our volumes number only three hundred thirty-three thousand. Give or take."

I stride across the marbled floor, intending to show the visitors that it is safe to venture deeper into the library. Though the volumes in the shelves are bright, they do not radiate heat or pose any other danger.

"What books are these, exactly?" the red-haired girl asks.

"The great works of world literature are represented here, but also so much more," I answer as the group begins to follow me into the stacks. "Ms. Ranislee, the long-departed curator, was apparently an enthusiast of many different canons and traditions. In addition to the classics—and, it must be admitted, several works of popular doggerel—there are also . . . pieces . . . in this collection that I have never been able to account for, or even to categorize. Pieces that leave me baffled as to how or why she found them suitable for housing here, permanently, for the use of our guests—much less to be sheathed in gold."

"How are the books organized?" the red-haired girl wants to know.

"That gets to the heart of the matter," I reply, edging still deeper into the golden stacks. "You know, I used to believe that they were not organized at all. You see no alpha by author, no decimal system at work. And these unique golden covers, they quite eliminate the possibility of identifying a book without opening it first. A serious problem, no? Yet time and practice have taught me that certain volumes do seem to be grouped by schools of thought, by the author's geography, or by chronology. But most are grouped by content. Every two books sitting side by side on these shelves share some connection. On more than one occasion, I have borrowed two consecutive books, read them, and then tried to puzzle out what that connection might be. Sometimes it is obvious—both narratives take place during the Crimean War, for example—yet other times I have had to puzzle for hours or days before my Eureka moment. In this way, the true work of art in this library is not the gold leaf or even the literary works within, but rather the chain of connections linking from book-to-book-to-book across the shelves and down the walls."

"Who is the librarian now?" the red-haired girl asks as she slowly turns in a circle, apparently enjoying the phenomenon of being surrounded by golden spines on all sides.

"It has never occurred to management to refill the position. In point of fact, very few guests want to borrow books these days. Most of our residents—even our long term ones—are not even aware the library exists; when in some cases, it's just down the hallway from their rooms."

"So there's no one here to tell us a story?" the red-haired girl presses, ceasing her rotation. "How sad."

"I wouldn't say that," I tell her. "This library is full of stories. They're just written down. Maybe you could read us one?"

"You want me to read you a story?" she asks skeptically.

I nod and smile.

"What story should I read?" she asks.

"That is entirely up to you," I tell her. "Why not select a volume? The identical dust jackets make reading each book like opening an exquisitely wrapped present, don't you agree?"

The red-haired girl considers this. Then—it is clear from her expression—she finds something agreeable in the idea. She smiles, squints, and puts her little finger to the corner of her mouth, pondering.

"Okay, I'll find a book," she says.

She strides determinedly across the library floor, passing stacks and stacks of golden volumes; their covers giving a deep, regal gleam in the electric light. Whenever the red-haired girl reaches a 'T' in the maze of books, she turns confidently either right or left, as though she were already sure of where to go. This is amusing as it is ridiculous, and so I make a point to follow her closely for fear of missing anything.

After I (trailed by the handful of other guests) have chased her for the better part of five minutes, the girl stops against a far library wall. Here, the books rise some twelve feet high. Undeterred, the red-haired girl looks left and right until she espies a movable staircase on wheels, resting quietly a few yards down the stack. She carefully pushes it to her chosen spot and climbs the steps to near the very top. (I am not worried about the consequences of her falling, but some of the other guests do cluck concernedly.) High above us, she selects a slim golden volume and brings it back down.

"There!" she pronounces. "This one."

"An excellent selection, I'm sure," I tell her.

She opens it and begins leafing through.

"Only a few small pages?" I say, reading over her shoulder. "Too bad. It appears to be doctor's notes of some sort. Handwritten, though with uncharacteristically clear penmanship for a physician. And something in the lilt of the letters makes me think the hand is female. A lady doctor, then?"

The red-haired girl refuses to be flustered by her selection. She returns to the first page, and prepares to begin.

"Don't worry," I tell her. "I once opened a golden volume to find that it contained a carefully cataloged set of notes written on bar napkins. There wasn't much in the way of narrative structure, but as bar napkins go, they were fascinating. It told the entire story of an affair in a few quick missives. These meandering poets we have today could have learned a thing or two from those barroom writers . . . whoever they were."

The red-haired girl raises an eyebrow to ask if I am quite though.

When it appears that I am, she begins to read.

From the desk of Emiko Ou, LCSW

John Weber
Patient Entry #1
Intake Session

John Weber, male, mid-30s, presents for initial consult. Patient is suffering from generalized anxiety and depression. Physician referral.

A lifelong Midwesterner, John moved here to Minneapolis from Carbondale five years ago. He is employed as an electrician. John has no children, but is divorced. Family resides in Southern Indiana and Illinois. John "feels like a failure" and wishes that he could have done more to save his marriage. His father was abusive and they have grown distant. Mother drinks heavily, also distant now. He has one sibling (a sister) who John characterizes as "more successful" than he (university-educated plastics engineer).

His disorder manifests in the form of anxiety, sleeplessness, and occasional on-the-job panic. John has taken sick days from work when overcome by feelings of panic. He has removed himself from social situations because of panic and anxiety. However, he has never thought about hurting himself or anyone else. He does not abuse any substances. He does not take any prescription medications, but has been administered Xanax (he thinks) in an Emergency Room when he presented with symptoms of a panic attack. During attacks, John would characterize his anxiety as a "high eight" on a scale of one to ten.

Recommend continued weekly sessions with me, which will function in coordination with visits as necessary to his physician, Dr. Greene. (Has never referred before. Do I know him? In-network for insurance?) John agrees to proposed treatment. At end of session, John remarks that he already feels better after initial consult.

Addendum—I feel extremely sure that I have seen or met John Weber somewhere before. I wonder if I may have encountered him in the course of his work as an electrician or simply in a restaurant or store. Perhaps it's from somewhere earlier in my life. Somewhere in my youth, even. Googling him has revealed nothing. We have lived in some of the same states, but not at the same time and in none of the same cities. There is no reason yet to assume that a conflict of interest will present itself, but I will be keeping an eye open. As Doctor Carthridge, my mentor, has advised me, I am expanding my patient session notes to include my own personal reactions and observations— which may not initially seem salient—in hopes of detecting larger patterns that may become visible over time. This unexpected and strange sense of knowing John Weber should present an excellent opportunity for this exercise.

John Weber
Patient Entry #2

Second session. John is reasonably happy to speak about his ex-wife and their divorce, but not the years leading up to their split. John talked for most of the session about the immediate days surrounding the end of their marriage. John says he and his ex-wife spent almost all of their evenings fighting (never physically) and arguing with one another. In passing, John remarks that he blames himself for becoming distant early in the marriage and spending too much time with his friends. He also says he ought to have made more of an effort to find shared interests with his wife and to participate in activities with her. He believes her parents—especially her mother—encouraged her to leave him for someone "more successful," by which John seems to mean someone with greater earning potential.

John appears to have deep neuroses about how much money he makes and how he is perceived by others in terms of "success" and "failure." There is more to be discussed here regarding John's marriage, his wife's parents, and his own parents. John agrees. Will follow up next week.

Addendum—I continue to feel certain that I have seen John Weber somewhere before. In addition, I notice that an aspect of his smell (aftershave? soap?) is hauntingly familiar. Can all this be as simple has his using the same cologne as one of my high school teachers, or something like that? I know that smells can trigger some of our deepest and most powerful memories. Yet this explanation feels somewhat insufficient. I remain certain that I once knew John, but where? I wonder if I will be embarrassed when I finally figure it out. As in, 'How could I have forgotten about HIM?'

John Weber
Patient Entry #3

Today John talked about growing up in Centralia and Saginaw, and his early family life. John's father was an itinerant factory worker who appears to have constantly shifted from good union jobs to very bad ones that paid little money, and then back again. His mother worked at a yarn store in Saginaw for a time, and also sometimes did odd jobs. John's youth was mostly periods of feast or famine. Some years, the family appears to have been

solidly middle class. At other times, they were apparently
close to destitute. I believe John's neuroses regarding his
divorce stem from status and housing insecurity dating
back to this period. John continually speaks of a vague,
generalized desire to somehow change himself—or
"redeem" himself—from what he sees as his failings.

Addendum—This is beginning to trouble me, as I still
cannot place him. It has been two years since my mother's diagnosis (early onset dementia). I understand that
I am at risk, but not for some time. I have been repeatedly assured by my physician that occasional forgetful-
ness is not anything to be concerned about. I will be my
mother's age (55) before I need to start being seriously
watchful. This is still twenty years away. I must make it a
point to disregard my own neuroses during our sessions,
or they may negatively impact my ability to treat John. I
will watch myself going forward.

John Weber
Patient Entry #4

This afternoon, John talked again about his wife and
their early marriage. (John says these sessions seem
to be helping his sleeplessness and panic attacks. This
makes me feel like we may be making progress. John
says he has experienced no panic in the workplace since
we began our sessions—nearly a month!) John spoke
of meeting his wife and their courtship as high school

students. In his community, many couples married early. I think John and his wife (Emma) may have been acting more out of custom than mature romantic feelings. I made this point to John, and he seemed to consider it for a moment, but ultimately declared that it did not excuse what happened to their marriage. He points to the couples he still knows from high school whose marriages remain successful. John tends to want to recount the exciting parts of their courtship (first sight, proposal, wedding, honeymoon) and the excruciating parts of their breakup (screaming, public arguments, her storming out of the house), but he is substantially less keen to go into the small and steady details contributing to the dissolution of their marriage. I have advised John that we should delve into this in our subsequent sessions, even if he finds it tedious or uncomfortable. He cautiously agrees.

Addendum—Still haunted by a sense of familiarity that I'm unable to place . . . or to shake.

John Weber
Patient Entry #5

During today's session, John dipped his toe into a real discussion of the issues that took down his marriage. I consider this progress. John recounted fights with his wife over money and time spent away, and jealousy over activities with friends. John seems to desire to remain convinced that his own financial and nonspecific "personal shortcomings" were the only reason for their split. I think there is more here than that.

Addendum—I've figured out how I know him! During the session—in the course of referencing the better days of his childhood when his father had work— John spoke of attending Camp Bluebird in Interlochen one summer while his family was living in Saginaw. I attended this same camp when my father was on faculty at Wayne State! This is the connection! Still . . . I have no clear memory of actually seeing John there. Apparently, we would have both been around twelve years old. I've looked online, but cannot find any information about our year there together. The camp website does not have camper photo galleries, or any related information. This is quite frustrating. Why does John bring back such strong emotions? Why do I have such a strong sense of . . . not exactly déjà vu, but something along the same lines. I will email my mother and ask if she has photos of my summers at Camp Bluebird that she could scan and send. Why does John feel important? I know he's not the first boy I kissed. . . . There's something though. We will wait and see.

Addendum to addendum—I must NOT allow my curiosity about our summer together to direct the course of our sessions. If John volunteers any additional information about his time at Camp Bluebird, fine. But it would be unprofessional for me to steer the conversation.

John Weber

Patient Entry #6

John seemed not to be in the mood for therapy today. He was reluctant to talk. When he did answer, it was typically in short dramatic bursts. I tried activities to induce him to speak more casually and get into a conversational flow—we played chess at one point—but nothing took. (I must remind myself that this is not unusual. Occasionally, my patients simply come in tired or distracted. They have 'bad days.' I've also found that increased drama during sessions can be caused by patients having watched television or film portrayals of psychotherapy, and suddenly feeling that—in order for it to be useful—their own experience on the couch should be as angry and yell-y [a word?] as what they have seen on television. For the moment, however, I will give John the benefit of the doubt and simply chalk it up to a sleepless night.) We will resume next week.

　　Addendum—My mother sent a few photos of me at Camp Bluebird, but none of them showed John Weber. (I'm pretty sure I could recognize a "younger him.") Mostly, they show me looking mosquito-bit, and either too hot or too cold . . . . And like I haven't had a shower in several years. Still, seeing the photos takes me back to those summers and I remember all the crazy things we did. I remember the girls who were my fast-friends for an intense two and a half months, and then who I never saw again. I remember the pen pals that gradually faded away. I remember the woodsy smell of the cabins and going swimming in the lakes and how it felt splashing through the creeks at dusk with a big group of kids. I remember swinging on the rope swing. I remember leeches, yes, but also the smaller, unidentified creepy-crawlies that seemed to get everywhere in your clothes. I remember scandalous rumors over who had gotten her period. I remember even more scandalous rumors over who had sneaked out late at night to do "stuff" with one of the boys. But I do not remember John Weber. I will continue to rack my brain for an explanation of his familiarity. I will also ask my mother if she can find any more material from my camp days to send. I never know what may jog my memory.

The red-haired girl stops reading and frowns down at the golden book in her hands. She plucks out a single yellow page that looks torn from a legal pad. It is covered in inky black handwriting. She holds it up for us all to see.

"This next page is different from the others," she announces. "It's not written on stationery. I don't know if that's important."

I nod down at her to say this distinction has been noted. She may proceed.

John Weber

Patient Entry #7

This was not a therapy session.

On Sunday afternoon I went mountain biking along a forest trail outside the city. I am good on short trips but still working on my endurance. This particular ride pushed me a beyond my usual limits. A little past the halfway point, I began to feel powerfully exhausted and pulled to the side of the trail. I was—I now realize—very dehydrated. This was foolish and could easily have been avoided. (Had only coffee for breakfast.) As I recovered beside the trail, I began to feel weak, nauseous, and lightheaded. I saw pinpoints of lights in the corners of my vision. In short order, I passed out . . . but first—right before it happened—I remember staggering against a tree and trying to stay upright. And in that moment, John Weber stepped out from the forest beside me.

I awoke a few minutes later on the ground next to my bicycle. John was still there, and he offered me cold water from his water bottle. I accepted it quietly, still feeling disoriented. John said I looked okay, but should watch out for heatstroke. It took a bit for me to feel well enough to answer him, but I eventually said 'Thank you.' Then I asked how he happened to be right there next to where I'd pulled over. John said something about going for a hike. He did not, however, seem to be in hiking attire. He was wearing dress pants and a golf shirt. It also seemed unclear where he was keeping his water bottle (just carrying it in his hand?) and how the water inside could stay so cold. (Had he just filled it? And if so, where?)

Just as I was gearing up to ask him a follow-up question, three other cyclists rode up and stopped beside us. They asked if I needed help. One of them identified himself as a physician, and John suggested he check me for heatstroke. The doctor looked me over and took my pulse. He said I should rest and consume fluids, but that I did not appear to have a dangerous fever. One of them went and got his car, and gave me a ride back to my own with the AC blasting the whole way. This very quickly made me feel better. I rested for the remainder of the day at home, staying off my feet and drinking a good deal of ice water.

Encountering John like this can be nothing more than a strange coincidence. Going for the ride was a last-minute decision on my part, made impulsively after a friend cancelled on me for the movies. Still, I can't shake the sense that something funny is going on. This is not a feeling I have ever had previously when chancing to encounter patients out in the world. This is likely connected to my inability to remember John from years ago at camp.

I must continue to watch my own emotions in regard to this patient.

John Weber

Patient Entry #8

John arrived enthusiastic and ready for our session today. He briefly mentioned our run-in on the bike trail and inquired as to my health. I assured him that I was fine and thanked him for his help. I reminded him that— as with all patients—I would never mention any of the details of our sessions in a public setting and that I would not even identify myself as his therapist unless he did so first. John seemed unconcerned about this, and we let the matter drop.

John wanted to speak about his relationship with his father. (While John began therapy to talk about his divorce, he is now delving deeper into his background and his formative years. Though John may be unaware of it, this also brings us closer to the underpinnings of his anxiety.) John told me about his strong feelings of affection for his father that were not consistently returned. His father's up-and-down emotions may have been the result of his employment difficulties, or even undiagnosed bipolar tendencies. John regrets that he and his father have become distant in recent years. I tried to redirect the conversation to his wife several times, asking if he thought certain patterns or modes of communication with his father might have impacted his later adult relationships. John did not seem willing to explore these connections.

Addendum—When I arrived home after work today, a package from my mother was waiting for me on the doorstep. Inside was a note from her explaining that the box contained everything from Camp Bluebird that she had been able to find in the house. Within the box, carefully packed in bubble wrap, were several items. A homemade wallet; an ornate paper mask; woven bracelets; my stretched-out Camp Bluebird t-shirt; an ancient visor and snorkel; an irreparably crushed "Indian" headdress made from cardboard and feathers and leather strips.

Then, at the bottom of the box I found it.

I did not know in that moment that it would be the thing to bring back the memories I'd been searching for. I have no idea how my mother chose to include it or even why she would have kept it in the house all these years. It was thick stick—about twelve inches long, covered in ancient, dried mud. It had bulbous knots—two at each end—making it look like a brown bone. Strands of red and yellow yarn had been wrapped around the center of the stick.

The memory was instant. As I turned the stick over in my hands, I began to recall a very specific evening years ago at Camp Bluebird. More accurately, it was a single scene from an evening. Twilight. Myself and two or three other girls sitting in a muddy pit inside a grove of trees. We are secluded—away from the other campers. . . . It is not somewhere that we are supposed to be. We are playing some kind of camp game or.... But no. It was not a game. It was closer to . . . a ritual.

As I sat in my kitchen and turned the familiar stick over in my hands, the memories washed over me.

There had been an older girl at the camp. A counselor. She must have been around sixteen or seventeen, but thinking back she feels like a full-fledged adult. She had taken a shine to me and my friends, and had told us about an activity the campers had enjoyed back when she had been our age. An activity that was now forbidden. (It could only have been five or so years prior, but that felt like a span of eons.) Camp Bluebird was big on tradition. The 'camp traditions' seemed to be referenced at every gathering and by nearly every camp employee. But this counselor went out of her way to tell us that a particular tradition had recently been discontinued . . . after something had happened.

The forbidden practice involved invoking a spirit who was said to inhabit the woods surrounding Camp Bluebird. I cannot recall the spirit's name—or anything else about it—except that the name sounded Native American. It was a protector spirit. A spirit that kept the campers safe. Since the founding of Camp Bluebird, there had always been a ritual at the beginning of the summer at which the campers asked the spirit to protect them and help them have a good and safe time together over the two and a half months that would follow. Then the spirit was invoked again at the end of the year. The campers thanked it for providing a healthy and happy summer, and asked for its blessing as they returned to their regular lives.

I could not remember seeing how there was much wrong with this, or why they would want to discontinue it. As traditions went, it sounded very innocent. (Maybe fundamentalist campers complained about being asked to appeal to a spirit from a different religion?)

But when I asked why it had been discontinued, the friendly counselor said it was connected to a death. A *camper's* death. That idea had made all of us shudder. We asked the older girl what had happened.

Officially, she told us, it had been a drowning. But unofficially, the spirit had been involved.

And...

And I am not able to remember more. I have been checking the Internet all over again for more information on Camp Bluebird, this time with the words "murder" or "death" added to my search terms. Still, I find nothing. I can't imagine that a camper dying would not have been reported in one of the local Michigan papers, but perhaps a record from so long ago would only exist on microfiche? How frustrating!

Yet the new memory does not fade. I can see it clear as day. My small cadre of summer friends—along with the older counselor—sitting together in this mud pit, surrounded by high trees all around and engaging in some kind of repeated chant. We are listening to the older girl say certain words and then repeating them after her in unison. And I can remember forcing my stick into the muddy ground and leaving it there.

Then the memory ends.

And here is the stick, once again, in my hands.

I will continue to research this. More than ever, I want to remember.

John Weber
Patient Entry #9

Impetuously, I left the muddy camp stick in my office during today's sessions. I have been carrying it around absentmindedly, idly transporting back and forth between office and home and not really paying attention to where it gets left. Leaving it out was not intentional. At least not completely.

Halfway through our session, I noticed John looking over my shoulder. At first I thought something outside my office window had distracted him (sometimes big hawks fly by), but no. He had noticed my stick resting on the window ledge. Now John's eyes returned to it every few moments. Several times, it seemed to make him lose his train of thought.

I hesitated for a moment, but knew that it was now or never. I must bring up our connection . . . or else forever remain silent.

"I see you noticing my art piece," I said. "'Art' is being charitable, of course. I made it myself at summer camp when I was about twelve years old. As a matter of fact, it was at Camp Bluebird, near Interlochen, which I believe you previously mentioned attending."

For a long time, John stayed silent. Would he now recall the way in which we knew one another? I was on tenterhooks.

Then John said something that was confusing and chilling at the same time.

"That's vaguely familiar to me, that stick," he said. "Maybe I made one of them. I suppose we made a lot of arts and crafts at that camp. Looking at that stick, it's like I'm trying to remember what it means, but I can't. Funny."

I nodded slowly.

"Anyhow, sorry for being distracted," he said. "Where was I? My father?"

I confirmed that he had been speaking of his parents, and John was able to refocus himself and continue. However, I must confess that—though I did take notes—for the rest of the session my thoughts were only of the strange way John had materialized during my bike ride, and of what our possible connection might be.

Was John telling the truth? Did the stick truly create the kind of fleeting memories for him that I had been experiencing? Or was he lying? Was he keeping something from me?

At the end of the session, as he rose from the couch and collected his things, I watched John take a final glance at the stick.

I still do not know what to think.

(John Weber???)
Entry #10

This is not a record of patient counseling, but of external events I believe may be related to John Weber.

After my session with John this week, I continued to scour the Internet for any information about Camp Bluebird which I might have missed. I finally discovered a very old webpage for Camp Bluebird counselor alumni. The organization seemed to be unaffiliated with the camp. Not much effort had gone into the site; it was poorly rendered and even more poorly maintained. It had not been updated in several years. Even so, several former counselors had their information listed, and—remarkably—I found one who had been a counselor at the same time the "ritual" had been discontinued. He listed Minneapolis as his hometown.

The site gave his email address, and I sent a message asking if he was available to meet or talk by phone. I did not disclose exactly what I wished to discuss, and only said that I was a former camper and had some questions. He answered quickly and in the affirmative, and on Sunday evening I drove to a suburban coffee shop to find him waiting for me.

His name was Norman. He was fortyish, with hair receded into a Phil Collins stripe and a bulbous nose. He was slightly overweight and had the rosy cheeks of a drinker.

We got our coffees and began to chat. Norman was pleasant enough. He said he now worked as a tax attorney, and had not thought about the counselor alumni website for a long time. When I contacted him, he'd initially thought/hoped it might be through his online dating profile. He was recently divorced, he explained, and looking to 'get back out there.' I apologized for confusing him and said I hoped he would understand if I was not looking for romance.

I got down to business, telling him I had heard stories about a discontinued ritual and a camper who had passed away just before my time. Norman seemed to understand what I was getting at. The question also apparently upset him. For a while, he looked out the window of the coffee shop as a mom unloaded her kids from a minivan, a distracted, painful expression across his face.

"I feel bad about what happened . . ." he finally said. "But I feel worse about how we handled it . . . the lesson it taught the kids."

"So what happened?" I asked.

"A camper drowned," Norman said. "Two boys went swimming together without permission. One went down below the waterline and got his ankle tangled in some roots. Couldn't swim back up. Later—the investigators—they said it looked like the roots had grabbed him. Like it was a hand holding onto his ankle that wouldn't let go."

Norman took another look outside at the minivan.

"That was just a tragedy," he said. "Very sad, but just a tragedy. An accident. Nothing more. But the *other* kid— the one who lived?—well. . . . He was the problem. He wouldn't stop babbling about Ininuway."

It hit me like a ton of bricks dropped on my solar plexus. "In-in-you-way." *That* had been the name of the spirit. *That* had been what we had chanted in the mud pit. Hearing the name again inside that coffee shop transported me. In my mind, I was once again sitting in the pit amongst my friends, rocking back and forth. Half kidding but half serious. Under some sort of strange spell of our own making. Above the strong smell of the coffee beans and the cologne of the unfamiliar man, I seemed to smell the mud and the chlorophyll of the woods around us, our own unwashed bodies, and the cool summer night air.

"That was back when we still did the welcome ritual and the parting ritual," Norman continued. "It was nice. Sort of bookended the whole experience. I'd heard that the founders of the camp had learned it from some local tribe. Everyone seemed to like it and almost nobody took it seriously. It was more on the level of an old ghost story you'd tell around the campfire. But there were always one or two kids who'd get obsessed with Ininuway. They'd ask the counselors all sorts of questions about it—that of course we didn't know the answers to. Half the time, we just made stuff up to keep them quiet. Made our answers boring as possible so they'd lose interest.

"Anyhow . . . here's the long and short of it: When the cops came, the kid who was still alive said the drowning was Ininuway's doing. He said the other kid—who, as I remember, was something of a husky bully—had invited him down to the water to 'show him something.' They had dived in and then the husky kid had started holding him under the water. The kid was never clear on whether it was attempted murder or if the other boy just wanted to scare him. Whatever the case, the boy said that Ininuway had made one of the underwater trees come alive and pull the husky boy off of him. Then it held him on the bottom of the lake until he stopped breathing."

"Jesus," I said.

Norman sort of shrugged.

"A tall tale, but I've heard taller," he said.

"What happened next? I asked.

"Well . . . if the kid had just cried and let his parents take him home, nothing would have changed," Norman said. "That would have been that. But the kid didn't go quietly. He told everyone who interviewed him about Ininuway. He screamed and shouted about it. How he was *sure* it had been the spirit protecting him from the bully. He told the doctors. The police. The social work-ers. The other kids, until we had to separate him. And he damn-sure told his parents.

"None of the local news outlets were reporting on it yet, but you could sort of smell the stink on the wind. Now that I'm older and wiser, I understand what the camp owners were thinking. How the media *could* have made it look. A summer camp where they brainwash the kids into believing in spirits, and the kids are dying and saying it was a Native American boogeyman called Ininuway? I don't exactly see that *increasing* applications for the next year, if you follow my drift.

"So the word came down from the leadership. No more Ininuway. Mention it again, and you're fired. At the end of the summer, we sent the kids home without the closing ritual. After a few years, the campers forgot all about it, I hear. Of course, by that time I had moved on to college."

"Okay," I said. "One more question. There's this guy . . . I'm not allowed to tell you how I know him, but he was at Bluebird with me, and now he's come back into my life. I'm having trouble recalling the particulars. His name is John Weber. Does that ring any bells? White guy. From the Midwest. No real defining features."

Norman shook his head.

"Nope," he said. "I can't remember anybody by that name. Have you checked online?"

"Yes," I said. "I haven't found anything. Do you think it would be worth contacting the camp directly?"

Norman shrugged.

"All they can do is say no," he told me.

We reminisced about Camp Bluebird for a few moments more. I was unable to discover any new connections. I thanked Norman for his help and left the coffee shop. (Over the next twenty-four hours, I received a voicemail and two emails from Norman saying he enjoyed our talk, thought we 'really connected,' and would like to take me to dinner. I emailed back and said I was in a relationship, even though I am not.)

I have decided to wait before contacting Camp Bluebird, as I'm not exactly certain what I would ask. If the drowned camper comes up in a session with John—maybe he heard about it too?—it can certainly be pursued as a legitimate line of therapeutic inquiry. However, I am beginning to feel like I should let the matter drop. I may never remember my time together with John at camp. Allowing connections with patients to intrude into a therapist's private life is not appropriate. I'm not even sure what I'm trying to find out at this point. In next week's session with John I must remain more focused on his needs. Probably, I can best do this by shutting off thoughts of Camp Bluebird completely.

John Weber
Final Patient Entry

Today's session with John Weber had ended productively—with John finally beginning to undertake a serious examination of the external factors that contributed to his ex-wife's lack of fulfillment in their marriage (including her relative youth and pressures exterior to John)—when we were interrupted by my former patient Jack Kedzie barging into my office. He was holding a knife, and he lunged in my direction.

(Jack had come to me seeking treatment about a year ago, presenting anger issues and a history of violence. After several sessions, I told him that I was referring him to a colleague more specialized in the treatment of anger-management. This parting did not go well. Jack felt rejected—not uncommon in the case of a referral—and repeatedly threatened me during the final session. I informed him that if he did not leave, I would call the police. He then grudgingly departed.)

Jack raised the knife and charged straight at me, but John threw himself between us. The two men fought, both falling to the ground in the process. I repeatedly tried to knock the knife out of Jack's hands, but he held it too tightly. The scuffle ended when John turned the knife around and started stabbing Jack in the side. Jack screamed and stopped moving. John climbed off of him and I called 911.

Jack died before the EMTs got there.

John and I were taken to the police station and interviewed. I then contacted Dr. Brown (colleague)—who had been treating Jack, or trying to—and he came to the station and also provided an account of Jack Kedzie's violent tendencies. (Dr. Brown apologized profusely to me, saying he never saw anything in their sessions to make him believe Jack would carry-out any of his violent fantasies against me. I accepted this apology, but cannot help but have mixed feelings.) After that, the police allowed us to go home. Within the week, it had been conclusively ruled a case of self-defense. John was never charged with a crime.

Obviously, our sessions together could not continue. For his part, John seemed to have some sense of this. He left me a voicemail in which he said he would be ending our therapist/patient relationship. Specifically, he said he "had done what he had come here to do." This was confusing, as John could have had no foreknowledge of my treatment of Jack Kedzie, or Jack's murderous intentions.

I am, of course, aware that patients often confuse a strong external event in their lives with therapeutic progress. Patients who survive a dramatic car accident or natural disaster often report no longer needing therapy, despite the fact that this event—however powerful—has not directly addressed the root causes of their disorders. (Even milder external changes, like the onset of spring weather, can cause patients to feel 'cured.' A therapist in his or her first year of practice will notice a significant drop in business after the first warm day of spring, and likely remain confused until it happens the next spring, and then the spring after that.)

A violent physical confrontation in which a patient saves the life of his therapist definitely qualifies as an event likely to precipitate feelings of a cure. For the moment, however, I have decided to take John at his word. I emailed him back, wishing him the best of luck in the future, and continued health and wellness.

Addendum—Has he come before? Will he come again?

Perhaps John Weber has made himself manifest in my life at other times—any time is possible, between now and our period together at camp—and I simply have forgotten it.

Perhaps there is something else entirely that I fail to remember.

If I am under the protection of Ininuway, will it continue indefinitely? Or am I allowed one get-out-of-murder-free card only?

I have noticed in the days—now weeks—since the trauma in my office, the familiarity I felt with John slowly fading away. In his presence, I was *absolutely sure* we had met before. Yet now that it has been almost a month since I have physically been with him, doubt overtakes. I begin to feel as if I may somehow be mistaken about having known him. I will never forget being attacked by Jack Kedzie, but the connection to John Weber already feels questionable.

For that reason, it will be important to preserve these notes.

The red-haired girl closes the golden cover with extreme care, as if the notebook pages inside are ancient parchment that could crumble under excessive pressure. She silently climbs the movable staircase and places the volume back onto the shelves with all the others. Within moments, I have lost it in the massive wall of golden books.

"A somewhat disjoined selection," I pronounce as the red-haired girl descends, "though not entirely unpromising. When read in the context of the volumes surrounding it, perhaps a redeeming quality reveals itself."

The remaining guests nod solemnly to say that the red-haired girl should not feel bad about her choice. She had no way of knowing what it would be.

"I thought it was sort of interesting," the red-haired girl says defiantly as she steps off of the movable staircase.

I turn in a circle and give the other guests an expression that says: "It takes all sorts."

"May we look at more of the books?" asks one.

"Ooh, yes," says another. "Can we, please? This place is so huge. I'm just dying to see more."

"By all means," I tell them. "I must point out, however, that the identical golden spines tend to get people turned around, especially on their first visit to the library. If this happens to you, my advice is to simply pick a wall and walk clockwise. You will eventually run into a staircase that leads back down to the lobby. Incidentally, this is the final stop on our tour. So when you feel you've seen enough, you can simply let yourselves out that way."

The guests smile agreeably at this idea. I can tell they are pleased to have made it to the library and are glad they did not choose to remain behind in a different room.

One says: "Thanks for being our guide tonight. I sure learned a lot."

I give a lightning-quick smile with the corners of my mouth to acknowledge this remark. (I never know how to deal with compliments. Not least, because they are almost always misguided or wrong. Those who believe they have learned something about the Grand Hotel from me are usually the mostly likely to have missed the point entirely.)

Normally, I would have a little fun with a guest like this. Probing them about exactly what fixture or feature they had found most pleasing. Tonight, however, I am too excited. The possibilities presenting themselves are too vast. Too unthinkable. Too wonderful.

I have waited here for so, so very long. It has not been an unpleasant interval. In point of fact, I would not have traded it for anything. (As if I could.) But all things want. Everything wants. Including me. I have waited so many years for the next one to come. I want this to happen. I can admit it.

Some of the guests mistake my reflective wistfulness for a sign of sadness at their departure. One even leans in to hug me, but I wave the burly man off. A handshake will do. And so it does.

The remaining guests head off in different directions to explore the remainder of the golden library. They disperse, revealing the red-haired girl standing perfectly still at the foot of the movable staircase. She smiles up at me, ready and confident.

It is time for another test.

I begin to stroll counter-clockwise along the library's eastern wall. I give her a glance that asks "Are you coming?" The click of her footsteps on the burnished floors confirms that she is.

I walk in silence, allowing the tension to build. For a time we hear the footfalls and whispered voices of the other guests nearby, yet soon they fall away, muffled by row after row of identical volumes.

More silence. The girl seems to sense that this is part of the test. Good.

"We could talk about the notes left by the therapist," I begin cautiously. "I suppose they are interesting . . . in their own way. But what makes me curious is how you would like to see someone talk about them."

The red-haired girl looks up at me.

"But let me stop being obtuse," I say with a smile. "What I'm wondering is this: If you were going to ask someone a question about the tale told in the therapist's notes, what would it be?"

"If. . . . If I were asking you about them?" she wonders.

I shake my head no.

"If you wanted to discern if somebody had taken away the correct lesson from the text, what would you ask?"

A few more counter-clockwise steps.

"This, of course, assumes that I already know that lesson," she observes with a grin.

"That knowledge is necessary, but not sufficient," I say. "But I think you understand me. Now. . . . What would you ask if you were the one conducting the . . . verification?"

The red-haired girl slackens her pace, but does not stop entirely. This is good. She is thinking. Taking it seriously.

For my part, I am so nervous that I can hardly keep down the bile rising in the back of my throat. I take deep breaths and count my lucky stars. Such as they are.

"In her first entry, the therapist said she was dedicated to taking better and more personal notes to help her improve as a therapist. So why did she leave out the . . . romantic . . . feelings she obviously had for John Weber?"

"Good," I say, my voice so strained with the emotion of the moment that it is almost a creak. "Yes. That's right."

And here—above and apart from her testing—the girl impresses me by showing mercy. She can hear my angst and sense the feelings about to overwhelm me. (Even if she does not understand why.) Accordingly, she does not force me to prompt her for the answer.

"That would be my question," she continues. "As far as an acceptable answer, I would want to hear a response indicating that all mental health practitioners are likely to feel varying degrees of attraction to patients. But in this case, it came through because the therapist had probably seen the patient somewhere before. And that it had faded, as romantic feelings often do. And as memories do. Whether or not she actually *was* John Weber's ex-wife . . . is another matter."

Her voice falls into a tone of concern.

"So. . . . Are you. . . ? Are you okay? Vi- Sir?"

I lift an arm and nod vigorously to say that my sobs and spasms will be under control in a moment.

They are.

Once composed, I resume pacing widdershins along the wall. I am silent. I can tell that the red-haired girl is waiting to understand what is happening. Waiting for the next step. But there is the real test, perhaps. Does she have any idea of what awaits her? And even if she does possess an inkling . . . will she be willing to accept what is hers? What she is?

"Very good," I whisper when the power of speech returns. "You have answered me correctly. Because of this, I will show you something that nobody has seen before. A secret part of the hotel. How does that sound?"

"I. . . . Good, I think," she manages. "Are you sure you're okay?"

How sweet, her concern.

"Yes," I tell her. "Actually, I have not been this well in quite some time."

We walk until we reach a white marble staircase leading up and away from the library floor. The red-haired girl is clearly confused.

"Is this a way out?" she says. "You said the staircase went back to the lobby. Does this?"

"No," I say. "This is a different one. It goes . . . somewhere else. Do you want to see?"

She nods cautiously.

"We haven't run into any of the other guests," she points out.

"They were walking the other direction," I remind her. "Have no worries. They will have all found their way back safely by this time. I'm almost sure of it."

"Well then," she says, placing her foot on the first stair. "What are we waiting for?"

What indeed.

King Vikram

The staircase winds onwards and upwards. Our footsteps make a reverberant clamor as we advance. Sconces along the walls hold bulbs that keep the way ahead bright and clear. The marble stair beneath us gives one the sense of advancing to a place of considerable importance.

"This feels like I'm walking into a bank or a courthouse or . . . a mansion," observes the girl.

I nod to say these are all reasonable extrapolations.

At the top of the staircase is a single door—heavy, jet black, but with gold leaf inlay and a conspicuous yellow keyhole.

Before the red-haired girl can ask, I pat my pockets and produce a large brass key. Instants later, it is in the lock and the door swings wide before us.

Beyond is a dimly-lit but pleasant set of rooms that may give the impression of a gentleman's lounge from another century. There are leather chairs (high-backed and regal), couches, teak end tables, and a stately fireplace with a raging fire. A billiards table it set into one corner and a selection of cues lines the wall nearby. In another corner is a fully-stocked bar. It is in this direction I first head.

"Can I get you anything?" I ask as the red-haired girl takes a few tentative steps within. "You're a bit young for cocktails, but perhaps some seltzer? I might even be able to do a glass of milk."

"Water will be fine," the girl answers absently. She is looking around, evidently unsure what to make of this place. She cautiously moves deeper into the room, her eyes probing a red tapestry on the walls. (The lettering is probably exotic and unfamiliar to her, but the image should be clear enough—a lord and lady sunning themselves on a hill, unaware of the tiger who stalks in the grass right behind them.)

Soon her eyes settle on the fireplace mantle where a magnificent sword is displayed in its wooden stand. When it was forged, the hilt and crossguard contained more emeralds and rubies than any sword ever made. (Of course, that was literally ages ago, and the record has now been surpassed several times.)

"Been in my family for years," I explain, returning briskly from the bar and handing her a glass of water. In my other hand I clutch a glass containing something significantly stronger.

"It's beautiful," she says, watching the gems reflect the firelight.

"Would you like to have a seat?" I ask, falling into one of the nearby leather chairs. "We've been on our feet for . . . I don't know . . . it feels like hours."

Still holding her water, she saunters to a chair a few paces from mine and sits down. The leather stretches underneath her with a funny, fuzzy noise. She smiles, sips her cool drink, and lets her arms drape on the armrests.

"These are your private rooms?" she says.

"Some of them," I tell her. "Everyone ought to have a place where they can retire and feel like themselves, don't you agree?"

The red-haired girl flattens her mouth and looks back and forth, indicating that the question had never occurred to her.

"You seem different all of a sudden," she observes.

I shrug to allow that it may be so, and have a sip of my own drink.

"Why did you bring me here?" she asks. "I mean. . . . Don't take it the wrong way. This room is very pleasant—in an old-man sort of way—but there doesn't seem to be . . ."

"Anyone to tell a story?" I finish for her.

She notices that now I am looking quite fixedly at the sword above the fireplace and the play of the firelight upon its jewels.

"Actually, there *is* a story here," I say, never taking my eyes from the glistening weapon. "I will be the one to tell it."

"Will I have to answer a question afterwards?" she asks, though on some level she must already sense that we are far past riddles.

I shake my head silently and stare deeper into the jewels and darkness and flame.

A long time ago, there was a king named Vikram, who ruled the city of Pratisthana in what is today South Central India. Though he was quite young, everybody said he was wise and strong beyond his years. His armies were fierce and feared. His lands were prosperous. His castle was as magnificent as it was formidable. Vikram conducted business from atop an impressive throne forged in the shape of a great cat. Though an untested king, he was assured by his attendants and flatterers that he possessed all the traits needed to ensure a long and prosperous reign. The young king saw no reason to doubt this.

One day during receiving hours, a naked monk came into the throne room. He said nothing but presented the young king with a small fruit. The king was equal parts mystified and amused. It seemed important to the holy man to make the presentation, so the king allowed it to happen. With a knowing smile to his court attendants, the king accepted the fruit and thanked the holy man, who bowed and went on his way. The next day, the holy man appeared again. Once more, he offered a piece of fruit, and then silently departed. Then he came the day after that. And then the day after that. Vikram remained genially bemused by the monk and his offerings. The monk's presentation of fruit became a daily occurrence in Vikram's court, regular as the rising of the sun.

One day the monk stumbled as he kneeled to present his piece of fruit. It fell onto the stone floor where it split open to reveal a glistening ruby inside, slick from the wetness of the fruit.

Vikram was astonished and said: "Monk, why would you place something so valuable inside the fruit you give to me?"

The monk answered: "One does not visit a king empty-handed. For lo these many days, I have hidden jewels inside each piece of fruit."

Vikram ordered his attendants to bring him all of the fruits ever presented by the monk. Soon they were arrayed in front of the king in a giant pile. The king opened them to find each contained a glimmering emerald, diamond, or ruby.

Vikram was delighted . . . but also confused. He turned to the monk, who silently watched these events without comment.

"These jewels are worth more than my entire treasury!"Vikram said to the monk."How can I possibly thank you?"

The monk said:"Your majesty, I will now disclose my true purpose to you, but it must be done in private."

With a few snaps of Vikram's fingers, the attendants cleared out. The king was alone with the monk. Vikram descended from the throne until he stood right beside the holy man.

The monk whispered his words in confidential tones.

"Your majesty, on the fourteenth day of this month, I plan to undertake secret rites and spells in the burning grounds on the banks of the Godavari River. If I am successful in this magic, I will obtain the eight great Siddhis, or magical powers. I will be able to make myself as small as an atom or as large as a mountain. I'll be able to weigh whatever I like—light as a feather or as heavy as an elephant. I'll be able to turn invisible, make other people do whatever I tell them to, have whatever I want, and be counted a Lord of the World. But for this rite . . . I need a strong, brave man to assist me. This man would be rewarded for his assistance, with powers like those of Death himself. I can't think of anybody as strong and brave as you, my king. Will you assist me in this matter?"

The king didn't know what to say. He had never dabbled in spells before and felt some trepidation about what he might be expected to do. At the same time, he could not deny that the holy man had already brought him wealth beyond his wildest imagination. Feeling he was already indebted, Vikram replied that he would help the monk.

"Good," said the monk. "Meet me at the edge of the burning grounds on the date in question. Come alone. Come at night. Bring only your sword."

Here, the red-haired girl takes another long look at the jeweled weapon above the fireplace.

My own eyes have never left it.

On the fourteenth day of the month, the king dressed all in black and, taking only his sword, journeyed alone to the burning grounds that abutted the Godavari. At the edge of the grounds he found the naked monk waiting for him. The monk smiled and watched as the king took in the strange and horrible sight before him.

Vikram had never been to the burning grounds, and did not know what to expect. What stretched before him now was a hideous landscape like out of a nightmare. Corpses littered the blasted earth. Sun-bleached bones stuck up out of the grounds like trees in a forest. Funeral pyres burned in great con-flagrations, and their smoke created an impenetrable mist so thick that Vikram could not see but a small way ahead. The stench of death and burning flesh was everywhere. Never in his life had Vikram seen demons, but knew that if they lived anywhere, it would be in a place like this.

"What must I do?" the king asked the monk as both squinted into the smoky gloom.

The monk pointed into the heart of the smoke and flame and mist.

"You must journey into the grounds just there, in that direction," said the monk. "Stay true to your course. After several miles, you will find a clearing where grows a single sinsipa tree. On one of its branches hangs an old corpse. You must bring that corpse back to me."

"That is all?" the king asked.

The monk nodded, yet something in the naked man's expression told Vikram there was more to it.

The king summoned all his courage and set off into the burning grounds. Inside, it was even more horrible than he had imagined.

The smoke was so thick that after a moment's march he could no longer see the monk behind him. The way forward was littered with mutilated dead, decaying pools of rotting flesh, and gleaming white bones. Rib cages were piled into pyramids. Amputated limbs had been stacked into columns. At one point, Vikram spied two human skulls that had been made into drinking goblets. He knew this was the work of demons.

From time to time, powerful winds whipped up the pyre-smoke, and ash blinded the king. It was easy to become disoriented, but Vikram forced himself to press on.

Vikram encountered trees draped in human entrails. Vultures perched upon their branches, feasting. He heard horrible, unnatural howls on the wind, and other sounds that were not completely human. As he moved deeper into the grounds, he had a hint as to their source.

Amid the fire and smoke, an arrangement of tables had been set up as if for feasting. Ghouls, goblins, and ogres cavorted all around them. Piled high for their indulgence was all matter of human flesh. The king stayed in the shadows to circumvent this disgusting carnival.

Finally, in the deepest part of the grounds, the king came upon a large, flat expanse where grew a lone sinsipa tree. And indeed, draped over its lowest branch was a blue, skinless corpse, awful to behold.

Vikram approached the tree and carefully took down the body. He threw it over his shoulder and turned around, ready to retrace his steps back to the mendicant monk. Yet no sooner had he started the return journey than the corpse began to speak! Vikram realized it was possessed by a genie. He had heard that this could happen.

"Listen up," the genie said into Vikram's ear. "Intelligent rulers fill their days with grand things like poetry and military arts. Stupid ones waste their time sleeping, quibbling, or being brutal. But what good is inheriting a regal position if you don't have the discipline to keep it? And what good is eloquence with words if you have nothing to say?"

Vikram remained silent. He thought maybe the genie's words were a trick.

"Listen, king," continued the genie. "I'm going to tell you a tale."

Vikram was surprised by this turn of events, but kept walking back toward the monk. As he did, true to its word, the genie told him a story. It contained a good deal of murder and betrayal, and the king found it exciting and reasonably easy to follow. When the story ended, the genie asked Vikram about how certain characters had acted and his opinion of one character in particular. Vikram saw no harm in answering and told the genie what he thought, right off the top of his head. The moment the words were out of the king's mouth, the corpse disappeared from his shoulder. Vikram was dumbfounded. He looked all around for the body, and eventually retraced his steps. He found the corpse back on the branch of the sinsipa tree.

"I don't know what that was about," Vikram said, taking the body down once more and putting it over his shoulder. "But you are still coming with me."

"Very well . . ." said the possessed corpse. "And I shall tell you a tale along the way."

The same thing happened. The genie inside the dead body told Vikram another story as the king stalked back through that wasteland of human offal. This one was about a beautiful woman who had three suitors. The woman was bitten by a snake and died. The three suitors mourned her in different ways. Then, miraculously, the woman was restored to life. The genie in the corpse asked Vikram who should have the young lady's hand in marriage based on how they had acted after her death. Vikram thought about it and gave his answer. When he did, the corpse again disappeared from his shoulder.

Vikram began to grow annoyed. He retraced his steps and found the corpse, once more, slung over the branch of the sinsipa tree.

The king took it down and said: "Are you going to do this every time I give a wrong answer?"

"To the contrary," said the genie. "Both of your answers so far have been absolutely correct."

"Ahh," Vikram said with a chuckle. "Then perhaps I should answer incorrectly, eh? Would you stay on my shoulder then?"

The genie only laughed—darkly and horribly. It was the most disturbing sound Vikram had ever heard.

The king suddenly understood that if he gave the genie an incorrect answer, he was going to die. Or worse.

With some trepidation, the king shouldered the corpse once more and set off into the blood-soaked burning grounds.

I take a deep breath and close my eyes for a moment, remembering.

The genie told the king twenty-four tales in all. Some were yarns of high adventure, others were tender stories of romance, others still were accounts of encounters with fantastic beasts and magical creatures. And at the end of each tale, the djinn asked Vikram a question. Each time, the king considered carefully—aware than his life hung in the balance—and answered truthfully. Each time the genie returned to the tree, and the king had to go back. And each time—ever so desperately—the king hoped *this* tale would be the last.

After giving his twenty-fourth answer, the inveterate king returned to the tree and took down the corpse. As he walked, the genie inside spoke to him once again.

"Great king, you have answered all my questions correctly. Your judgment, wisdom, and temperament are truly beyond reproach. So now I tell you the twenty-fifth and final tale. It is your own.

"You were asked here by a holy man who promised there would be great power for you—and for himself— if you brought this corpse to him. He flattered you with blandishments of your own mightiness and perspicacity, saying that of all in the land you were the most fit to undertake this quest. But the secret you did not know is that the holy man is a charlatan. A dark wizard. A warlock. When you arrive with the corpse, he will perform sacred rites upon it. These rites will require your involvement. He will ask you to prostrate yourself on the ground beside the corpse. When you do, he will kill you."

"If that's how it is, then I will run this wizard through," Vikram cried, reaching for his sword.

"His magic is too powerful," said the genie. "He would strike you down with a spell before you even got close. But there is another way to win. Play dumb when the wizard asks you to prostrate yourself. Tell him you are a king and have bowed before no man. Ask him to show you how it's done. When he kneels, you must cut off his head.

"Or not. After all, it's your story."

The king thought about this as he stalked through the bloody boneyard back to where the naked monk was waiting.

When Vikram arrived, the hoary old man was overjoyed. Just as the corpse had foretold, the monk began a strange ritual and told the king that he must prostrate himself beside the corpse for it to work. Vikram did not hesitate, but told the naked monk that he did not know the correct way. Would the monk please demonstrate?

In his haste to complete the ritual, the monk agreed. He fell to the ground in front of the king. Vikram wasted no time, but drew his sword and beheaded the traitor with a single stroke.

"You have done it!" cried the genie. "The gods are pleased. Now ask me a boon and I shall grant it."

King Vikram thought for a moment, then said: "My wish is to be a good king. To protect my people. To bring prosperity to the land. To be fair and just, and to rule in glory."

"And so you shall have it," said the genie.

With that, the corpse disappeared once again. The king was left alone at the edge of the misty burning grounds next to the decapitated body of the wizard. The first light of dawn began to creep over the horizon. The king walked away from that awful place, never to return.

In the years that followed, the king's attendants declared that they had been right all along about their lord, for Vikram ruled always with might and wisdom. His lands prospered and his people loved him. His policies and decrees were uniformly successful. He ushered in an era of peace that lasted a hundred years.

Vikram was content in his reign, yet often felt puzzled by his encounter with the genie.

It was not until many years had passed—and the king had grown very old—that he finally guessed that there might have been no supernatural power at all to the genie's blessing. And, rather, that his prosperous, peaceful reign might have arisen from his own good decisions made by drawing upon the lessons in the genie's twenty-five tales.

That the genie had been a teacher, and that the stories and riddles themselves had been the true boon.

I drain the remaining contents of my glass and set it on an end-table.

"That's a good story," the red-haired girl says.

I shrug to say it might have been an okay one.

"I like the idea that the genie's stories were lessons to help the king be a good king," she says. "But parts of it are still a little . . . weird."

"Old stories often are," I tell her. "And that one is *very* old."

"What I can't see is why the genie couldn't have just told the king what he needed to know flat-out. Why did the genie have to make the lessons into mysteries and riddles?"

I nod, seeing where she is going with this.

"The king would not have been receptive," I say. "He would have probably been insulted, actually. He was a powerful king, after all, and he already thought he was very smart."

Something occurs to the red-haired girl, and an obstreperous gleam comes into her eyes.

"You have quite a command of the details in that tale," she says. "Your knowledge seems almost . . . firsthand?"

She lets in hang.

How I love this little one. She is all that I have ever hoped for. She will bring so many wonderful things to this place.

"Do you think that I have divulged too much?" I ask her. "Tell me, is there a place where I could have possibly done less? Said less?"

"Perhaps if you were the king," she answers.

Here she raises her glass. Perhaps copying me, she drains the remnants in one final gulp. Then she sets it down and looks me squarely in the face.

"But you are the genie."

A new ripple of pleasure courses through my spine.

Of course, it is not technically "mine." Yet the effect is nonetheless satisfying.

"Truly, there is nothing I can keep from you," I answer. "My name is Vicrakindrin. I am a spirit that is nearly two thousand years old. Perhaps you have seen the way my skin holds an indeterminate darkness . . . something wholly divorced from pigment. You have observed the way I tend to hang in the shadows. Indeed, though it is only my latest vessel, the body I inhabit has not drawn natural breath in many, many years."

The red-haired girl is pleased to be correct in her hypothesis.

"For you, it is a very different case," I say. "You have been dead for only a few hours, if I am not mistaken."

I am not.

A look of consternation crosses the girl's face. Her brow furrows and her eyes go from left to right. So very clever, and yet this possibility has somehow not occurred to her.

Tut-tut.

"Place your hand over your heart and count the beats," I tell her, getting up to fix myself a second drink.

I will need it. I thought she had figured this much out. Apparently not.

The girl obeys. Her expression of alarm grows. Soon she is gripping madly at her wrist.

I pour the drink slowly, watching the amber liquid fill my glass.

"You probably do not remember the incident that brought you here," I tell her. "People seldom do. No one, I think, in the group tonight had any real inkling. You drowned yourself in the river, during your secret excursion, a little past six this evening. Something about your family. You would have been a king yourself—or a queen—of sorts. But now you are something else. You were always destined to be something else. Something more, in my opinion. So many spirits. . . . When they come to the other side, they do not find their usefulness. They fade away or else become distracted with the mundane. But you are special. I have not seen one of your kind in hundreds of years. And I have never seen one so . . . suitable."

The girl looks at me. Terrified. Awestruck. And still wonderfully resolute.

"I have never used the word protégé, but I can think of nothing that more finely suits the arrangement I envision."

She looks up at me harshly.

"What are you?" she asks in a trembling voice.

"A genie, as you yourself said," I tell her. "A spirit. A special spirit, just like you. Genies are very rare, you see. The universe only burps one out every few hundred years. I do not insist that you feel 'honored' to be among our ranks, but it would not be an inappropriate reaction."

"What is this place? What exactly do you do here?"

I take a sip of my drink and rejoin her near the fire.

"What do all the permanent guests in the hotel have in common?" I ask.

She thinks for a second.

"They've had something unusual happen to them," she answers.

"Yes . . . every person in this hotel has had something unusual happen. Every one of them is trying to make sense of it. To make sense of their stories. My job is to help them do that. No more, no less. I prompt them. I ask them about themselves. I bring them audiences. The more I can make them talk it through—to tell their stories again and again—the more they can come a little closer to understanding why it happened and what it means. To moving on."

The girl nods.

"That's what a genie does. Tells stories. Asks questions—the right *kind* of questions. And, now and then, it helps somebody realize something."

"Like how to be a better king?" she asks.

"Sure," I say. "That's one of them. King Vikram was probably my most celebrated client, but I'm not in it for the fame."

"So what exactly do you want from me?" asks the red-haired girl.

"I am very, very, very old," I tell her. "I feel that I have served my usefulness in this post. I, myself, am ready to move on. To go to whatever and wherever—and perhaps whenever—is next. Hundreds of years ago, I took this charge from another. Now I am ready to offer it to you."

"But you've only known me for one evening," she says.

"I know enough," I tell her. "My own 'audition'—such as it was—passed even more quickly than yours."

The girl considers this for a moment.

"Do you think I'm ready?" she asks.

"You're ready," I tell her. "Whether you are willing, is, of course, another matter. No one can be forced."

The red-haired girl rises absently to her feet, evidently deep in thought. She stands beside the fire. Perhaps she is warming herself. The bejeweled sword glitters behind her—one end to either side, from my perspective—as though it has run her through. She takes a deep breath.

"If these are to be my quarters, then those old couches will have to go," she pronounces. "Some of the chairs as well. And the walls are in need of something entirely different. These draperies and hangings of yours are . . . strange."

I try to not take this personally.

"Will you require me to remove the sword as well? It is a tad militaristic and morbid, I expect."

"Oh no," she responds. "That will need to stay. It reminds me of my favorite story."

★ ★ ★

As the years pass, the Grand Hotel will welcome her in its own ways. Of that, I have no doubt. And she, in turn, will come to influence her new home. If I chance to pass this way again, I may find these familiar halls transmuted completely. I may not recognize the Grand Hotel at all. It may not even be a hotel.

This will all be well and good.

I am not afraid of what comes next, for I am ready. To depart. To fade away. It is time for that.

But as I leave the red-haired girl alone in my salon—already, she has taken down and put away my favorite porcelain animal; this place will now be increasingly hers and less and less mine with each moment that passes—the only thing that nags me is the question of her appreciation for the role.

I go now into the fade—to the other side—and still there is no surcease of concern. Nothing tells me it will go one way or the other. I have done my best, but there may never be a way that I can know for sure.

Does she truly understand what happens here? What this place actually is? Does she really grasp the importance of her work?

These questions will ever haunt me.

I fear some riddles are unanswerable.

Author's Note

Significant parts of this work are inspired by *The Five-and-Twenty Tales of the Genie*, a story cycle arising in the oral traditions of ancient India and first put into Sanskrit around 1200 AD by an author named Sivadasa. (This version is still generally available today, and in a variety of translations.)

Very little about Sivadasa is known, but recent years have seen an expansion of scholarly inquiry into his writing. With interest in the *Tales* mounting, I am cautiously hopeful that this trend will continue.